Jasmine SKIES

SITA BRAHMACHARI

Albert Whitman & Company
Chicago, Illinois

TJ

Library of Congress Cataloging-in-Publication data
is on file with the publisher.
Copyright © 2012 Sita Brahmachari
First published in 2012 in the UK by Macmillan Children's Books
Published in 2014 by Albert Whitman & Company
ISBN 978-0-8075-3782-4

Printed in China.
10 9 8 7 6 5 4 3 2 1 BP 18 17 16 15 14

Cover design by Jenna Stempel
Cover image © visual7/E+/Getty Images

For more information about Albert Whitman & Company,
visit our web site at www.albertwhitman.com.

In memory of Dad—
Dr. Amal Krishna Brahmachari
Written with love for Mum—
Freda Brahmachari—
and my whole family

Kolkata Airport

✿✹✿

I can't wait to grab my suitcase and walk through to the other side.

It's hard to believe that I've finally arrived in India, and that I, Mira Levenson, made it here, all by myself…against all odds. You'd think your mum would *want* to encourage you to visit the place where your granddad grew up. But it feels like it's been me who's had to make it happen…well, to be precise… me and Priya, my second cousin, who's the same age as me. And if we hadn't got in touch with each other through Facebook after Granddad died, I don't suppose I would be standing here now.

I don't care how many times Mum tells me that the only reason she hasn't been back to India since she was my age is that her and Priya's mum, Aunt Anjali, "just lost touch"…I don't believe her. When I finally persuaded her to start talking to

Anjali it seemed to take them hours and hours of phone calls till they could sound anything like normal with each other. Then, when Mum finally agreed I could make this trip, she kept switching between over-the-top happiness and nervousness. What was it she said to me?

"You're going in Granddad's place, Mira. If I could go with you, I would."

But I didn't believe that either, because if she really wanted to go, then what's been stopping her for all these years…or Granddad for that matter? When I asked him when the last time he'd been to Kolkata was, he said it was when his ma died, which was thirty years ago. I didn't even know my own great-grandma's name was Medini till he told me. The more I think about it, the more I know it can't be true that the reason why no one in our family's been back to India for so long is that everyone was "working too hard," "couldn't afford it," or "just lost touch." There are kids in my year at school who go to the other side of the world *every year* to see family, and it's not like they're rich or anything or not hardworking.

It's sad really, because not long before he died, Granddad seemed to decide that he wanted to go back "home." I remember that's what he called it, because it made me wonder how long you have to live in a place before you think of it as home.

"If I get better, you can come to India with Nana Kath and

me!" he told me in that way he had of making you think that anything he said would actually happen. But he never did get better. I suppose it's because he's not here anymore that I felt like I had to answer Priya's email, like I *needed* to keep some kind of connection to the place where Granddad was born… for both of us. But arranging to visit India has been such a struggle: getting Mum and Anjali to talk to each other in the first place, then persuading Mum that I'd be all right flying with an airport chaperone (I am fourteen!), then Anjali convincing Mum that I'd be well looked after, then getting the time off school (mainly because I said I'll be working in Anjali's children's refuge and organizing an art project), then the luck of Priya being picked for a dance gala so she only has a couple of hours of lessons a day. I think it's probably fair to say that me and Priya have been on a mission to wear down any objections, but even after all our planning Mum was still wavering. I think it was Dad who finally persuaded her that it was a good idea for me to come here. I overheard them talking one night…

"Let her go, Uma. I remember when I was her age I got so into tracing my roots. I drew up this whole journey of my dad's family from Poland to the East End. It's why I became interested in history in the first place."

Good old Dad!

"I suppose I did visit at her age…so it's only fair to let Mira go too." Mum sighed as if a part of her was actually afraid to let me come here. I don't know why, but I intend to find out.

Now here I am, crushed up close to all these people yelling instructions over each other's heads, scrambling for cases and trolleys, I'm being jostled backward and forward, but mostly backward…

The air-conditioning is either switched off or broken and sweat patches are spreading embarrassingly under my T-shirt. Jidé says boys sweat, girls glow, but I reckon whatever spin you put on it, it's the same. There's no way I can meet Anjali and Priya looking and smelling like this.

Gradually people start to steer their trolleys, laden with cases, back out through the crowd so that I catch sight of the conveyor belt for the first time. No sign of *my* case yet. Suddenly my stomach tenses into a nervous knot of excitement…I know it sounds a bit sad, but I've loved everything so far—the takeoff, the hot towels, and even the moment when I handed over my passport to the sour-faced uniformed woman sitting behind her glass screen. She checked me against my photo a couple of times and for a second I thought she wasn't going to let me through, but then she handed my passport back to me and said, "Welcome to Kolkata," without even glancing up.

I take another look at my passport photo. I suppose I do look different now. I was only twelve when this was taken. Jidé laughed his head off when I showed it to him, remembering me like that. I've got jet-black hair (no sign of dye) tucked neatly behind my ears and I'm wearing no make-up (not even eyeliner or lip gloss). No dangly earrings either, just neat little gold studs. My braces must have just been fitted, because my mouth looks all pouchy, like I'm struggling to stretch my lips closed over them.

"Have I changed that much?" I asked Jidé as he handed the passport back to me.

"Smile!" he said, snapping a photo on my dinky digital camera, the one Mum and Dad gave me for my birthday. "What do you think?" he asked, laughing and showing it to me.

It's a good photo…It actually makes me look like I've got cheekbones! The best ones are always when you don't expect them to be taken, but I still can't get used to myself without my braces. They only came off a few days ago. I scan from Jidé's photo to the passport picture. It's still me…the eyes are just the same, but I look so little girly compared to now, and my hair's so neat! I can't believe Jidé liked me when I looked like that! I stow the camera and my passport safely back in my bag and feel around for the photo of him I always carry around with me. I don't know why I love this one so much, but it was taken when we first met. I can't believe how young he looks either! Just thinking of Jidé makes me feel a very long way from home. I wonder where he is now, probably on his way to France on the bus, winding up through the mountains.

Maybe it will make it easier to be away from him, not being able to be in touch for at least two weeks.

Maybe…

﹏ ✛ ﹏

I glance over at an old couple who are waiting patiently for their cases. They arrived in baggage claim just ahead of me, so maybe there's no need to panic…yet. They're not, anyway. The woman's sitting on an empty trolley and the old man's standing next to her, one hand resting on her shoulder. The woman idly unravels her tight gray plait and the old man lifts his hand and runs his fingers from the top to the bottom of her silvery waves. She tilts her neck backward and rests her head in his hand.

"My Iris," I hear him whisper to her. She looks up at him and smiles, and he struggles to bend toward her to kiss her on the lips. I don't know why it's so embarrassing for two old people to show that they love each other *like that*, but it just is. You hardly ever see that sort of love between people their age. Jidé and I have been together for two years, nearly, and that's way longer than any of our friends. I wonder how long those two have known each other. Probably most of their lives, like my Nana Kath and Granddad Bimal. Poor Nana Kath—it must be so hard for her to live on her own now. She said she would come with me, and I believed her, but she's not well enough. Now I think of it, the person who was happiest that I was coming here was Nana Kath.

"I spent years trying to persuade your granddad to take time off work to go back and visit his family. You're going to love Kolkata. And you must send my love to Lila," she told me.

Apparently Nana went to Kolkata for the first time after she and Granddad got married, and she loved it, meeting my great-grandma and getting to know Granddad's sister Lila, who taught her how to cook the best curries and sweets. Nana Kath is the most amazing cook. Just thinking about her curry makes my tummy rumble. Granddad always used to joke that his English wife was a better cook than any of the Bengali wives he knew!

It's actually quite weird how much the old man with the trolley reminds me of Granddad. With his thin V-necked sweater, striped shirt, tie, smart trousers, and shiny shoes, he looks just like he's stepped out of Granddad's wardrobe.

I must be staring, because the old man catches me watching him and nods in my direction. How embarrassing is that! I quickly look away. I never mean to stare, but sometimes it feels like I'm in a sort of trance, as if I'm watching a film being acted out in front of me and I forget that *I'm* actually part of what's going on and that I can be seen too! I get so caught up in people-watching that I forget that it's really rude to stare. I suppose what I try to do (because it wouldn't feel right to take an *actual* photo) is take a photo in my head so I can pluck it out of my memory and paint or draw it later. Jidé says I'm always staring. He usually gives me a nudge to snap me out of it.

The old man is still watching me as I turn back to the carousel and pretend to be interested in the same parcels, cases, and rucksacks I've been watching for what seems like forever, going round and round on the dull gray belt. Some of them are so well sealed, their surfaces plastered with addresses in permanent marker, I get the feeling that whoever packed them didn't really believe that they would arrive. Then the dreaded "what if" thoughts start to bombard me. What if my case doesn't turn up? What if I've waited here for so long that Aunt Anjali and Priya have given up on me and aren't there on the other side of that wall? What if Priya and me don't get on? I mean, I hardly know her—all we've done is Facebooked and Skyped and the odd phone conversation. What if…?

I take my mobile out of my bag to call Anjali, but I can't seem to find a network. What if they've left and I can't get in touch with them? Suddenly my heart's racing. I know I need to keep calm, but this is exactly why I exploded at Mum. Since Granddad died she's been getting Nana Kath to teach her how to cook Indian food, and the day before I left she made this unbelievable feast all by herself. Not as good as Nana Kath's curry, as my little brother Krish couldn't help pointing out, but still tasty. The thing that got on my nerves though is that she kept trying to use the meal as a sort of rehearsal for me.

"How do you say…that was delicious?" Mum drilled me for the hundredth time. But all the words she thought she was teaching me I'd heard Granddad say anyway, and I remember them.

"*Khub bhalo*," I said, just to get her off my case.

I don't know what her problem was, but for the last few days before I left she was so stressed and uptight. Dad said she was just worried about me flying alone, but it wasn't just that. She kept telling me what I had to wear, what I had to pack, what presents I had to give to who, and what I should say to Anjali. It was as if she was trying to make up for lost time and give me a crash course in all things Indian or something. She just went on and on at me about stuff that wasn't that important…and the things that would have been really useful, like sorting out my phone, she didn't get around to doing. I just got more and more wound up until we had a huge fight. In the end I didn't even hug her at the airport or say good-bye properly. We don't really argue that much, me and Mum, not compared to most people I know, and when we do we always make up really quickly— usually by sending each other "sorry texts," even if we're both in the house, so it feels even more wrong to have left things the way we did.

I shove my mobile into the little pouch in my bag, but something's stopping it sitting snugly inside. I feel around and pull out a tiny parcel of white tissue paper, sealed with a red ribbon and a tag…

Sorry earrings! Peace offering!
Love you, Mum x

A lump forms in my throat and a wave of tiredness washes over me. I feel mean and guilty and wish I could "sorry text" her back, but my stupid phone won't work. I wish I could text Jidé too. Just a silly, nothing text like we ping-pong back and forth all the time. It just feels so weird not to be in contact with anyone. I take a deep breath to stop the tears welling up, walk over to a bench, and sit down. The argument wasn't really about anything much and now it feels stupid to have gotten so angry. After Mum's over-the-top supper I wandered into her bedroom to ask her if I could borrow her earrings—*these* earrings—she never wears them anyway. She was sitting on her bed looking at some old letters. I didn't think anything of it so I just sat by her side and peered over her shoulder…

5TH NOVEMBER 1981
Dear Uma,
    I can't believe that you are actually coming to see us, after all this time.

I quickly scanned to the bottom of the page and read…

There will be no more time to write now before you

come, so instead of waiting for your letters, as I have done for all these years, now I am waiting for you.

Your cousin,

Anjali x

I thought she was about to give this and all the other letters and photos to me, but I couldn't have been more wrong. As soon as she realized I was reading over her shoulder she jumped up off the bed, gathered everything up, and bundled it into a faded cloth-covered album that I'd never seen before. Then she placed it inside her old wooden chest at the end of her bed where she keeps all her precious, *not-to-be-messed-with* things. She gave me no explanation. Nothing! So all I did was ask her a few questions about when she went to India at my age and what she and Anjali got up to. She's told me bits and pieces before, so I wasn't expecting her to go off into a rant—telling me it was none of my business and to stop digging up the past, whatever that's supposed to mean. What's weird is, normally she loves sharing stories about when she was growing up.

It felt like she was shutting me out when I just wanted to understand more about Kolkata. I don't think it was that outrageous of me to ask a few questions, considering I was about to fly halfway round the world on my own to meet my family for the first time.

That's why, just before we left for the airport, I snuck back into Mum's room and took her letter album. Jidé was right to tell me to put it back. I should never have taken it, because ever since then it feels like Mum's letters are burning a great big guilty hole in my conscience.

Maybe, just maybe, I can do something to put things right. So here's my deal: if there's such a thing as what I call Notsurewho Notsurewhat, what some people call God, good karma, bad karma…whatever forces are out there operating in the universe…

I'm going to go to the loos to freshen up and *if*, when I come out, my case is on that carousel I'll put Mum's letters away and never read them. When I get home I'll place them back in her old wooden chest and hopefully she'll never know I took them. No harm done. Bad karma reversed. Maybe…

I stand up as a tall moustached man wearing a military-looking uniform walks past me. I take a deep breath from my belly like I've learned to do in singing lessons, so my voice doesn't come out all weak and wonky.

"Excuse me, my case hasn't arrived…"

His eyes travel down my bare legs and I find myself tugging at the bottom of my denim miniskirt. He glances upward again but doesn't look me in the eye.

Instead he swipes something off his shoulder, as if I'm an insignificant insect that's been bothering him.

"Wait, little longer. Takes time," he finally mutters before wandering off.

Now I wish I hadn't bothered asking Creepy Guard anything. I scan the carousel again. There are only a few bags left, but none of them are mine.

Another wave of tiredness hits me and my stomach is well and truly tied in knots. I have got to get myself together before I meet Priya and Anjali. I walk over to the loos and lock myself in. It's like an oven in here! I start to undress and I take out the lemon wipes Mum packed for me. I wash the staleness of a night's traveling off my skin. I spray on some deodorant and begin to feel less grim. I fold my miniskirt and T-shirt into my bag and take out the soft cotton salwar-kameez, the one Granddad's sister, Lila, sent for me, the one I said I wouldn't be seen dead in...because Mum was going on and on about how important it was that I wear "appropriate clothing." The fine cotton is paper thin and a rich autumn orange, with a paisley black and red block print all over it. Orange is my favorite color and the cloth feels soft and cool against my skin. I can't believe I was so mean to Mum about it now.

I come out of the cubicle and look in the mirror. I take out my eyeliner and draw a black sweep over the top lid, arching slightly upward, and a thin line on the bottom lid like I always do. I comb my hair and then bend forward and throw it back again so it doesn't look too tidy.

As I open the door the old lady I saw earlier brushes past me and a wave of her gray hair sweeps across my shoulder, wafting along with it the sweet smell of lily of the valley perfume.

Because I'm looking backward and walking forward, I fall straight over a trolley that's neatly stacked up with cases. I just about manage to save myself from falling flat on my face, but I drop my bag and *everything* spills out across the floor. I grab my new camera (it seems to be OK) and my passport. The old man, who was pushing the trolley, is bending down now, helping to pick my things up and chuntering his apology in Bengali. I look at him blankly and he suddenly gets it that I don't understand. Now he's this close to me I realize he's wearing the same Old Spice aftershave that we used to buy Granddad Bimal for Christmas and birthdays. It makes me shiver how that smell brings me to feeling close to Granddad.

"Sorry!" He smiles at me as I try to collect myself together, along with all the "just in case" stuff I slung into my shoulder bag before I left. I'm so busy picking up tweezers, eyeliner, period stuff, mobile, iPod, *Wuthering Heights*, a photo of Jidé… that I completely forget about Mum's letter album until the old man hands me one of her postcards. I check around the floor to make sure nothing else has gone astray and then I hold out my hand for the old man to pass the card back to me, but he's busy inspecting the stamp.

He reaches in his pocket for his thick-rimmed spectacles and holds the postcard up closer to his eyes. The image is of a sculpture of a mother feeding her baby, the umbilical cord wrapped around their bodies like a vine.

"This takes me back...I thought so, yes, this is it," he says, tapping the card excitedly with his finger. "Nineteen sixty-six... Now that was a great gathering." The old man seems to have forgotten I'm even standing here.

I glance over to the empty luggage carousel and my heart sinks as I watch it slowly grinding to a halt. I suppose that's decided it. No case, and a stranger is holding one of my mum's precious cards in his hands. My stomach coils into an even tighter knot.

The old man is looking up at me as if he's waiting for an answer to a question.

"Dr. Nayan Sen," he's saying, handing me back the postcard and shaking my hand. "You know, I went to this very conference."

"My granddad was a doctor," I blurt out. Why am I always so awkward with strangers?

He looks at me with new interest.

"His name?"

"Dr. Bimal Chatterjee," I answer automatically.

"I don't believe it!" he says, his eyes bulging in surprise. Suddenly he laughs so hard that he starts to cough and splutter. He's wheezing as his wife comes out of the loos smelling even more strongly of perfume. She leads him over to a seat.

"Iris, Iris...this is *Bimal's* granddaughter. Can you believe?

Such a shame we lost touch. Remember Bimal and Kath?" he asks, shaking her plump arm and making her whole body wobble.

"Of course I do," Iris smiles. She has a matter-of-fact Yorkshire accent. "Kath and I were practically best friends, but that was a very long time ago. Are you…Uma's daughter?"

I nod, feeling a bit weird that these strangers seem to know my family so well.

"Never! Seems like yesterday your mother was born. You do look a little like your granddad, something here about the eyes…" Iris says.

A bit of me wonders if this is actually happening. I feel like I've entered some sort of weird no-man's land. The faster I get out of here the better…I don't want to have to tell them about Granddad, and Anjali and Priya will be starting to worry, and I've still got to report my case missing…but I can't think of a way to cut this short.

"And how is my old friend Bimal? Taking a well-earned break, I hope."

It's too late now.

"Granddad died last year," I almost whisper. Even though this old couple are strangers to me, it still feels awful having to tell them…almost cruel to bump into someone by chance and then have to give them bad news.

Tears fill Nayan's eyes. Iris takes the handkerchief out of his pocket and hands it to him.

Although I haven't cried about Granddad for ages, Nayan's tears make my throat tighten and there's nothing I can do about it, my eyes well up too, again.

"Sorry! Sorry!" Nayan sighs and pats my knee. "Just so many memories. Happy memories really, and it feels like yesterday that your granddad and I were sailing to England together. Isn't that so, Iris? Time just goes like that." He clicks his fingers and his wife smiles fondly at him as he trumpet-blows his nose to pull himself together.

"Here…take my card. Kolkata and London address," he says, rummaging in his pocket. "Tell Kath you met us. We would very much like to reunite with her one day, catch up with news for old time's sake and…Here, you can write your home number and address in my book! Maybe we'll send Uma and Kath a card from Kolkata." He hands me a small green leather address book with a matching mini pen tucked in the side. It's the sort of "quality item" Granddad used to have. "Put it under B for Bimal and then I'll know where to look!" says Nayan, smiling at me.

I write my home address and phone number and swap the book for his card, which I place in my purse.

"Would you like us to wait with you?" asks Iris, glancing over at the luggage carousel.

"No thanks, I'm fine!"

I've rehearsed the moment when I meet Priya and Anjali so many times, and walking through to Arrivals with old friends of

Granddad Bimal and Nana Kath's is not part of my plan, no matter how nice they are.

"What a strange twist of fate to bump into you like this! A pleasure to make your acquaintance, Bimal's granddaughter…" Nayan raises his eyebrows in a question and holds out his hand for me to shake again.

"My name's Mira," I say.

He nods and smiles as he keeps my hand in his, as if he can't believe that we're parting so soon.

I do feel a bit weirded out as I watch the old couple wheel their trolley away. That's why the *tap, tap* on my shoulder makes me jump right out of my skin.

"Sorry! I am wandering around looking for miniskirt, not Indian girl in traditional dress!" Creepy Guard laughs at his own joke. "Your family are waiting for you, worrying where you are. Baggage may be lost. Make some report. Better not wait more, or you may be lost too." He fires these orders at me then goes off through customs. I suppose I have to follow him.

Now he's sitting behind a desk.

"Probably your case is traveling in other direction," he chuckles, not exactly kindly.

I nod without looking at him and start to walk past.

"One minute! Quick check of hand luggage," he demands.

I open my bag, feeling slightly sick that I have to let him paw over my belongings.

18

"What is this?" He asks, pulling out Mum's letter album.

"Personal letters," I explain.

He looks up at me with a mischievous glint in his eye and begins to pull them out one by one: photos, cards, and letters. He lays them on his white Formica table, just for his own amusement, I think. A photo of Mum and Aunt Anjali I've never seen before, hugging each other and grinning happily, catches my eye.

"This is you?" he asks.

"My mum and aunt," I tell him.

"Looks like you!" He smirks, glancing down at my covered legs, as I gather up the letters and place them back in the album.

A few minutes ago I could have put these letters away forever, but now, after all that stuff with Granddad's friend and Creepy Guard putting them on display, it feels like I don't have much choice anymore. There is no way I will be able to stop myself from reading them now. Bad karma or not.

As I walk through to Arrivals I hold on to my silver bracelet, twisting its small artichoke-heart charm round and round. I don't think I've ever felt such a mix-up of emotions as I'm feeling right now, as I take my first steps into India on my own.

Meeting Priya

✾✾✾

"Mira! Mira!"

I suppose that must be Priya leaping up and down, hollering and waving. She looks nothing like she did last week on Skype…I'm sure she had long hair. As I draw nearer she vaults over the barrier and sprints toward me with her arms opening into the widest and warmest of hugs. The tears that have been threatening to spill over for the last half-hour suddenly cascade down my face. To meet a whole side of your family in the flesh, for the first time in your life, is the strangest feeling in the world, sort of like coming home.

Anjali steps forward and enfolds me in her graceful arms and the soft folds of her cotton sari. Her hair's pulled back into a tight bun, and without wearing a spot of make-up she still looks beautiful. She takes my head in her hands and studies my face. The tears are rolling down her cheeks too.

"So pretty, like your ma at your age." She smiles at me and kisses my cheek. "We were getting so worried about you. How was your journey? Tiring, na?" She sighs, wiping my smudged eyeliner away.

"Ha! You didn't even recognize me!" Priya laughs and scruffs up her hair, which is now a pixie crop with hennaed red tips. "And look at you, all trad! Anyone would think *I* am the London chick and you are the Hindu princess!" Priya wafts my *chunni* scarf over my shoulder, blows an egg-sized gum bubble, then pops it with her tongue.

"Priya!" scolds Anjali.

"Want some?" Priya grins and hands me a piece.

The peppermint feels fresh and cool in my mouth.

I can't wait to brush my teeth properly.

"Well, thank goodness you're here safely. We thought you were lost, let me take...but where is your case?" asks Anjali.

"Is that *all* you brought?" Priya gasps, taking my shoulder bag from me.

"Priya! Give Mira a chance to breathe! You should know, Mira, that *all* of this"—Anjali points to Priya's hair, and then down to her skinny jeans and what look like brand-new red Converse—"all of this is done in your honor!"

"I was cutting my hair anyway, Ma. I told you that *ages* ago." Priya shrugs, then turns to me. "So where's all your stuff?"

"My case is missing."

Anjali claps a hand to her forehead in a gesture of total despair. "Typical!" she snaps and then strides over to an official. But, by her increasingly passionate hand gestures and his crossed arms and shaking head, I can tell that she's not having much luck. After a while she comes back toward us, smoothing her damp hair away from her face.

"Don't worry, Mira. If it doesn't turn up, we have everything you need here. It'll be a great hardship for her, but I am sure my Priya won't mind taking you shopping!" Anjali laughs, trying to put a bright spin on things.

"That'll be *such* a chore! I hate shopping! But I suppose I *could* just make an exception for you, coz! I'll take you to the mall. You'll love it. All the shops you've got in London and more!" boasts Priya.

"But I brought presents for you all." I can hear a wobble in my voice and I swallow hard.

"Forget about presents! *You* are the present. Come on, you must be exhausted. Let's take you home. I'll call about the bag later." Anjali sighs, then walks toward the exit, gesturing for me and Priya to follow.

I can't bear the fact that all my clothes are missing. All the T-shirts Jidé's given me—my favorite Banksy one with the girl with the red balloon, and the one with the peace sign on it that he bought for me in Brighton last summer. And *what* was I thinking, packing Jidé's note in my case?! It seemed like a good idea because whenever I'm feeling stressed I just read Jidé's words and I can't help feeling happy again. I miss him so much already…Even though I know it by heart, if that note's lost I can never replace it. If he wrote me a new one, it wouldn't be the same. Maybe losing it is some sort of payback for taking Mum's letters.

"What were you going to give me anyway?" whispers Priya, breaking into my thoughts.

Anjali overhears her then turns and shoots her an "I'll deal with you later!" look. I wonder if *all* mums, wherever you live, anywhere in the world, have the same silent repertoire of reprimands.

Priya takes my arm and squeezes it tight. Walking arm in arm with her feels so natural, like we've been friends forever. It's only now that I realize how nervous I've been about meeting her, and Anjali, and how relieved I am that they're so lovely.

A flock of tiny birds shoots ahead of us, swooping low; shaving the air millimeters from my head. I automatically duck down.

"Only airport birds," says Priya. "They're always passing through, just like all the other international travelers! That's going to be me one day. New York, Paris, London…" She sighs as we watch the birds dart between people and luggage.

"And I'm *never* having kids," announces Priya, shaking her head at a little girl who's throwing a tantrum. Her mum looks exhausted. "Don't see why I should add to this crazy population! I'll just travel, like you, Mira, free as a bird…"

Anjali smiles knowingly at Priya's chatter. "Never is a very long time!" she says, catching my eye. For a moment a look of sadness sweeps the smile from her face. She quickly turns away and walks briskly toward the exit.

The electric doors open and I step out of the airport and into the fierce furnace of Kolkata. So the air-conditioning wasn't broken after all. No amount of Mum warning me how hot it was going to be and trying to persuade me that Christmas was a cooler time for me to come here could have prepared me for this. I open my mouth to gulp some air, but the heat's already curling its way down my throat. Only five steps out of the airport, and my face, back, and legs are literally dripping with sweat.

"Don't worry, you'll get used to it," sighs Anjali, taking a handkerchief and wiping her own brow. She waves to the driver of a sparkling-clean white car that's drawing up next to us. A man with a head of thick silver hair jumps out and opens the trunk. Anjali must be telling him that my case hasn't turned up, because he shakes his head and slams the trunk closed again. Then he opens the back door and ushers me and Priya onto the wrinkly beige leather seats. Inside the car it smells of beeswax and incense.

"This is our friend and sometimes driver, Manu," Anjali tells me. "Manu, this is my cousin's daughter, Mira."

"Pleased to meet you, welcome to my Ambassador!" he says, grinning widely.

Priya raises her eyes to the sky. "This car is Manu's pride and joy!" she whispers, stroking the seats in mock adoration.

The engine starts up, but just as we turn out of the airport and onto the main road, we find ourselves surrounded by traffic and splutter to a standstill.

"I told you we should have taken the metro!" Priya groans.

Manu calls someone on his mobile, tuts, and then turns off his engine. "Apparently there's been an accident on the road ahead of us." He sits with his arms folded on top of his round tummy and closes his eyes.

Priya nudges me and grins in Manu's direction. "He's meditating," she says. "When the traffic moves off again, you have to tap him on the shoulder or he'd just sit there all day!"

Priya's English is almost perfect. I can't believe she's only fourteen and can already speak it so fluently. She goes to an American school where all the lessons are taught in English. It makes me feel ashamed that I can hardly speak a word of Bengali.

"And Ma's taking relaxation lessons from him." Priya laughs, nodding toward Anjali, who also has her eyes closed.

"Music's *my* meditation," she goes on, taking out her iPod. "I'll show you mine if you'll show me yours?"

She grins, holding out her hand for me to pass over mine. I do and then she hands me hers.

I've got such a random collection on it, especially all the stuff that Jidé loaded on for me. *What's* she's going to think of me?

"You might not like some of it." I say apologetically.

"Maybe you won't like mine either." Priya shrugs, plugging herself into my earphones.

I press shuffle, landing on something I've never heard before. It's a mixture of street sounds, people talking and children playing, fusing into classical Indian music with a dubstep, heavy bass thing building underneath.

"That's my own mix," says Priya, moving closer to me and listening in. "But check out some of Sukh Knight's sounds—they're totally awesome!" She takes an earphone and searches through for me, choosing more and more tunes for me to listen to. "And what about the Engine-Earz…if only we could mix it up like them." She sighs wistfully.

"We?"

"There's a few of us experimenting with dubstep."

"I know people who listen to stuff like this for hours," I tell her, thinking about my friend Ben.

"Been to Fabric or XOYO?" she asks excitedly.

"Not yet. I mostly do festivals!" I tell her.

"So we can go to Fabric together when I come to see you in London!" She plugs herself back into my iPod and I realize that I haven't got anything anywhere near as experimental as this. What I do is get completely obsessed with one or two

26

artists for a while—it's Adele, Florence, and Bombay Bicycle Club at the moment—then I sort of listen myself out and start on someone new.

"Joplin!" says Priya, closing her eyes and waving her hands around in the air. She lifts her bum off the seat and gyrates her hips as she sings along, as if she's in music heaven. The suited man in the new-looking estate car that's pulled up alongside the Ambassador is laughing his head off. Priya notices and pops a gum bubble toward his window, as a grand finale. She just doesn't care who's watching her. I suppose, because I knew she was into classical dance, I thought she'd be all quiet and serious, but she's the complete opposite! I wonder what she thought I'd be like.

"Soooooo retro! Haven't heard this in *ages*!" she sighs as she scrolls through the rest of my playlist. If I'd thought the first thing Priya would do was listen to my iPod I would have cleaned it up a bit, but it's too late now. She skips over all the mainstream stuff, but at least she seems to be finding some tracks she likes…

"I'm not the best singer!" she laughs, but she's so confident it doesn't even matter that much.

"Jidé loaded that on for me before I left," I mumble.

"Sounds like he doesn't want you to forget him!" Priya smiles and unplugs herself. "Mind you, from the Facebook photos I've seen of him, you're not likely to do that. He's drop-dead gorgeous! Got any more pics?"

I rummage in my bag.

"Nice camera," Priya says as I switch it on and scroll through a few photos I took of Jidé before I left. She wolf-whistles.

I can't help laughing, because I know he's good looking, but I just don't go around saying it! I suppose we've been together for so long, sometimes I don't even think about what he looks like anymore.

"A great way of finding out who someone is, is listening to their iPod! Let me guess…with that big laugh, you're really a quiet one, storing it all up! A bit romantic, retro, arty, on the hippy side, the lyrics get you every time! Am I right?"

"Pretty much!" I laugh again.

"Smile!" I say, holding up my camera to take a photo of her. I haven't got used to using it yet, and it takes me a few seconds to switch it back to photo mode. By the time I do, Priya has managed to produce a great big green bubble!

"My first photo in India!"

"Now it's your turn! What does my iPod say about me?" Priya asks, slumping back on the seat and waiting for my answer.

"You're into dance music, bass, dubstep, fusion…a bit radical. I don't really know how else to describe this!" I say, plugging an earphone back in.

"And that's just the music!" She winks at me.

She's the kind of person who makes time fly. Whatever happens on this trip, it's definitely not going to be boring. We've already been sitting in this queue for over an hour, but it feels like only ten minutes have passed.

As I look out of the window at the city skyscape, I wonder what Kolkata will be like. I've got a guidebook and I looked some stuff up online, but the pictures that have stuck in my head are all from Granddad's stories. He brought the place alive for me—telling me about the streets around where he grew up, the food he ate and the people and places that were important to him. The strange thing is that Granddad's memories have become the most real things about Kolkata for me, if that makes any sense at all, but his memories of Kolkata were of how it was over thirty years ago.

So now that I'm actually here, looking out of the window at these high-rise flats and swanky new office blocks, it's a bit of a shock, because it doesn't look anything like how I imagined it through Granddad's eyes.

One of the skyscrapers is for a huge telephone company. It makes me think of Nana Kath. If she suspects she's being called by someone in India she always wants to chat. They'll be ringing to ask some marketing question and she starts by proudly telling them that her name's Chatterjee and then they make the mistake of commenting on the name and she tells them all about how she and Granddad were married and that he was from Kolkata… she just launches into one…and after a while you can always sense them desperately trying to find a way of ending the call. It

29

makes me laugh, because Nana Kath always has the last word. "Well, actually I think you'll find that *you* called *me*. What was it you wanted to ask me, anyway?"

Me and Nana Kath watched a program once where a girl from a village just outside Delhi was being trained to work for one of those call centers. She had to learn to speak in a Yorkshire accent, just like Iris's.

It showed the girl walking to work alongside some cows and cramming onto a crowded train heading for the city. She had a screen in front of her telling her what the weather in Matlock was like. She had to learn "local knowledge" about what cricket matches were on and even what a Yorkshire pudding was (though neither of us could work out how that would ever come in handy).

"I'm never fooled," Nana Kath said after the program finished, "because if you listen, there's always a little delay at the beginning of the call that gives the game away—a tiny pause that says, 'this is pretend.' And pretending's not a real connection."

I think she was right. It seems like the weirdest way of being connected, people pretending to be who they're not and where they're not, in order to make someone trust them more.

When I look out of the window at the land around the airport I get the same feeling of things not being joined up, like one of those thousand-piece jigsaw puzzles my brother Krish insists on buying from jumble sales. He spends hours making them, only to find that there're always swathes of the jigsaw missing—whole chunks that don't piece together. This landscape is like that too. There are no proper pathways or pavements leading from the road to the grand entrances of the high-rise blocks. I wonder how people actually get into work. They must have to walk across the scrubland, past all the slum dwellings that line the roads, to get to their brand-new sparkly offices. To me the new buildings are like giant glass flowers and the slum dwellings look like weeds, with heads of blue tarpaulin…but they're both growing out of the same scrubland. Under the flimsy plastic roofs I see makeshift kitchens, bathrooms, and bedrooms. It feels wrong that these slums are reflected in the new, mirrored surfaces of the swanky high-rises, like a really old jigsaw and a really new one have been flung together. These two worlds shouldn't exist side by side. It feels like the old world should become extinct before the other is allowed to grow. Or maybe that's what will happen eventually. Granddad was right, he said, "when you go to India, Mira, your eyes will pop out of your head, and I know *you* don't miss a thing."

In one corrugated iron shack, a mother is plaiting her daughter's hair. The girl wears a clean white shirt and a pleated bottle-green skirt. Priya catches me staring at her.

"Uniform! *Such* oppression. I don't suppose you have to wear those in your school," she says.

"Actually, we do."

She looks a bit disappointed. I think of all the times I've complained about the boring black skirt and white shirt we have to wear for school. But looking at this girl wearing her clean, crisp uniform makes me see it differently somehow. You wouldn't be able to tell, when she's at school anyway, whether she's rich or poor, at least not by the way she looks. So I suppose in that way the uniform gives her a sort of freedom.

As the girl stands up, her mother inspects her nails and rubs a cloth over her shoes, smiling her approval at her daughter before the girl heads off down the road lined with giant glass buildings, away from the weeds and the dirt shack that's her home.

"*Work hard at school, Mira. The greatest freedom is the freedom to be educated.*" Granddad used to say that all the time and, looking at this little girl, I think I understand what he meant.

Huge billboards tower over us. Four men arrive wearing nothing but thin lungi cloths wrapped around their bottom halves, like Granddad sometimes wore when he was relaxing. Between them they carry a giant scroll of paper rolled around long bamboo sticks. Toddling next to them is a little boy. He has huge eyes, a mop of black hair, and the sweetest dimply smile. He catches me watching him and waves excitedly. I wave back, but Priya grabs hold of my arm and lowers it.

"*Don't* encourage him!" she says sharply.

"OK, sorry," I mumble, not really knowing why.

The boy walks barefoot among the rubble and the dust of the

road. He's only wearing a dirty piece of cloth around his bottom. He climbs onto the bamboo poles and the men shout at him. When he refuses to get off he's shaken and unceremoniously dumped on the ground, covered in a coat of white building dust. For a few minutes he stands and watches as the men unpack their bundle of poles, construct some makeshift scaffolding and begin to climb, barefoot, up toward the Bollywood beauty whose ice-white smile, silken locks, and glinting eyes are beaming down at all of us. Climbing on each other's shoulders like circus artists, the men pull down the superstar and replace her with another poster, this time of a glitzy-looking couple dancing together. The men sing as they paste up the new billboard stars, and the little boy beneath starts to dance along to a song he seems to recognize, moving his hips this way and that, making the exaggerated curvy movements of a Bollywood diva.

Priya laughs. The boy senses her moment of weakness and turns to her; his outstretched hands open and waiting. As soon as he's at the window Priya's smile fades and she fixes her gaze straight ahead, as if the boy has suddenly become invisible. When he can't get her attention he runs around to my side of the car, almost colliding with a moped, horn blaring as it weaves its way through the stationary traffic.

"Look forward," orders Priya.

I do as she says and ignore the *tap, tap, tap* of the dusty little hand at my window; the same-size hand as my little sister Laila's. "Ma'am, ma'am, little money, ma'am," I hear him say, his voice muffled by the glass.

The traffic whirs slowly back into motion around us. Dust Boy is gone from my window, but when I close my eyes I can still see his pleading face.

The car stops again almost as quickly as it started up. I'm beginning to think we'll never get to Priya's flat!

I look out of the windscreen and see that a naked man is lying in the island junction of a crossroads, alongside a thin dog. A policeman wearing a khaki uniform directs the traffic around him.

Anjali turns around, smiles at me and follows my gaze toward the naked man and dog.

"Is he sleeping?" I ask.

"Impossible to tell," Anjali answers sadly. "These people live on the streets and sometimes it happens that they die on the streets. That's why we take in only children at the refuge. When they're still young there is a chance that we can help them get off the street...to try to escape this kind of fate. You'll see." Anjali sighs, looking away from the naked man.

"But how long will he be left there?"

"He'll be moved on, eventually," says Anjali. "Anyway, you'll be coming to the refuge soon enough to help out and meet some of our wonderful children and staff."

For the moment I'd completely forgotten about the refuge, even though I know that going to work there is the only reason my school gave me permission to take time off. Anjali sent them all this information about the children's refuge and now I'm supposed to be out here as some sort of ambassador, writing a report on how my school and Anjali's refuge could become partners. Everyone else in my year is off on a geography trip to France looking at glacial scenery, and I would have been sitting on the top of a mountain in the Alps with Jidé too, but I managed to persuade my teachers that this was a one-off opportunity. I said I'd be teaching art at the refuge. I even said that when I get back I'd do some sort of presentation about my time working there, just so I could get an extra week off school. What was I thinking? It's so easy to promise stuff like that, but then reality hits and the truth is, now I'm actually here, I'm wondering what can *I* actually do to help children like Dust Boy? I can't even speak his language.

"Ma! Give her a break. She's only just arrived. Typical! There's no escape, Mira—she makes *everyone* do something for her beloved refuge! Look! Look! There's the new mall I'll take you to tomorrow." Priya sits up and points at a huge glass building in the distance. "I'll call my friends and we can hang out for a while. You'll find everything you need in there."

But when I think about Dust Boy and that little schoolgirl, and the man lying in the street, I wonder what I actually do *need*, compared to them. This all makes me feel guilty and pathetic that I care so much about losing my suitcase, but I just do.

We sit in silence for a while as I take in the "hotchpotch" (that was a Granddad Bimal word) of buildings, modern and old together. Even the pavements are jam-packed, with stalls selling things, people drinking tea, huge cauldrons of food being cooked up. *Mmmmmm*—delicious samosas are being dropped into bubbling-hot oil. I open my window and the tempting smells hit my nostrils and travel down to my belly, which rumbles greedily. I realize I haven't eaten for hours, because I couldn't bring myself to eat the mush that was the so-called "vegetarian option" on the plane. I'd like to ask Manu to stop the car so I can jump out and grab a packet of spicy samosas. Granddad always used to say that one of his strongest memories when he was a little boy was eating bubbling hot puri from street-side stalls. Sometimes he said he used to dream of the time he walked along a beach on holiday in Digha and had hot sticky jalebi sweets cooked up for him for breakfast. He used to make me laugh, the way he licked his lips when he told that story as if he could actually taste the memory. I think I know what he meant. I love being here in this street. It's not like any street I've ever seen. I think I've probably inherited Granddad's love of food, because tasting all the street food is one of the things I've been looking forward to the most.

"Hungry?" Anjali asks.

I nod, feeling a bit embarrassed that my tummy is gurgling.

"Promise me not to eat off the street! You won't have the stomach for it," Anjali says, as if she's reading my mind.

"Stop fussing, Ma! I'll look after her." Priya rolls her eyes at me.

"That's what I'm worried about!" jokes Anjali.

"But you like spicy food?" Priya asks.

"Yes! Granddad used to think it was hilarious to pretend that chilies were a kind of fruit and watch me bite into them and then go running for the tap. After a while I got used to the taste and now I love them!"

"He sounds fun. I wish I'd met him." Priya wraps a comforting arm around my shoulder.

"He was a great man." Anjali says, turning around and smiling sadly at me.

We pull into a dirt road, with a bony-bottomed cow ambling down the middle. In a really weird way its slow, steady walk makes me think of Granddad's! I don't think I can ever remember him hurrying anywhere. We always used to groan when we went anywhere with him, because even just a trip to the post office could take hours while he stopped every few minutes to talk to his patients. He always had time to talk to people about their worries. It's a bit strange how Granddad is so in my thoughts. I suppose it's inevitable I'll be thinking about him lots, now I'm finally here, in India, but somehow I can't shift the feeling that it's more than that…maybe it's because of bumping into his old friends at the airport.

Manu beeps his horn, and the cow slowly turns its head and blinks at him with its big brown eyes and long lashes, as if to say, "*What* is your problem?!" I swear that cow's got attitude. It doesn't move an inch, so Manu has to slowly maneuver around it, narrowly missing the precariously stacked fruit seller's cart on the corner. The mangoes look delicious.

We turn into a wide tree-lined street with electricity lines strung between well-looked-after buildings, like wire bunting. I feel like I've stepped into a different world.

Anjali smiles. "Welcome to our neighborhood."

Priya's Flat

✺✺✺

We draw up outside a small apartment block with a wrought-iron arch, painted pale green, at the entrance. It looks quite retro, probably 1930s. Through the arch is a leafy green garden that must be watered all the time to keep it looking so lush. A thin brown dog dozes on a metal swing chair.

When Priya flings open the door the dog springs up and bounds toward us.

"Ah! Bacha, Bacha, Bacha!" Priya giggles, stroking the little dog and snuggling it to her. "Bacha belongs to no one, but for some reason he thinks I'm his owner!"

"He recognizes a kindred spirit!" Anjali smiles.

"What? Moi? Very funny, Ma! *Bacha* means naughty!" explains Priya.

We climb the stone steps to the second floor, where a metal balcony overlooks an enormous tree that has glossy green leaves and orange flowers. Its branches reach up and up to the top of the three-story block.

Priya and Anjali take their sandals off on a communal landing. I take mine off too.

"Those are awesome!" she says, picking up one of my Converse and inspecting it closely.

Jidé calls them my "hippy feet" because of the hundreds of tiny flowers, hearts, rainbows, swirls, multicolored bindi patterns…anything really I've doodled all over them.

Priya puts my shoe back down and then places her hands on my shoulders and steers me through their front door and into an airy living room that has an archway off to the right. I look through and see a tiny kitchen with silver and copper pots hanging from hooks all over the ceiling and walls. We walk past it and into the living area, which has two sofas, a dining table and also a little computer desk, just like ours at home. I look behind it for the embroidered Rajasthani wall hanging that I saw when I Skyped Priya. And here it is, with its hundreds of tiny mirrors glinting back at me. The difference is, now here *I* am, on *this* side of the screen, and that does feel quite weird. When you're looking into a room from the other side of the world, you can think that it's just next door, but now home—Mum, Dad, Krish, Laila, and Jidé—feel a million miles away.

What I couldn't see through the screen, to the right of the

hanging, is some beautiful French windows that open out onto a balcony shaded by a canopy of leaves. "That's my bedroom," says Anjali, pointing down a corridor.

"By the way, Dinesh sends his love. He's sorry to miss you, but he couldn't rearrange his business trip. Anyway, hopefully this visit will be the first of many."

Priya is walking farther down the corridor.

"There's the bathroom, and *this* is our room," she says, pointing to the last remaining door. She grabs my hand and pulls me into her bedroom. "All mod conveniences here, en-suite and everything," Priya jokes, opening a door into a tiny shower room.

I look up at the little window high above the bed, which is covered by a leaf-patterned metal grid. The combination of the leaves rustling on the tree outside, the ceiling fan whirring and the cold marble under my bare feet make me feel sleepily calm.

"She has the best view," says Anjali, peering through the window to the enormous tree outside.

"Actually Janu's got the best rooftop view!" corrects Priya, pointing to the ceiling. Somehow I didn't think of the adopted boy Janu as still living here because of working at the refuge, but I suppose he must only be sixteen.

"This flat's an oasis from the heat and the chaos for all of us," says Anjali, "except for the racket that comes out of this room, of course!"

"I keep telling you it's called *music*, Ma!" Priya shakes her head.

41

"Mira, maybe you want to shower before eating," suggests Anjali. "I expect you could do with getting out of those clothes too."

I'm just about to tell her that it's not long since I changed into them, but then I realize that my top is already damp with sweat. The thought of having a cool shower and fresh clothes to step into is just about the best thing I can imagine right now.

"Priya, you'll find something for Mira to wear?" asks Anjali, wandering back into the living room. Priya casts Anjali a look as if to say, "Have you actually *seen* me compared to Mira?" Priya is tiny. I'd say she's smaller, and just as skinny, as my little brother Krish, who's only twelve. Even though we're the same age, I'm about two heads taller than her but, as Jidé likes to point out, I've got curves. In fact I'm probably closer to Anjali's size than to Priya's.

When I first started to grow I was so embarrassed that I kept trying to cover up with big sweaters and cardigans, but then I sort of got used to myself. My best friend (after Jidé!), Millie, and me made a pact that we weren't going to get hung up on the whole weight thing. There are girls in my class who will actually make themselves faint from not eating. It's so weird that people can be starving all around the world, and then people I know starve themselves because they want to be a size zero. Anyway, as Jidé says, being obsessed with how you look is about the most boring thing in the world. Even so, I would prefer it if I could borrow something of Priya's, but her clothes just won't fit me.

"Maybe you could ask your mum if she's got something she could lend me." I suggest.

"Poor you! I'll try to find something that's not *too* awful!" Priya mutters, wandering off toward her mum's room.

~ ✣ ~

The shower is icy bliss. I let the water run over my hair, face, and body, washing away the journey with sandalwood soap and shampoo. The warm, spicy smell takes me to Nana Josie's flat. She's burning sandalwood joysticks and dancing around the room with a paintbrush in her hand. The cold water streams over my face. I open my eyes to look down at the charm bracelet Nana gave me when I was only twelve, just before she died…that seems like such a long time ago. At least I didn't pack *this* away in my suitcase. I twist the little artichoke charm around and around. Holding on to it makes me feel like everything's going to be all right, just like Nana used to make me feel. It's a strange thing, memory…People say it fades over time, but I never want to forget the way she always used to know how I was feeling. The way I could always be myself around her.

I step out of the shower, wrap myself in a long white towel, and twist a smaller one into a turban shape around my head. Then I take a hand towel and pat dry the tiny silver leaves of my charm. I hear Nana's voice in my head, talking about the layers of the heart and love. I suppose if you love people who have died, but you still love them as much as you did when they were alive, then in your memory your love can actually keep them alive. Maybe that's why I keep thinking of Granddad all the time. I take a deep breath and look at myself in the mirror, towel-turban wrapped around my head. "Come on, Mira," I say to myself, "Step into the room." That's what Jidé always says to me when I'm daydreaming.

Priya has laid out a midnight blue and silver salwar-kameez for me and some knickers (still in their packet). It didn't even occur to me that I'd have to borrow *underwear*.

"Sorry about the underpants—at least they've never been worn!" Priya jokes. "First thing tomorrow, you and me are going shopping! But the salwar-kameez is OK. Ma says she's never worn it because the waist's too tight for her."

Priya's tall wrought-iron bed is like a work of art, with silk and mirrored cushions and bolsters at either end that make it look like a sofa. It's covered by the most beautiful quilt, made out of hundreds of random shaped pieces of cotton and silk, all different colors. Each bit of material is stitched together using an intricate pattern. When I think how long it took me to sew a bookmark in cross-stitch for

Mum once, I can't imagine how many hours it would have taken to make this quilt.

"You can sleep on my bed, and I'll sleep down here." Priya points to a roll-down mattress on the floor. "I don't sleep much anyway! I'll leave you to it," she says, closing the door behind her. I think she can tell, even though I'm trying to put a brave face on it, what a nightmare it is for me not having my own things.

I quickly dry myself and put on more deodorant—I'm starting to feel a bit paranoid about "glowing" on this trip! I step into Anjali's cotton trousers, tying them with the drawstring at the waist. They're tight at the bottom and they cling to my calves and ankles. Next I tug the long blouse over my head, and zip it up at the side. It's fitted at the waist. I walk into the bathroom. There's no full-length mirror, but standing on my tiptoes, from what I can see, it actually fits. I smile at myself in the mirror, I'm still getting used to the sight of me with no braces. It's like I've been hiding behind them for so long that now they're not part of me anymore I feel a bit exposed. I tie my wet hair back into a scruffy ponytail and walk out into the living room.

Priya whistles at me and looks down at my legs. "Love the churidar. You look amazing!"

I can feel myself blushing at the compliment.

"What a figure!" says Anjali, standing between me and Priya

45

and wrapping an arm around each of our shoulders. "My beautiful girls…I told Uma, while you're here, Mira, you're like a second daughter to me. There is *nothing* you can't ask of me, OK?"

"OK!" I say, wondering what would happen if I came straight out with the questions I asked Mum a few days ago. *How come you two lost touch for so long?* I ask the question in my head and it seems to hang in the air, waiting to be answered.

Priya and I sit on the benches around the little wooden table, drinking hot sweet chai as Anjali lays out a feast. There are spicy chickpeas, rice, dhal, fried fish, samosas, chapattis, and yogurt. My mouth waters and I eat until the fitted waist of Anjali's top feels a bit tighter than it did half an hour ago! Then, as if she's been waiting for this moment, Priya jumps up from the table and produces a platter of sweets.

"In honor of Mira!" She starts tucking in.

Anjali taps her hand and tuts. "At least tell Mira what's on offer before you wade in."

Actually I know most of them, rosogolla, sandesh, jalebi, ladoo…

"What's this?" I ask, picking up a small clay pot.

"*Mishti doi*—sweet yogurt," Priya mumbles through a mouthful of the set creamy yogurt, the kind that Nana used to make for Granddad by straining the curd through muslin.

"Don't forget you have to dance in a few minutes," Anjali reminds her, "So don't eat too much."

46

"Please, Ma! Can't I just have *today* off?" pleads Priya.

"You know you can't. It's too close to the gala," says Anjali sternly.

Even though Anjali's really kind, she's got this bright, sharp look about her that makes me think she could be quite tough if she wanted to be. I suppose doing the work she does at the refuge, she has to be strong.

Priya sighs and takes her left hand in her right, as if she's battling with herself…her right hand tempted to grab a sweet; her left hand holding her in check.

"OK, OK! But save some for me!" She laughs. "I'll be back in about two hours." She grabs a bag and dances out of the door.

I get up and start to clear away the pots, but Anjali puts her hand on mine to stop me.

"Not today!" She smiles. "You must rest now."

I feel like I should argue with her, but I'm suddenly so tired that I know that if I don't lie down soon, I'll keel over.

"We'll Skype your ma later to tell her you're here safe and sound," Anjali says, pointing toward the computer.

I nod and wander through to the bedroom. That's something I'm not looking forward to. I don't know if I can face Mum yet. The only person I really want to talk to right now is Jidé.

Priya's Room

❁❁❁

I really love the colors of this flat: pale greens and lilac blues. Priya's room is a sort of mint green.

If Priya were a color she would *definitely* be peppermint. I don't know what I was expecting of her, but it wasn't this punchy peppermint Priya, all fresh and sparky and full of surprises!

I feel a bit like I've been holding my breath since I left London, so it's a relief to be on my own now. I walk round Priya's room, just taking it all in. Her beautiful bed is under the window at the far end of the room and right next to it is a low wooden table. One wall is covered by a white storage unit, with a desk and shelves built in, and to its right and left are floor-to-ceiling wardrobes. Even though I know it's nosy of me, I walk over and open one side of the doors. Clothes come piling down on top of me. I *thought* it looked suspiciously tidy in here. I have to stop myself from laughing, because this is exactly what I do when Mum tells me to sort out my room. Maybe it's what everyone does! I quickly stuff the clothes back in and wedge the door shut.

I hardly dare open the other wardrobe, but when I do it's like discovering a whole new Priya. There's a flash-looking music deck, earphones, and hundreds of CDs all stacked in alphabetical order. The way it's all laid out so carefully gives me the impression that Priya would know if anything was moved so I close the door without touching a thing.

I slowly walk along the only free wall in the room, where Priya's stuck CD covers and bits torn from magazines, mostly stuff about bands I've never heard of, but mixed in with all this are photos of her dancing, holding the most amazing poses. I hardly recognize her. She looks so classical and…like she could be out of any period in time.

At the end of her bed is an ancient cupboard, carved and painted in flaky fading orange, green, and gold paint. It's about my height. I run my fingers around the cornice. I've never touched such beautiful carving. It's a shame about the one small piece of wood missing that breaks the pattern, but even so I love the way the leaf motif repeats and repeats. The cupboard is split into two, with a wooden slat down the middle and two thick shelves on either side. There are holes where hinges for doors used to go. It looks like the sort of cupboard that you would want to store precious things in, so it feels right that Priya has filled it with big coffee-table books about classical dance and all her dancing trophies. It reminds me a bit of Mum's wooden chest, the one I took her letter album from.

I lie down on Priya's quilt and look up through the tiny window, I can see blue sky glinting through the chinks in the canopy of green leaves. The worn lace curtains gently waft toward me, along with a faintly sweet smell. I close my eyes, but all I can think about are Mum's letters. No matter how terrible I feel, I know I'm going to have to read them and this time on my own is my chance to get it over and done with.

I pick up my bag and walk through to the shower room. I lock the door and take out the faded album. I look closely at the embroidered dancers decorating the cover. I take a deep breath and unfold the first letter.

Stolen Letters

✿❀✿

There are lots of cards in the album, because Anjali and Mum share the same birthday, 30 May, 1966. That much I do know because Granddad used to say how strange it was that Anjali and Mum were born on the same day and that mine and Priya's birthdays are only three months apart. I suppose that is quite a coincidence.

It's sweet to see the tiny, wobbly handwriting and funny little drawings by six-year-old Anjali (who was obviously obsessed with monkeys!). As the years go by the cards grow into letters and sometimes postcards, like this one Anjali sent from Khajuraho. The picture on the front shows naked sculptures in all sorts of positions. Thankfully this one didn't fall out at the airport or get leered at by Creepy Guard. It's funny to see Anjali's handwriting change over time, from baby scrawl to swirly grown-up script. I turn the postcard over…

To ARRIVE FOR 30 MAY 1980 (Here's hoping!)

Dear Uma,

A birthday card from our holiday in Khajuraho! It's all sex sex sex!

Prem is trying to make me embarrassed. Keeps asking me to explain how the positions these statues have got themselves into are possible! I told him, they're sculptures…they can get themselves into any position they want! They call them "erotic" statues! What do you think?!

Happy big 14th Birthday,

Love,

Your cousin,

Anjali

How embarrassing is that! You just don't want to think of your mum and your aunt having those sorts of thoughts.

I put all the letters and cards in order. There are only three actual letters—I thought there would be more than that. The first card is handmade and dated 1970, which would have made them four years old. There's a picture of three cheeky monkeys.

It just says in big babyish letters: *These are my monkeys. Love Anjali x;* with a drawing of a family of monkeys.

It's so sweet to see the wobbly writing, like Laila's.

There are tons of cards and letters from then all the way to

1981 (that must have been after Mum's visit), but then there's a massive leap across time to just one card in 2011, which has got a photograph of the most beautiful kingfisher on it.

6 JANUARY

Dear Uma,

We are all so sorry for the passing of your father. He was a wonderful, caring man. I remember his hearty laugh, his humor, and his warm nature.

With very much love even across all this space and time,

Anjali, Dinesh, and Priya x

Does this mean that Anjali didn't write to Mum for all that time? Maybe they just talked on the phone, but it's strange that they would go from writing several times a year to... nothing. There's not even a card for Mum and Dad's wedding here.

This kingfisher card feels like a sort of olive branch. So I was right—these letters must have something to do with why Mum and Anjali weren't in contact for so long, and, looking at the dates, maybe whatever happened between them was something to do with Mum's visit to Kolkata. I'm trying to wind my mind back to work out when Priya first sent me a Facebook message. Before I got to know her, the only contact we had with India was through Granddad's sister Lila, Priya's grandma, because she came to visit when Granddad was ill. I remember how excited Granddad and Nana Kath were when Lila arrived, and how much they enjoyed taking her up to meet all Nana Kath's brothers and sisters in the Lake District. Mum kind of named my little sister Laila after her because Lila came to see her the day after she was born. She was so happy holding baby Laila in her arms, and she sang her a song in Bengali. After Lila left Granddad started talking about going back home to see everyone and taking me with him. Lila called Mum after Granddad died, and I remember it clearly because she hardly speaks any English and Mum doesn't speak much Bengali so they just cried and cried together on the phone. Afterward Mum said it had made her feel better to cry with Lila. Now I think of it, maybe it was Lila who suggested to Priya that she should email me? It was just after Granddad died that Priya started Facebooking me.

Looking at some of these photos of Anjali and Mum, when they were teenagers, Creepy Guard was right, it could actually be me and Priya in these photos. The only thing that really makes Priya look different from Anjali is her short hair. It's sort of comforting to see these old photos. I don't understand why Mum wouldn't share them with me. I start to read the earliest letter.

3 JUNE 1979

Dear Uma,

As you've asked I will try to describe to you my (our) grandmother's house. It's in old Calcutta on a street called Doctor's Lane.

I don't know what you'd make of the narrow lanes, hidden away from the busy roads. I love wandering down these old mud streets that are crowded with rickshaws and bustling with people selling anything and everything. I don't expect cows walk down your highways, but they roam freely here. The roads are lined with grand houses, but most of them are slightly crumbling now. The paint is flaking away, leaving the old brickwork peeping through as though a layer of skin has been grazed off.

Have you heard the story of our great-grandfather? His name was Pran. He used to give medicine out to the poor, and that's why our family has a special connection to this road. Pran died when your father was still a boy, but he always thought Bimal Uncle would be the next one in the family to treat the sick in Doctor's Lane.

Grandmother's house, where we live too, to help look after her, is one of the British-built houses, with shuttered windows and iron balconies on every floor. It goes up and up for four levels and on the top there's a roof terrace where Grandmother grows fruit trees. I always think the

55

branches growing above the top balcony make the house look alive.

The front door is my favorite on the street. It has two huge sandstone pillars that have swirly patterning at their tops, and above them there's more wooden carving, painted green with tiny orange flowers scattered across its surface. The door itself is heavy as a tree and has great metal hoops for turning. On either side of the handle are panels full of grand bouquets of flowers. It's our Uncle Shudi who carved and painted this door. He made it for Grandma's last birthday. I wish you could have seen her face when they brought her slowly down the wooden staircase through the house, past the floor we live on and out onto the street.

She looked up at her precious door, and you know what she said? "This door will last for longer than you and me and longer than this house even. It's a work of art." Then she walked back up the wooden stairs, past the shop where Shudi Uncle does his carving (and before that Great-Granddad used to have his doctor's surgery), past the kitchen, and up, up, up, back to her bedroom.

I will paint a picture of Dida, your thakurma, how she was on her eightieth birthday.

She settles on her huge metal bed, propped up by cushions. She's sitting on a cream quilt and wearing her thin white sari with gold edging, and a small blue cardigan rests over her

56

shoulders. She sits cross-legged in the middle of her mattress, like a tiny frail doll, and her thin strands of white hair are pulled into a tight bun.

"Dance for me, Anjali, on my birthday," she whispers in her dry crackly voice, and then she asks me to turn the little silver key with the heart-shaped end and open her sari cupboard. She says that it's the most beautiful piece of carving Shudi Uncle has ever made for her. Inside the cupboard are all her saris, hundreds and hundreds of them, in every color and style of silk and cotton.

This is our game. When she plays it she doesn't seem so frail and sleepy anymore. She likes me to choose a sari to wear to dance for her. I pick a turquoise one and I prance around the room to her old-fashioned sitar music. She taps her hand on her knee as I dance and her eyes begin to sparkle with happiness.

You asked me to tell you about the house, and I have ended up telling you about Dida. I suppose for me it's impossible to describe the house without the people in it. Probably what I have said is just how your father describes it anyway.

You should come and see it for yourself.

Your loving cousin,

Anjali x

When I finish reading I realize that my heart is beating too fast. It's strange how close I feel to Granddad, Mum, and Anjali reading these words. I scan over the same lines again and again and, as I read, my guilt for taking these letters starts to simmer up into anger that Mum wanted to keep all of this from me when she was asking the same questions herself!

Granddad used to talk to me all the time about his childhood in the house in Doctor's Lane. When he knew he was too ill to fly to India he told me that the place he would have liked to go to more than any other was his old home. "You should go there, Mira; it was a beautiful house," he said.

"Are you OK in there?" calls Anjali through the bathroom door.

"Fine!" I shout back, jumping up and shoving everything back into my bag. I turn on the taps to pretend I'm washing my hands, hang the bag on the hook on the back of the door and then step out into the bedroom.

"I've just got to pop down to the refuge. Won't be more than an hour. It's very safe here. Manu's wife is only downstairs and Bacha's guarding the door! Unless you want to come with me?"

"I'll be fine here," I reassure her. All I can think about is getting back to the letters.

~ ✦ ~

I climb on the bed to look out of the high window and watch Anjali walk quickly down the stairs, appearing and disappearing, until she reaches the street below, where the golden-brown cow is still ambling around. It's so strange that in the middle of a city like this, with all the cars and shiny glass buildings and technology, cows still wander the streets.

Now that I'm here I'm starting to feel closer to the stories Granddad used to tell me. Like the time he talked about Partition, when the British left India and there was so much chaos and bloodshed that all the medical students were sent to treat the wounded passengers fleeing their old homes and coming in off the trains to Howrah Station. I'll never forget the way he described helping a woman in one of the carriages to give birth, and there were people around her already dead, and then she died and Granddad carried the baby out into the city to an orphanage. He said that the pavements smelled of blood. He remembered everything in so much detail it was as if it had happened yesterday. "I often wonder what happened to that baby," was the way that Granddad always used to end that story.

I know that it's really gruesome of me, but knowing that my granddad was connected to that moment in history made me want to read everything I could about Partition and Indian Independence from the British. I wouldn't have known so much about it otherwise, because it's not like they teach you about it in school. Sometimes I think about what it must have been like for his family in India when Granddad married an Englishwoman and stayed in Britain instead of coming back home.

Nana Kath's told me all sorts of stories about how difficult it was for them to marry in Britain, how the priest wouldn't marry a Hindu man in a church and what a shock it was for her parents at first that she married a "foreigner." She also tells me that gradually Granddad charmed everyone. I can believe that.

I think these stories about where you come from and the history of your own family help you to see where you stand in the world. I suppose it's because of Jidé telling me about what happened to his family in Rwanda that made me understand him better. I think I have a right to know about what happened in my own family and reading these letters seems the only way to do it, seeing as no one will tell me the truth.

As Manu's Ambassador turns the corner I step off the bed, lock myself in the bathroom again and open a thin pale blue airmail envelope addressed to:

Uma Chatterjee
2, Mill Lane
York Way
York
North Yorkshire
UK

I didn't even know Mum had ever lived in York. It sort of jolts me into a place that always makes me feel a bit weirded out, thinking of my mum as a Chatterjee not a Levenson"—her life before Dad, and before me. I would *never* give up my name. It would be like giving up half of myself.

6 OCTOBER 1980

Dear Uma,

I can't believe that you're actually coming to see us, after all this time. Ma's gone crazy preparing for your arrival. I'm telling you, if ABBA was touring India and coming to stay at our house, there would be less fuss than my ma is making of you!

Dida has ordered Ma to buy a silver service of knives and forks in your honor. You know, she just sits on her bed now at the top of the house like a queen and waits for the daughter of her "shudurer putro" (her "faraway son") to arrive. She says it will be the highlight of her older years to see the daughter of her beloved son Bimal sit on her bed beside her and sing.

Sorry! That's my fault. I told her about your voice, and you'd better be prepared because you are not going to get away with visiting your thakurma unless you sing to her! (In answer to your question, that is what you, as the son's daughter, should call her, and I call her Dida, because I'm her daughter's daughter.)

I didn't even know Mum had a good voice. With all the singing I've been doing recently, why wouldn't she have told me that she used to sing too? I've never heard her, not even in the shower!

If it's any consolation at all, I have to dance for her every day, so you and I can be the all-singing, all-dancing act together! You won't believe the pleasure it will give her. She has photos of you all around her bed, like a little puja (prayer).

We've been painting the walls, a mint-green color, Ma chose it; she said it would make you feel cool in the heat. On every single surface Ma's placed a fan, and when I came in from school yesterday I couldn't hear what anyone was saying to me over the noise!

So I guess we're just about ready for your arrival. You'll find everything that I've described to be more or less exactly as I told you, but I want to warn you about something.

You and I have been writing for so long that, in some ways, I feel like we know each other so well, but there are a few things that maybe I haven't described exactly as they are. You see, I've always felt free to say anything I wanted and occasionally I've told you things that I wanted to be true. You must realize by now that those six wise monkeys jumping in through my bedroom window every day were a creation to entertain you!

I don't remember Baba dying (I was only two), but Ma says the monkeys arrived soon after that.

So, what I'm trying to tell you is that nothing will be quite as you pictured it.

Now I'm writing this by candlelight because we've had another one of the electrical power surges I've never told you about. They can happen at any time of the day or night, and if they happen at night the city blacks out, but there's something I like about the way the darkness shrinks the whole city into one room; suddenly the birds go mad, as if to say, "You humans have switched off all your noise. Now it's our turn to take over."

There will be no more time to write again before you come, so instead of waiting for your letters, as I have done for all these years, now I am waiting for you.

Your cousin,

Anjali x

I could read these letters over and over again, just taking in every detail. I love the feel of the thin airmail paper, almost like material, and the sound of Anjali's fourteen-year-old voice, which is so full energy and excitement, like Priya's...These letters have so much history in them that I'm starting to understand why Mum wanted to keep them safe.

I take out the final letter.

6 March 1981

Dear Uma,

Thank you for your kind letter about Dida. We will all miss her so much.

What I want you to know is that I will never tell anyone, not your family or mine, that it was your idea. No matter how much they press me for the truth. And even though you ask me to tell you, there's no point in dwelling on what happened after you left.

It's awful. I don't want to upset you, but I just want you to know that we should both have thought more carefully about what we were doing. I should have made you understand how it is here...that some things are unjust and some people have nothing...and, even though we don't like it anymore than you do, it's not easy to fix. In many ways I feel responsible, because it was such a crazy, spur-of-the-moment act—I suppose I just wanted you to know that I care as much as you do. But how we tried to help was foolish and thoughtless and wrong.

I can't tell you, when I remember the sadness in our grandmother's eyes, how sorry I am for what we did, but I have not written to you to cause you pain.

I just don't know what there is left to say to each other at this moment in time. Of course, I will always hold you in my heart. I'm not blaming you—we are both equally responsible for running away with our imaginations.

I think we should stop writing to each other for a while.

I hope that one day we will meet again when the pain of this has passed.

Anjali

I search through the pile again, but there is nothing else until the condolence letter for Granddad in 2011. I read this last letter over and over, trying to work out what could have happened to make them stop talking for thirty years. There's no way the silence between them could have been "just losing touch," and I feel terrible now because it's obvious that the reason why Mum was in such a state before I left has something to do with what happened between her, Anjali, and my great-grandmother. I know Granddad went to Great-Grandma's funeral but then never returned to India after that. I feel like a thief stealing into someone else's house of memories. I suppose it serves me right for taking the album in the first place, because now I won't be able to let things lie until I know what really caused that silence. And I can't ask Mum or Anjali for the answers.

I stand up, go over to the sink and stare into the mirror. I didn't notice before that the frame is decorated with hand-painted cheeky-faced monkeys. I wonder if this mirror once belonged to little-girl Anjali. I look into it at the deepening rings of tiredness under my eyes and wonder if anyone else will be able to read on my face how guilty I feel. I take Mum's earrings out of my bag and push them through the half-closed-up holes in my lobes. It hurts, and I think maybe that's right, it should hurt, because I was so vile to Mum before I left, and she obviously felt bad about the argument…What if me coming here is all part of Mum's sorry to Anjali for whatever it was that happened between them all those years ago? What if…without even knowing it, *I'm* the olive branch?

I unlock the bathroom door, walk over to Priya's bed, and lie down, looking up through the great arching branches of the tree…All the images from Anjali's letters and a stream of questions bombard my mind as I read the letters over and over again.

When I can't read anymore I take out my iPod and listen to Jidé's playlist and it makes me wish more than ever that he was here with me…"Summer Breeze"…I've never heard this song before. Jidé spends hours trawling through old stuff on YouTube, and he always finds the perfect song for my mood. Lately he's been picking out songs he thinks I could sing. I think it's his way of encouraging me to write and sing my own stuff. He's always going on about what a great voice I have and that I should record it, so that I'm forced to believe that I'm good. But he would say that, wouldn't he?! I close my eyes and let the music wash over me, feeling the whisper of a breeze through the window, wafting that sweet smell toward me again. The tune is really pretty. I sing along to the refrain. It's catchy, the sort of thing that keeps floating through your mind.

My Lips Are Sealed

❀ ✹ ❀

Dust falling.
Dust through light,
Dancing glitter.

I try to catch the tiny specks, opening and closing, opening and closing my hands, reaching up toward a distant light. I look down. My hands are full of ash pouring between my fingers. Sand sifting through time. My head is numb and empty; the thoughts have drained out of me and all that's left is colors, hundreds of silken rainbow colors spiralling through the air, cascading toward me, length after length of colored silk shining through the darkness.

"Mira, is that you? Climb up!" calls a voice from above. That gentle lilting voice I know.

I climb and climb the lengths of cloth from pink to green to red and gold, up through turquoise blues and mustard. My arms ache so *badly I stop and try to catch my breath, but the air is full of ash, filling my lungs.*

"Only a little way to go!" says the voice in the darkness above my head, so I reach out for it and find myself clasping Granddad's hands.

"Be careful where you place your feet!" he says, pulling me to safety.

I nod at him and look down, down, down to the crater below, swirling with dust.

"What is that?" I ask him.

"History…takes time to settle." He smiles at me. "You know, Mira…as long as there are memories to hold on to, nothing ever really dies."

Then I feel his hand slip out of mine.

"Granddad!" I call, but nothing but my own voice echoing comes back at me.

❧ ✤ ☙

I'm trying desperately to search for where I am through a fog of dust, endless clouds, and a constant thudding in my head.

"Thought you would *never* wake up…" Priya grins. The doors of her wardrobe are thrown open and she's got something cranked up to full volume.

"What do you think of this track?"

"Heavy!" I mumble, but I'm obviously not that convincing because she turns it off.

"It's metal, punk, dubstep…crossover. They're all over this in the States, but maybe not the best to wake up to! Ma wouldn't let me disturb you, but I've waited all this time to meet you. I couldn't let you sleep anymore! Sorry! So much to show you, so little time!" Priya grins again and offers me a stick of gum at the same time as throwing three pieces into her own mouth.

"So this is the hub," she says proudly, spreading her arms wide. "It's where the magic happens! I'm just messing around really, learning to mix it all up."

I nod, but I'm finding it difficult to get my head back in gear. That dream sort of pulled me into somewhere deep, and now I feel like I'm having to climb back out again. I think Priya realizes I'm still groggy, because she walks over and sits next to me on the bed…and that's when I see, too late, that Anjali's letters are still strewn everywhere. How could I have been so careless? I gather the pages as fast as I can, but Priya's already holding one in her hands.

"This is Ma's writing, isn't it?"

I suppose there's no point in lying to her.

I nod.

"It's weird! So retro! I mean who writes letters these days anyway? Did your mum give them to you?" she asks.

"Not really. I sort of borrowed them," I whisper.

"Rebel!" teases Priya, casting her eyes carelessly over the letter. "Ah! The house in Doctor's Lane…Well, the door's just about still standing. I wouldn't ask Ma about the old place though if I were you. It's one of her sore points."

"Why?"

"All I know is that the family had to give it up after Boro-Dida—old Grandma died. We had to move out because my other grandparents were ill, so we lived with them for a while. I think Shudi Uncle and his wife, Anishka, stayed on there for some time. You know, he was a carpenter and he had a workshop there, but apparently Anishka was keen to move to a modern flat. No one wanted to sell the house but no one wanted to live there either. I think Ma tried to have the refuge there, but it was not possible. So it got sold to developers. Ma calls them sharks waiting to eat up the whole of old Kolkata. If you ask her about it she just says that we all need to stop living in the past. She'll tell you she doesn't want to go back to the house because she wants to keep her memories sacred. Anyway, trust me, she's so stubborn you'll never get anything out of her unless she wants to tell you." Priya hops off the bed and tugs me to my feet. "Doesn't your ma get like that from time to time, all emotional over nothing much?"

"I suppose so…Have you ever asked Anjali why she and Mum lost contact?"

"I did, when you and me started Facebooking, but she just said that they were both so busy." Priya shrugs, as if she hasn't really thought that much about it.

"You won't tell your ma about me taking the letters, will you? I'm planning to put them back when I get home so she'll never know I took them." I smile nervously.

"My lips are sealed!" Priya says, sticking her tongue through her most enormous bubble yet and making it pop. "Look at us! You've only been here for a few hours and we're already, what's the phrase…thick as thieves? Keeping secrets is something I *can* do…you'll see!" Priya smiles mysteriously and then collapses back onto the bed. "You know, this is the best thing that's happened to me in ages, having you here, and I love that we made it happen ourselves—with a little help from my didima."

"I can't wait to see her again. Does she live in this block?" I ask Priya.

"Ma would love her to, but she's far too independent. Anyway, this place is not her style at all—far too retro for Didima, you'll see!" Priya laughs. "She'll probably take you to her apartment. She's on cloud nine since she heard you were finally coming. Like you being here is her personal triumph or something. I suppose in a way it is, because she wouldn't stop going on at me until I Facebooked you!"

So Lila *is* behind me and Priya getting together. I suppose Lila must know about whatever it is that happened in the past. Granddad must have known too. Perhaps that was also why he didn't want to come back to India until Lila came to see him.

"You know, my big plan is to make this a regular gig! Next time it's my turn to come and stay with you in London," says Priya, wrapping her arm around my shoulder. "We could hit the clubs, make some contacts." She laughs.

As if! I think to myself. Like my mum would let us go out clubbing together!

"How was your dance rehearsal?" I ask, changing the subject.

"OK! Same as ever. The choreographer's a total dragon!"

"But you like doing it?" I point at the photos pasted all over her wall.

"The hours of training I could do without, but when I'm actually performing I *love* it! Do you dance?"

"No!" I never feel comfortable dancing, even in a really crowded place, unless I'm with Jidé. He'll make a joke of it and prance about, dragging me around with him.

"Well, to start to learn Kathak you don't even have to move! Here, I'll show you. It begins with the eyes. Stare at me without blinking for as long as you can!"

After a few seconds I'm blinking already, but Priya goes on staring for ages. Then she does one huge blink, and starts flicking her eyes from left to right, up and down until I can't help laughing.

"I call it the 'demented goddess' exercise. It's supposed to strengthen the muscles in your eyes!"

I can see how she would be an amazing dancer, because she's got this brightness playing about her face and an easy grace in the way she moves that makes you want to watch her. If she was an animal she'd definitely be a cat—you get the feeling that at any moment she could spring from a standstill to a great height.

"Anyway," she carries on, "no rehearsals tomorrow. So shopping, shopping, shopping all day long…bliss! Then where do you want to go?"

The truth is, I want to see everything I can in this city, but the place I want to see more than anywhere else is the house in Doctor's Lane, and now reading the letters has made me want to go there even more, but after what she's told me, I don't feel like I should ask. Not straight away anyway.

"I circled loads of places," I tell Priya, handing her my guidebook.

She flicks through. "All the usual suspects! I knew you liked art, so I guessed you'd want to check out the galleries."

I nod. There is so much I want to see. I can already tell from the tiny glimpses of the city I've seen so far that three weeks will never be enough time here.

"After the mall I'll take you to somewhere that's not on your list," says Priya mysteriously. "It's going to blast your mind! And Janu says he'll take you to Kumartuli, where they make all the clay idols for pujas…gods and goddesses. Janu's into all that. You should have seen his face light up when I told him you're a proper artist!"

"Not really!" I mumble, feeling terrible that I haven't asked after Janu yet. In fact, I'd almost forgotten all about him. Granddad mentioned him a couple of times, and Lila showed us a photograph when she came to see us, but really all I know is what's written in the leaflet Anjali sent me. It says that he was the first baby Anjali took in at the refuge and that now he's graduated to working there.

"Is Janu here?" I ask, feeling slightly stupid for not knowing.

"He lives half here, half at the refuge these days. He's a work addict like Ma. Never stops. I'm always telling him to lighten up a bit...act his age! He's sixteen going on twenty! Anyway you'll meet him soon enough." Priya shrugs. "But while we're on our own I want to hear all about this love of yours. No one I know has been going out with a boy since they were twelve years old. It's like you're married or something! He must be more than a pretty face!" Priya sits on the bed and crosses her legs in a yoga position, both feet resting easily on the tops of her thighs.

I sit on the edge of the bed next to her, I'm not sure what to say. "He's sort of my best friend," I start, trying to find the right words to describe what Jidé is to me.

Priya raises her eyebrows as if to say, "Yes! *And...*"

"Well, we've been through a load of stuff together, and he knows me better than anyone else...and now I'm here I can't believe how much I miss speaking to him every day."

I can tell by the look on Priya's face that I'm not doing this very well, but I've never tried to explain to anyone before how I really feel about Jidé.

"Me and Bacha have been through *stuff* together!" she laughs.

"Well, he's…he makes me laugh, he's clever and he's got this gentle smile…and a good heart, and I told you we're best friends. Here!" I say, rummaging in my bag. "It's my favorite photo of him. I carry it everywhere." I hand it to Priya.

"Sweet! But he's changed a bit since this!" Priya laughs. "More juicy details please!"

"He's a good kisser!" I giggle and now Priya jumps up on the bed, pulls me up too, and starts to dance around.

"Now you're talking. *And*…?!"

"He does sweet, thoughtful things like load random songs onto my iPod."

"If music be the food of love…" laughs Priya. "And…?!"

"What?"

"Is it love?"

"I think so." It's what I've always thought but neither of us has actually used the word.

"OK, I'll try again. Is it forever?"

"How do I know?"

I've never really thought of that before, but just the idea that it might not be forever makes me feel odd.

"Let's Skype him and I'll interview him! See if he's good enough for you," she jokes.

"We can't. Not for nearly two weeks anyway. He's gone on this geography field trip to the Alps. And they're not allowed to take mobiles or laptops. He gets back a week before me, so you'll have to wait till then!" I say.

"Shame! But what's that saying? 'Absence makes the heart grow fonder,'" she teases, her eyes pirouetting around their sockets in a suggestive "You know what I mean" dance. But suddenly I can't bring myself to laugh anymore because the image of Jidé's lost love note floating somewhere between here and London fills my mind and right now I would do anything just to hear his voice.

Priya must sense that I'm close to tears because she squeezes my hand and changes the subject.

"So what's your favorite song right now?"

"This one. I was listening to it before I fell asleep." I hand her my iPod and shuffle to "Summer Breeze." I've only just heard it, but somehow the fact that Jidé chose it for me makes me feel closer to him.

Priya takes one earphone and hands the other to me and we listen to the track together. She closes her eyes and her body sways. When she listens to music, she seems to slip away somewhere else. She starts to sing along and I join in. It's a while before I realize that she's taken out her earphone and is listening to me.

"You didn't tell me you can sing!" She smiles. "My ma said Uma had a great voice too."

"I don't know. I'm not that sure about it yet. I only started singing lessons last year," I tell her. "But what I like best is writing my own stuff."

"Take it from me, you can sing!" She laughs, standing on her tiptoes, reaching out through the window and plucking a tiny cluster of white flowers from a vine, which she hands to me.

"Jasmine, just like in the song...smell that!" she orders. "Janu grows it on the balcony upstairs."

So that's the sweet smell that's been wafting through the window.

"You know sooner or later you're going to have to sing for me, like it or not. I want you to write me something with that sort of beat. I could use it...Give me a few days to experiment, then I'll record you and mix it all up. I think it could work. The drop could come right...here. Let me just listen a few more times."

"I don't know. I've never been recorded before," I mumble, but my words are lost on Priya because she's already plugged herself back in. I watch her sink into her pillows, close her eyes, and roll onto her side. After a while I think she's fallen asleep.

There's a gentle knock at the door and Anjali walks in. I feel as if guilt is written all over my face.

"That bed's supposed to be for you! Typical of Priya—she'll go on and on and then suddenly she's out like a light!" Anjali whispers. "It's all the dancing she's doing, it wears her out."

"I'm fine sleeping on the roll-up bed," I whisper back.

"I Skyped Uma for you earlier, because you were fast asleep. She was happy to hear you've arrived safely. She wanted to know if you've got her 'sorry'? She said you'd understand."

I put my hands up to feel my earrings still in place. I smile and nod at Anjali. At least I don't have to face Mum tonight.

"Want anything to eat or drink?" Anjali asks me.

"No, thank you."

"Well, sweet dreams then!"

It's midnight and the whole neighborhood is quiet now. I watch Priya sleeping on her bed. I don't know if it's just because we're family that I already like her so much. Maybe when someone is family, even when you come from different worlds, you're just not so scared to give a bit more of what's really inside you. That's how I already feel about Priya, and I would hate *not* to know her from now on. Mum and Anjali obviously once felt like that too, and so it must have taken something really big to have pulled them apart.

The words of Anjali's letters scroll down and down through my mind, and somewhere in my gut I know that the answers to my questions are buried in the house in Doctor's Lane.

Abra-Kadamba

✤✣✤

I look over to Priya's empty bed, with the covers thrown back. By the light coming through the window it feels quite late. The last thing I remember hearing is the dawn chorus in the tree outside the window.

"Get down, Bacha!" I hear Priya shout from outside.

I stand on her bed and watch Bacha's front legs resting on Priya's shoulders as he dances around the garden with her!

"Hi!" I call from the window.

"Ah, the sleeping beauty awakes!" Priya pushes Bacha off her and legs it up the stairs. The way she runs at everything reminds me of my brother Krish. As she disappears up the second flight of stairs I reach out to touch the spreading leaves of the tree.

"Beautiful, isn't it?" says Anjali, coming into the room. She places a hand on my shoulder and sits on the edge of the bed beside me. "You know, that was the reason we bought this flat."

"What kind of tree is it?" I ask.

"It's called a Kadamba—a tree of truth…people say it even has some health-giving properties. Every day I wake up I'm thankful to live under its shade—it makes me feel so far away from all the chaos of the city."

"It's my magic tree!" says Priya, springing into the room and launching herself, limbs splaying in all directions, onto her bed. "Abra-Kadamba! Make a wish, Mira, a secret wish."

I wish…I wish that I get to see the house in Doctor's Lane.

Anjali takes my hand and one of Priya's. She has an effortless warmth about her that you're just drawn toward.

"I used to make up stories about the magic powers of the Abra-Kadamba for little Priya," says Anjali, "because I could never get her to sleep. Still can't! What are you organizing now?" she asks Priya, but she's completely zoned out as her fingers move at lightning speed over the keypad of her mobile phone. She's the fastest texter I've ever seen!

"No, Priya's never been much of a sleeper. Even now, she'd spend half the night texting her friends if I'd let her!" Anjali confides in me. "Who are you texting?" she asks, tapping Priya on the shoulder to get her attention.

"Just arranging for the others to meet us at the mall later," Priya says, throwing her mobile on the bed.

"Sari shopping first, for Mira's welcoming party, remember?" Anjali reminds Priya as she wanders out of the bedroom.

"Ma's got it into her head that you'd like to go to one of those Park Street sari shops. I don't know why. I could understand it if your ma was here, but it's not as if you're going to wear a sari, is it? Just say the word and I'll put her off," Priya whispers.

"I don't mind what I do," I say with a shrug. I feel like my little sister, Laila, when I take her to a toy shop! I just want to see everything. I'm actually really looking forward to seeing all that colored cloth in the same place. I imagine it would be like walking through Mr. Bird's art shop, which is one of my favorite things to do at home. I love just taking in all the colors. But I don't want Priya to think I'm weird!

"Ma's just desperate to show you off to Didima and Prem Uncle and all the cousins. Are you sure you're up to all the admiration?!" Priya laughs and squeezes one of my cheeks.

Anjali reappears in the doorway holding an old wooden case the size of a toolbox. It's covered in smears of paint.

"Janu thought you might want to borrow these to make up for losing your case," she says, placing the box on the low wooden table. She undoes the rusty catch and opens the lid to reveal pastels, charcoals, gouache, and oil paints all neatly arranged in a color-coded rainbow arc.

"These belonged to your granddad's brother, Shudi."

"The one who carved the door...Granddad used to talk about?" I ask, probably a bit too keenly.

Anjali nods. "He made so many pieces of beautiful furniture. It's a shame we don't have more."

"Ma...Mira wants to see the house. I'll take her if you want," offers Priya in the gentlest of voices, as if she's afraid of upsetting her.

Two deep furrows appear between Anjali's eyes. "There are so many places to take you, Mira. That old house is nothing like it used to be. It's just a ruin now. No point going there."

"It's just...Granddad was always talking about it...and Mum does too sometimes," I lie.

Anjali's expression suddenly hardens. "Well, it's a very long time since your mum or Granddad saw that house," she snaps.

Something about the way her mood has switched reminds me of Mum, the day she snatched her letters away from me. I'm not going to argue with Anjali, but the truth is, ever since Granddad started telling me stories of living in that house I've wanted to see it.

Anjali takes a deep breath before she speaks, as if she's trying to compose herself. "You know, Mira? My Uncle Shudi left his art box to me—in those days I was a keen artist. Priya's not interested and so Janu uses them now, but he says you're welcome to use them while you're here." She's staring down at the box. "You can buy a sketchbook and some paper when you go shopping later." Her voice sounds a bit shaky. She smooths her hands over and over the quilt on Priya's bed as if touching it calms her.

"We're not doing *that* sort of shopping, Ma!" Priya groans.

"There'll be time for everything!" Anjali says with a sigh, a sharp edge creeping back into her voice. Then she smiles and turns to me. "Sorry, Mira. Priya always acts as if the world's about to come to an end today."

"Fine, we'll buy some paper, but I'm *not* having a new sari dress or anything. All I need is a new pair of skinny jeans, maybe some trainers, and a few CDs."

"Is that *all*?" Anjali laughs. "Remember you're supposed to be shopping for Mira! I washed that orange salwar-kameez for you last night, Mira, so at least you'll have something of your own to wear until you get some new clothes."

"Thank you." I could put on my miniskirt, but after Creepy Guard staring at me I've sort of been put off wearing it.

Anjali walks out of the room and Priya calls after her, "Ma, just so you know, I'm *not* buying anything trad!" It's weird watching the two of them locked in all these little tug of wars that are so like Mum's and mine.

I take out one of the paints and squeeze a tiny bit of gold onto my finger. I wonder if these were the same colors used on the door in Doctor's Lane. What did Anjali write that the colors were? Orange, green, and gold. The same faded colors as on Priya's trophy cupboard. They must have been Shudi's favorites.

"Typical of Janu." Priya sighs. "So thoughtful, but I don't know when he thinks you'll have time to use this stuff. Kolkata is for experience. You can take photographs and paint them when you get home!"

I nod as I place the gold paint back in the box and close the little rusty catch. I can tell that Priya doesn't want me to spend time painting when I could be chatting with her, but if I had some paper or a canvas here right now, I don't know if I would be able to resist trying out these colors. I can't believe that these once belonged to Granddad's brother. I imagine that using them might feel like it does when I paint on Nana Josie's easel. I wonder if you can inherit something like being good at art. I always thought it was because Nana Josie painted with me from when I was little that I'm so into it. It's never occurred to me before that I could have inherited it from someone on this side of the family.

The Sari Shop

✿✿✿

"No argument. I've already told Uma that this shopping trip is our gift to you." Anjali smiles as we settle into the back of Manu's car. "But I'm warning you—Priya can shop till she drops!"

"Like I said," Priya complains, "if we didn't have to do this whole sari-shop ritual, we'd have even longer!" She blows an enormous bubble and pops it. "See that?!"

"How could we miss it! Make sure you spit that out before we get in among all the cloth." Anjali sighs impatiently.

I'm snapping away at the hundreds of tiny scenes that unfold every few seconds on the street here, but if I'm honest I'm also hiding behind the camera to avoid getting involved in the conversation.

"Ma! Mira's never worn a sari in her life. If we don't wear them, why should she?"

"We can have a sari dress or salwar-kameez made up for

her, and I thought maybe Mira could help to choose a sari for Uma. She'll know better than me what her taste is. You know, when Uma came to visit, this was the first place my ma brought us."

"Did Mum buy a sari?" I ask.

"My ma bought your grandmother Kath a sari for Uma to take back home. It was very pretty, pale blue silk, with soft golden embroidery…the same color blue as your grandmother's eyes, and I see from photos that your brother has inherited the same color, but Indian almond shape, na?"

I nod. Out of all three of us I look the most Indian. Krish's eyes are massive, but they're Nana Kath's forget-me-not blue color and he got her fair skin, and Laila is somewhere in between. Sometimes I used to ask Granddad how it all worked with the genes, and he always used to say that would be "a good field to go into!" But even if I was that way inclined, I hate the thought of experimenting on animals.

"I think, if I remember, Uma bought a little embroidered folder from the sari shop, for letters and things."

The letter album! Priya looks at me and raises an eyebrow. I feel terrible, as if I've been found out.

"So if Mira doesn't want to get anything for herself, you're not going to force her!" asks Priya, grinning.

"No, of course not, this is supposed to be a pleasure," sighs Anjali. I feel a bit sorry for her. I think of Mum, and how I've told Anjali that I don't want to Skype home just yet. I can't face that, but I think I'll email her tonight, just to try to make things more normal between us. But being in contact with Jidé is the thing that would make me feel so much more settled.

"Don't take any notice of Ma," whispers Priya. "She's the worst shopper in the world. The minute we get into the mall she wants to know exactly what shops I'm going into, what I want to buy and what time *exactly* we can be out again. The only kind of shopping she likes is sari shops, emporiums, and markets, and then, be warned…you can't tear her away."

Anjali doesn't seem to be listening; she's just staring out of the window at the crowded pavement outside. My head is full of images and words from the past floating around in my mind. I think that the blue sari must have been the one that Nana Kath wore to Granddad's funeral. The color matched her eyes exactly, and she looked so beautiful, like she'd dressed up for him.

"Meet another of my Ambassadors, a bit older, like me— retired but still works OK. Only occasionally little creaky here and there!" jokes Manu, peering at Priya and me in his mirror.

In the front of the dashboard there's a tiny incense burner with a sandalwood joystick streaming perfumed smoke. Manu's bright white car is decorated inside with a banner dangling with plastic figurines: Ganesha, the elephant god I recognize and bright blue Shiva. Nana Josie would have loved this taxi—she'd probably have painted a picture of it. I think I will too.

"My protection on the roads!" adds Manu as he notices me looking at the little figures.

If I was going to drive in Kolkata I think I would want some protection too. We're heading down a wide open road jammed full of every kind of traffic: rickshaws, motorbikes, bright yellow taxis, smart estate cars, bikes loaded up with recycled rubbish, cycle rickshaws (like you get in Covent Garden), tuk-tuks, carts, and even a limousine…all weaving in and out, in and out. A hundred different horn blasts blare out. At first, the way I jump at every beep makes Manu smile.

"You must learn to close your ears and even sometimes your eyes to the mayhem of the road," he says. "And when you do you'll start to really feel at home in this city."

The traffic moves so slowly that I sit back and watch the strange scenes unfolding in front of me: a man's making puri in an enormous spitting frying pan, a child runs past on the way to school and swipes one. I wonder if little-boy Granddad ever did that! The man cuffs the boy around the ear, but I see him laughing to himself as he hands his next customer a brown paper packet. The man's bulging belly peeping through his shirt already looks stuffed full of puris.

After seeing all this, the streets at home are going to feel so empty, so lacking in color and life. It's like here, the street is where people are heading to but at home the street's just where you have to walk to get to your door and close it behind you. Granddad always used to say that it's the weather and the landscape that form people's characters and the way they live more than anything else. I suppose that's like Cathy in *Wuthering Heights*; a part of her was that wild moorland. Before I came here I expected to be excited about being here and seeing everything, but what I wasn't ready for is the way that every sense in me is zinging with energy and ideas at the newness of everything that's bombarding my mind.

There are pretty bunting flags everywhere here; even in the most grimy-looking street someone has hung a garland or a poster, as if a party's just about to start. On the other side of the road there are lots of people walking into the glass skyscrapers that line the street. Some of the women are wearing saris and others bright salwar-kameez. Some wear shirts or pretty tunic tops and jeans, others are in formal black, gray, and navy suits. Compared to London, people don't seem to be in such a hurry here. Maybe it's the heat slowing everyone down. I feel like I'm going to pass out in this car, with Manu's sandalwood incense streaming down my throat. Just as I think I can't stand it any more Manu pulls over. Anjali steps out, grasping my hand and reaching for Priya's.

"Ma! We're not children!" complains Priya as Anjali steers us into the busiest road I have ever attempted to cross. If I wasn't clinging on to her hand, there is no way I would dream of joining this carnage of cars, buses, humans, dogs, rickshaws, and mopeds. My heart's beating so fast it feels as if I've been running. Anjali's chin is pointed imperiously upward as she pulls me across the road. Now Priya's broken away from us and is dancing between vehicles, her hands raised in the air, conducting the traffic to stop and start. I hear her tinkling laugh as she dodges between a cycle rickshaw and a yellow cab. Horns sound, but the traffic stops for her. Anjali shakes her head at Priya, who is waving to us triumphantly from the safety of the pavement.

Now Priya's holding open a sparkling glass door and I'm being ushered into the most amazing shop I have ever been into in my life! "Ta-da!" she mock announces, like a magician opening a magic box. The shop has wall-to-wall dark wooden shelves stacked layer upon layer with colorful saris: pink and lime and mustard and gold and green and copper and orange and silver and turquoise…every color you can imagine, all folded neatly in piles on the shelves. Mum must have known I would love this place. Why didn't she tell me she'd been here? Anjali adjusts the green silk sari she's wearing and takes a seat on a low wooden bench. She looks so elegant today, and she's wearing gold earrings and bracelets, whereas yesterday she only wore her shell bracelet, like the one Nana Kath has always worn, to show that she's married. It was a wedding present from Lila. I think Anjali might have dressed up for the occasion. It's the first time I've seen her wearing the sindoor, vermillion powder through her parting, and the great red teep between her eyes.

"First customers. That's good." She smiles, glancing around the shop and kicking off her chappal sandals.

She raises her eyebrows at Priya and nods toward her bright red Converse but Priya shakes her head, refusing to take them off.

"Mira, *you* will need to take off your shoes—you don't want to damage the cloth." Anjali looks down at my feet and takes a second glance at my shabby, doodled trainers. She probably thinks it's a bit weird of me, liking things that are so old and worn.

"Don't fight it!" Priya whispers in my ear. "Just find something for your ma quickly and then we'll have more time at the mall."

A tiny man in a mustard shirt appears through a purple curtain. He presses his palms together in a formal namaste greeting. Anjali namastes him back. By the way that they chat together it's obvious that they know each other well. Then he turns to Priya and me. I copy Anjali, but Priya just says, "Hi!" Now Anjali is pointing out cloths and chattering away to Sari Man. He pulls each one she's interested in off the shelf so that she can inspect the patterns and the quality of the silk or cotton.

"What do you think?" asks Anjali as the man unravels a black and white fabric with a geometric border design.

"This one is latest fashion design," he says.

"Gross!" groans Priya, screwing up her nose.

"I was asking *Mira*!" says Anjali, obviously getting annoyed.

I smile politely but shake my head.

"How about this? Khub bhalo modern design," says Sari Man, wafting open a shocking pink cotton with a silver border.

Priya tuts.

"I'm not very keen on pink," I say apologetically, because he's trying so hard to find something I'll like.

Now Anjali's having words with Priya. I can tell enough from their hand gestures and the stony tone of Anjali's voice that she's not happy with Priya butting in.

"Is it for special occasion? Let me guess, maybe the young lady's sixteenth birthday?" Sari Man interrupts Anjali and Priya.

"No, no, she's only fourteen," says Anjali.

"You're lucky. No one ever thinks *I'm* older than I am," complains Priya.

"We're looking for a sari dress for Mira," explains Anjali.

"This is shame I have nothing made up at the moment—so

many wedding orders, you know—but if she can find material she likes I can take measurements and make something, no problem!" Sari Man smiles.

"And we want to find a sari for her to take home to her ma," Anjali adds.

"OK, this is good. I can start with Tussar silk—slightly heavy...handwoven, georgette...pretty because no shine, crêpe...very light. Depending what she likes for flow and fall. For borders I have brocade, Zardozi...*very* beautiful, hand-embroidered with jewels! Special gift."

For every kind of sari he names, he takes something off the shelf and throws it toward us in a dramatic flourish. A sea of colors unravels in waves in front of our eyes.

Priya leans into me. "Just choose something quick, or he'll go on and on like this all day!"

"Here is example of handwoven, very subtle!" he says. "A little worn, but still beautiful." He smiles at Anjali. I think he might be flirting with her! She ignores him as she reaches out and touches the fine embroidered cloth. The actual sari is cream silk but the border is a sage-green color, with little bits of faded orange, turquoise, and gold. When I look closer I see that there are tiny clusters of white flowers scattered everywhere. I can't help it—I just have to reach out and touch it. The stitching is so detailed and beautiful.

"Mum would *love* this," I say.

"Excellent choice." Sari Man nods, clapping his hands together like he's clinched the deal.

"Na, na." Anjali is shaking her head and wagging her finger at Sari Man. "Uma should have a new sari, a modern design, and this is not suitable for a sari dress."

"No, no, not for sari dress—of course it cannot be cut," agrees the man, looking outraged at the idea, "but if she thinks her mother would like it..." He raises his hands in the air as if to say, "But it's completely up to you."

Anjali doesn't answer, so Sari Man turns to me and holds out a length of the cloth so that I can inspect it again.

"See! Only a little damage on the pallu," he mumbles, running his fingers along the largest section of embroidery. "This is very rare indeed, to find something this old in fine silk. Probably this sari is over a hundred years old. Sorry to say, expensive choice though."

Anjali is starting to look annoyed, but Sari Man's on a roll. "We have more old saris I can show you, only for your interest. Just look at the work in this Kanchipuram sari," he says, walking over to a cabinet, taking out a little key, opening the lock and pulling out a pile of red and gold...see...true craftsmanship."

Sari Man drapes the cloth over his arms, presenting it like a waiter serving the most delicious dish. "Should be in museum really...Many times I think to myself, if this sari could talk... telling stories of all the brides who wore it...You know, it is becoming quite fashionable now for daughters to wear their mother's and grandmother's saris for their own weddings," he says, pointing to Priya and me.

"Good thing traditions change then!" Priya whispers in my ear. Somehow I can't see her ever wearing Anjali's bridal sari!

Sari Man catches the slightly bored look on Priya's face, sighs, and places his precious sari back in the cabinet. As he's locking it up he turns to Anjali. "What I can't understand is how anyone could let go of such a beautiful family heirloom!"

Anjali doesn't answer him. She's staring at the cupboard, but she looks distant, as if she's been transported somewhere else.

"Ma!" Priya shouts at Anjali, tapping her on the shoulder. "You look as if you've seen a ghost!"

"Ghost?" she asks vaguely.

"Take a seat, take seat," says Sari Man. Anjali slumps down as if she's been drained of all her energy. Bring some refreshment," the man shouts, clicking his fingers at a boy who's standing watching from a doorway. He must be about my age and looks just like Sari Man, but taller. Maybe he's his son. The boy springs into action and reappears with a cup of steaming hot tea for Anjali, which she sips without saying a word.

The tea seems to have given Anjali a new spurt of energy.

"Sorry, Mira!" she says, shaking her head. "I think I've been overdoing it a bit lately. Of course, if this is the one you think Uma will like, we will buy it. Perhaps we'll come another time to choose for the sari dress, or maybe you and Priya can buy something from the mall for the party tomorrow." She sips her tea slowly.

"I can wear this," I say, holding out mum's sari.

"Why would you do that?" whispers Priya.

"It might speed things up a bit!" I tell her.

"OK!" She winks at me and grins.

Before I know what's happening Sari Man is offering me his hand and helping me onto a little wooden stage.

"Why not try it, so you can see how it will look? Ever worn a sari before?" he asks. I shake my head. Sari Man moves like an opera star...all flourishes, bows, and grand gestures! Now he kicks away the reams of cloth so that my feet find the wooden boards underneath and he fixes a belt around my waist. Anjali steps onto the platform too and begins to dress me. I'd thought she'd be pleased if I said I would wear it, but she doesn't seem to be. The strange distant expression has returned to her face.

I catch my reflection in the mirror and hardly recognize myself.

I watched Nana Kath putting her sari on, the day of Granddad's funeral. It's weird to think that the letter album and Nana Kath's sari were both bought in this shop. I remember I was impressed that she could put it on so well by herself. She said Lila taught her years ago. Anjali wraps the sari around me and makes the folds. The truth is I've always fancied wearing a sari, but Mum can't put them on and even if she could, when and where would I wear it? It wouldn't feel right wearing it back home but here, in the middle of this shop in Kolkata, it feels like the only thing I should wear.

"You look like film star!" Sari Man says, grinning at me in the mirror. He's so over the top I can't help smiling back.

"Much better!" He laughs. "Why you are wasting this lovely smile?"

"Suits you!" Anjali agrees, stepping back and looking me up and down. She seems more herself again.

Priya is sitting on the wooden bench flashing her eyes as if to say, "Finally we can go!"

I really want to go to the mall to buy some clothes and meet Priya's friends, but I could also spend hours in this shop, sketching the patterns. I love the vintage saris best. Sari Man is right…looking at the fineness of the stitching makes you wonder whose hands from another time pulled through all the tiny threads. I feel like I want to know what stories they stitched into the cloth while they were sewing day after day after day.

"The choli blouse my tailors can make up within two hours," Sari Man tells Anjali as he takes my measurements.

We're just about to leave the shop when Anjali walks back toward Sari Man.

"Ma! We have to go!" Priya moans.

Anjali ignores her and carries on speaking with the man. He

goes into the back of the shop and comes out with a huge burlap sack. His son carries it out to the car and Manu puts it in the trunk.

"It's for our quilt maker at the refuge," explains Anjali. "She made that lovely kantha stitch *lep* on Priya's bed out of old bits of sari. Now she has more commissions than she can cope with. In London the double bedspreads are sometimes selling for five hundred pounds each, and I'm not even sure that's enough money for the work that goes into them. Now we're planning to set up a workshop cooperative for her, and she's teaching some of the other girls the many wonderful arrangements of the kantha stitch. I intend to take lessons from her myself," Anjali tells me proudly.

❧ ✤ ☙

In the car on the way home I try to do what Manu said and "forget the road," because I feel as though I can't take anything else and I haven't even been to the refuge yet or thought up my art project.

It is so hot today, my clothes are already damp with sweat. When Manu drops Anjali off at the flat I think about asking if I can have a quick shower, but by the way Priya practically pushes Anjali out of the car I can tell she's not planning to hang around.

"She can't wait to get rid of me," laughs Anjali as Bacha jumps up at her and tries to lick her face. "At least someone loves me!"

The Mall

✿ ✿ ✿

We are waiting at traffic lights *again* when the tiny hand is thrust through my half-open window. At first I feel so shocked that I can't work out what's going on, but now I see that a woman is forcing her baby's hand through the gap. She's clutching its wrist so hard that the skin is turning white. The baby wails and wails, its other arm flailing in the air. No sound comes from the mother's mouth, but her face speaks loud and clear; it says, "Pity me, help me…give me and my baby money."

Priya tries to close my window slowly, but the woman refuses to pull the baby's hand away.

"Why don't we just give her something?" I say.

"*Dut!*" shouts Manu, making me jump as he leans over into the backseat and winds up the window, missing crushing the baby's fingers by millimeters.

The woman holds her baby against the glass in a pleading

gesture. It has a cross scored into its forehead and flies gather around the wound. I notice that the woman has one too, but hers has healed into a scar.

"What's that mark on their heads?" I ask Priya.

"Probably made on purpose. Like branding an animal. It shows that they belong to the same begging ring. Anything you give her she will be forced to hand over. It's hopeless." Priya sighs.

She looks thoughtful and sad as she glances at the baby, who must be about six months old. "That's why I'm *never* having children…I've seen so many of them suffering," she says. "At least if they come to Ma's refuge there's some hope, perhaps even a way out, but if you hear the stories they tell you…" she shudders.

Now Branded Woman is tapping at the window, just like Dust Boy tapped, in exactly the same place. I feel awful because all I want is for the traffic to start moving again so that I don't have to look at this poor woman and her baby for a second longer. Eventually the light turns green and we move off, drawing up outside a huge building, like a sparkling glass palace. It's strange how you can feel like you're moving between worlds here just by taking a turn onto a different street. When we set off shopping this morning, I couldn't wait to get here and find some new clothes to wear. Now, after seeing Branded Woman and her baby, I'm not sure I have the stomach for shopping. I feel like I've only just arrived and my whole world has been turned upside down. I need to write and paint and find a way to filter all of this. It's not the feeling I have at home, when I stand in front of my easel and have to think about what I'm going to draw…it's like all these images and mixed-up emotions are pressing in on me, and I know I'm going to have to find some way of letting it out and making sense of it.

We walk past two security guards standing at the entrance to the grand glass doors of the mall. I wonder what they would do if Branded Woman tried to come into this air-conditioned, spotless glass dome. Suddenly it feels like I could be in any of the shopping centers I've been to at home. So many of the stores are exactly the same, and a part of me quite likes that. It's a relief, just for a while, to be in a place that feels familiar.

As we wander around the shops, Priya chatters on to me as we pick up a few T-shirts, long-sleeved cotton tunic tops (they're called *kurti*), chunni scarves (Priya insists I buy five different plain colors and five patterned ones), cotton leggings, and underwear. Occasionally she'll pick something up and say, "like?" but I get the feeling my taste's a bit tamer than hers. She picks up a short red leather jacket and slings it around her shoulders.

"Suits you," I tell her.

She checks out the price tag and whistles. "Mad world, isn't it?"

I know she's thinking of Branded Woman too.

When we get to the checkout and everything's rung through she turns to me. "Are you sure you don't need anything else?"

I shake my head.

A text beeps into Priya's inbox. She reads it and laughs. "Fancy grabbing a coffee with some of my friends?"

～❖～

We walk into a Starbucks, an exact replica of the one Jidé and I always go to. Priya takes a running jump into the arms of two tall boys who look identical. They catch her, as if this is how she always makes her entrance.

"Princess Priya!" says one of them as he lowers her onto a chair and ruffles her hair up. Both boys have spiky black hair, slightly downy moustaches, and are willowy thin.

"Meet Chand and Charbak," says Priya.

I look from one to the other in total amazement. I have never seen two people look more alike, except that one of them is wearing a stud earring in his right ear. He sees me looking at it.

"Just remember, Charbak is the one wearing the earring! He's the only boy in our school that the teachers actually thanked for having his ear pierced, as long as Chand doesn't do the same. Then they're both in trouble!" says Priya, hugging me to her. "Everyone, this is my cousin Mira!"

"Priya has told us all about you. It's great to finally meet you," says Charbak, smiling and gesturing for me to sit down.

"And these are my friends Paddy and Priti." Priya continues with the introductions, waving in the direction of two girls perched on the seat opposite me. "Cappuccino?" Priya asks me.

"Yes, please!"

Priya goes off with Charbak to queue at the counter. They're chatting away happily in fluent English, which makes me feel sort of inadequate. I still only know a tiny bit of Bengali.

"Bad luck about your case. How did the shopping go?" asks the girl sitting on my left, with the crazy, wavy hair.

I nod and lift up the bags to show her, suddenly feeling a bit shy without Priya around. She introduced everyone so quickly I can't remember who's who, which I think the girl senses because she smiles warmly at me. "I'm Paddy—short for Padma!"

"It's not shortened if it's the same number of letters." Chand says in a deadpan voice.

"Well, no, it's not *technically* shorter. Chand takes everything literally!" Paddy laughs, rolling her eyes.

"So you're Priti?" I say turning to the incredibly beautiful girl on my right, who has the shiniest plait of hair falling down her back.

"She's the priti-est!" bursts out Chand.

Priya and Charbak stroll back over with the drinks.

"That's a matter of opinion!" laughs Charbak, winking at Paddy.

Paddy shrugs as if she couldn't care less. In fact, I get the impression that she wouldn't want to be called pretty. She's wearing all black: black leggings, black T-shirt (with some band name I've never heard of), black high-tops, and a huge piece of skeleton costume jewelry around her neck.

"I like what you've done with those," she says, inspecting my Converse.

But before I can thank her, Priya stands up.

"Mind if I leave you with the Pod for a few minutes?" She doesn't wait for an answer before she dashes back into the shopping center.

"She's always up to something!" Paddy smiles at me.

"What's the Pod?" I ask.

"Us three! Priya, Priti, and Paddy…three *P*s in a pod! It's what our English teacher used to call us at school because we've always been so close!"

"It's a great name!" I say. "Do you both dance with Priya?"

Priti smiles. "Strictly speaking, we dance in her shadow."

"And *we're* just the musos!" Charbak chips in. "What Priya calls the Rhythm and Blues section—Chand's on sitar and I'm the rhythm!" He demonstrates by drumming out an impressive beat on the table. When he's done he takes a huge glug of his coffee.

"You've got a froth moustache!" Paddy laughs, handing him a napkin to wipe it off. I get the feeling that Paddy and Charbak like each other.

Priya strides back with a shoebox under her arm, which she

hands to me. I know what's inside as soon as I see the slim brown cardboard box with the star logo.

"They're not actually for you!" says Priya. "But would you personalize them for me, like yours? Don't tell Ma though—she'll go mad at me for buying another pair. She doesn't really get fashion." Priya places her foot next to mine. Even though I'm taller than her, our feet are more or less the same size.

"Don't worry. If Anjali finds them, I'll say they're mine," I tell her.

"Thanks, coz!" She grins and grabs my hand.

"Come on. We should be heading back. You'll see this lot in action at the gala." She pulls me to my feet and says bye to her friends in a whirlwind of hugging and high-fiving.

"Can I have a photo?" I ask.

They jump into about five different silly poses, grinning and waving, and Paddy, Priti, and Priya even strike some dance positions. I suppose they *are* performers!

"It was great to meet you all," I say as Priya springs out of the photo and drags me toward the door.

"Bye! See you soon, Mira," they chorus back at me.

We walk along an avenue of ornate fountains, the sort of thing you would expect to find in a grand park rather than a shopping mall. She dips her hand into one of them and splashes me. I shiver. I'm not wearing enough clothes. It actually feels *too* cold in this air-conditioned world of the mall.

"Where would you prefer to shop? Camden Market or

somewhere like this?" asks Priya, staring up at the enormous glass chandelier above our heads.

Priya knows so much more about London than I know about Kolkata. Mostly because she's always googling stuff and watching films and clips on YouTube about bands and clubs. But I still feel a bit embarrassed that I don't know more about the place where a whole side of my family is from.

"Camden...I think," I say, hesitating for a second because I don't want to offend her.

"Me too, but don't tell Ma!" She smiles and takes my arm in hers and together we walk out of the mall, back into a wall of heat.

Homespun

✿❀✿

I wake to the sound of hammering and glance over to Priya's empty bed. I open the lace curtains and watch tiny brown birds flitting around the Kadamba tree. A chipmunk leaps from branch to branch, offering up a high-pitched stuttering call. I try to catch it on video, but it moves so fast that all I see is a disappearing tail! It's so strange to see chipmunks running wild, but I suppose they're no different to the playful squirrels I see every day when I walk across the Rec to school.

"Come and see!" shouts Priya, suddenly appearing in the doorway, grabbing my arm and leading me out onto the landing.

I can't believe it. The entrance to the flat is decked in garlands of marigolds and roses, as if there's going to be a wedding or something. The marigolds are the background and the white roses spell out the words *Welcome, Mira.*

"Well, what do you think?" Priya asks, hopping up and down in excitement.

I don't know what it is about being here—at home whole days can go by when everything feels more or less normal, but here my emotions are all over the place. I can feel like laughing one moment and crying the next, and now my throat has gone all tight and my eyes are blurry.

"I thought you'd be happy!" Priya flings her arm over my shoulder and hugs me tightly.

"I am," I tell her, hugging her back. "Thank you!"

"To be honest it was Janu's idea as well. It was him who organized it with our friends from the flower market."

I don't know why, but all the time I was arranging to come here I kept forgetting about Janu, and even now that I'm here I can't really picture him living in this house, but that's probably because I haven't met him yet. He seems to spend more time at the refuge than here. I know Anjali told Mum that she couldn't run the place without his help. Even so I'm not sure how much a part of the family he is. All I know is that he's already been so kind to me, offering me the paints and now these flowers.

"Get ready for Didima and the aunties and Prem Uncle to arrive! And definitely get ready for lots of *this*!" Priya squeezes both of my cheeks between her fingers and thumbs. "At least my new hair will take some attention away from you." She smiles and runs her fingers through her short red spikes.

I've just stepped out of the shower when I hear Anjali and Priya's voices outside the bathroom door. They're having a raging argument. I think about turning the shower back on, but that would probably seem weird. So I go to the sink and let the tap run for a few seconds, but when I turn it off they're still going at it so I haven't got much choice. I pull on Priya's dressing gown and walk into the bedroom. Priya switches from Bengali to English, for my benefit, I assume.

"I'm *not* wearing a sari dress, Ma! I told you that yesterday!"

"OK! OK!" sighs Anjali. "You can wear one of those pretty tunic tops I bought you instead."

"I'm wearing jeans and a T-shirt," insists Priya, stomping off to take a shower and slamming the bathroom door behind her.

"I don't suppose it really matters," Anjali mutters under her breath.

My sari is laid out on the bed, and along with it a matching cream blouse and underskirt.

Now Priya's not getting dressed up, I'm regretting saying I'd wear this sari, but Anjali's gone to so much trouble I don't see that I've got much choice. I turn away from her and pull on the underskirt, tying it at the waist. I shrug off Priya's cotton dressing gown and try on the blouse. I'm struggling with the little hooks and eyes at the back, so Anjali comes over and helps me close them.

"You know, Mira, you coming here has brought back so

many memories of your ma and me when we were your age." Anjali wraps the silk sari around me, tucks it at the waist and starts to fold in the tiny pleats. She's lost somewhere deep in her own thoughts as she readjusts the folds she's already made and half unravels the silk again; folding, pleating, and undoing, tutting and starting again—folding, pleating, and undoing once more, even though it looks perfect to me every time.

"I think this is finally coming better now," she says, standing back to admire her work. "You were right, Mira—the detail on this pallu is gorgeous!" She smiles as she drapes the long piece of cloth over my shoulder.

"I love vintage clothes," I tell her.

"What is this 'vintage'?" Anjali asks.

"Old things. My Nana Josie loved them too," I say, looking down at the silver charm on my wrist.

"Ah! *Acha*, antique," she says, inspecting my charm. "Very pretty. What is it?"

"An artichoke heart," I tell her.

"I see. Layers of leaves…beautiful heirloom." Anjali sighs, sitting down on the bed and stroking Priya's sari quilt. I see her eyes are glistening with tears.

"Mira, our whole family is charmed by your visit, especially my ma," Anjali continues, opening her arms. I walk into them and she holds me close. I can feel the emotion welling up inside her.

Priya springs into the room wrapped in a towel.

"What do you think of Mira?" Anjali asks her, pulling me gently to my feet.

"Very traditional. But rather you than me!" Priya has an amused expression on her face as she wriggles into her skinny jeans and pulls on a bright red T-shirt with a black star print all over it.

"Well, I think she looks gorgeous!" says Anjali. "Wait! Let me take a photo of the two of you for Uma!" She goes off to find her camera.

I slip my feet into the pretty leather sandals she brought for me. She says they're made by the children in the refuge. I can't believe that the youngest sandal maker's only seven.

"You look like a proper traditional girl," says Priya. "Janu will approve. He's into homespun!" She grins and picks up the edge of my sari, inspecting the border pattern more closely. Something about the way she talks about Janu makes me feel slightly nervous, like it's important to her that he likes me.

I can hear people arriving and the sound of voices filling up the flat.

"Let's get this party started!" laughs Priya as she walks toward the living room. I take a deep breath and then follow her.

As soon as I enter, people start to hug me and—Priya was right—squeeze my cheeks! There's a whirlwind of introductions and then I hear a high-pitched voice screeching my name. Her arms are flung into the air in greeting—here comes Lila with a huge smile on her face. It's four years since I saw her, but so much has happened since then. Nana Josie dying and now Granddad Bimal…Lila walks straight up to me, chattering away as she smooths her fingers over my brow. She's saying my name, and she's running her hands over my shoulders and down to my waist as if she can't believe how much I've changed. She says, "Kath, Laila baby, Uma, Sam…Krishan…" I know she's asking after everyone at home, and the very last name she says is "Bimal"…as the tears roll down her cheeks. Even though I can't understand what she's saying now, I can tell that she's trying to find some of Granddad in my face, just like his friend Nayan did at the airport. When Lila's finished inspecting me she moves on to my sari.

"Not so little girl wearing sari! Old sari," Lila says, raising her eyebrows and patting Anjali on the shoulder. Anjali nods and both women trace their fingers over the embroidery of the pallu.

Priya comes bounding up, and Lila gives a little yelp of surprise at the sight of her hair. Then she pulls her granddaughter close to her and laughs, shaking her head and feeling the spiky dyed red ends. She says something to Priya as she runs her fingers through her new hairstyle.

"Didima says I look like the washerwoman hedgehog she saw in the Beatrix Potter museum when she went with your granddad and grandma to the Lake District!"

"Acha, hedgehog." Lila laughs.

"Ma!" calls Anjali, pointing her camera in our direction. Lila draws me and Priya close to her. Anjali clicks the camera and when I inspect the photo all three of us are wearing the same wide Chatterjee smile.

"We can send this one to Uma," says Anjali, going off with the camera to snap everyone else in the room.

Lila takes hold of my face, just like Granddad used to, and looks straight into my eyes as she speaks and Priya translates for her.

"Didima says her ma used to call your grandfather her 'shudurer putro.'"

It feels all wrong that I've read this already in Anjali's letters, like I've stolen other people's thoughts. "It means," Priya continues, "'her far away son.' She's saying that now he is too far away, but you, his granddaughter, have brought something of him back here in your soft smile."

As Priya speaks Lila touches my cheek again and then carries on talking. Not being able to speak Bengali makes me feel like I'm trying to cross a bridge but can only get so far, because to reach the other side it's not just the words you need to understand, but also the tones and colors; the way of thinking and seeing the world that are all locked inside the language.

A tall man enters the room. He looks a bit like Anjali.

"Ma!" he calls to Lila and walks over, wrapping his arm around her shoulder and kissing her on the forehead.

"My shudurer putro," says Lila, kissing him on both hands.

Priya takes a running jump at him and he swings her around like a little girl.

This must be Prem, Anjali's brother who lives in New York. Lila and Priya chat to him excitedly, talking over each other in Bengali. I hear both of them say my name and Mum's name and Granddad's name. Prem scruffs up Priya's hair and places her back on her feet. He turns to me with his arms outstretched and takes my hands in his.

"Hi! Great to meet you, Mira!" he says in a strong American accent.

"You too." I smile at him.

He has sparkly dark eyes and shaved-short hair and he reminds me a bit of my Uncle Rohan. It's ridiculous of me, but I do feel embarrassed at the thought of him teasing Anjali about the sexy sculptures they saw on their trip. I wish I hadn't read that postcard.

Lila is still talking to Prem and says something that makes him laugh.

He turns and explains to me. "Ma says you wear the sari well. She thinks maybe Priya could learn some lessons in ladylike behavior from *you*, Mira!"

"Joker!" laughs Priya. "I'm ready for NYC! Just waiting for the invite!"

"But is New York ready for you? That's the question!" Prem

smiles and scruffs up Priya's hair again, tutting at her new style. "How's our wild child?"

Priya shrugs and jumps into a Kathak pose, tapping out a lightning rhythm with her feet, her hands and eyes telling their own separate story.

"I don't see how you're going to be a classical dancer with hair like this!" Prem laughs.

"I don't know how they dance in NYC, but here we don't dance with our hair!" Priya jokes.

Prem taps his head as if to say, "she's nuts." Lila laughs, kisses Priya on the hair, and leads Prem away.

Priya turns to me. "Didima's so happy to have her beloved Prem and you at the same party! The way she goes on, you wouldn't guess she gets to see him every three or four months when he's here on business."

Priya strolls over to the desk to line up some tracks on her laptop. "Not my sort of thing this Bollywood stuff, but the family like it!"

Granddad would have loved to be in this room surrounded by all this warmth and laughter and the smells of delicious food cooking. Now that I'm here with all the family it's hard to understand why he didn't come home for so long, whatever may have happened…

A few of the younger cousins have come in and—it's just as Priya warned me—I'm the only person of our age wearing a sari. They must all be looking at me and thinking how weird and old-fashioned I am. It's not even as if it's a modern design.

One of Anjali's cousins comes over and offers me a plate of bhajis, vegetable samosas, and spicy lentil cakes. I take a bit of everything and then sit next to Lila on the sofa. She watches me closely, as though to see my reaction to each taste.

"*Mach-bhaja?*" she says, offering me some fried fish from her plate.

I shake my head.

"Oh-ho! *Tumi niramish?*" Lila laughs.

"No meat or fish, Ma," says Anjali, coming over with a tray. "Uma says rasamalai is your favorite sweet. I prepared this for you myself." Anjali smiles. But instead of handing me the bowl, she passes it to Lila, who takes a spoonful and feeds me like a baby. This *should* be really embarrassing but no one seems to take a second look.

"Delicious, na?"

"Khub bhalo," I reply. If it's true that Lila is the real reason I'm here, and the reason Granddad would have finally come back home if he'd lived long enough, then the very least I can do is try to speak a few words of Bengali to her.

She cups my chin in her hands and kisses me on the forehead, just like she did to Priya.

"Looks like you're a hit," says Priya, winking at me. "Come on, let's dance!"

She moves around the tiny rectangle of green carpet, prancing around with a plump boy of about seven who she spins round until she lets him drop to the floor in a dizzy heap. Now she's guiding me around the room and the aunties and uncles begin to clap. I try to follow what she's doing, but she's so graceful she makes me feel clumsy. I'm also worried in case my sari gets stepped on and it falls off! Thankfully someone walks into the room and Priya runs toward the door, abandoning me and the little dancing boy. He looks up at me hopefully for a second as if *I* could take over from Priya, but then he clocks my sari, thinks better of it, and wanders off.

I lean back on the arm of the sofa for a minute and glance at the door. Priya is chatting away to a tall man with a thick mane of hair pulled back from his face in a shoulder-length ponytail. He searches the room and when he finds my face he smiles, nods, and flicks away a strand of hair that's fallen over one eye. When he smiles his face looks younger, more boyish. He has huge almond-shaped eyes surrounded by thick lashes. It's only the eyes that I recognize from the photos Lila showed us when she came to London. He's wearing traditional cotton kurta pajamas and he's just about the most beautiful person I've ever seen in real life. Now he's walking toward me and smiling with his hand outstretched…

"Mira, this is Janu." Priya smiles, inspecting both of us for a reaction.

I can barely look him in the eye as he offers me his hand. His skin is rough and he has a bandage covering one finger.

Priya is watching me like a hawk. "I'm always telling him he's got the hands of a builder; I say, if you're going to be a carpenter you could at least remember to cut wood and not your fingers!" she jokes.

Janu takes my hands in his and smiles at me until I'm forced to meet his gaze. And when I do it feels like he's looking straight into me and reading my thoughts. I only have to glance down at my chest and feel the heat traveling up to my face to know that I must be blushing.

"So, you are Mira. I have...I mean...Priya has told me so very much about you," he says.

His voice lilts up and down with a low melody. He has a stronger accent than Priya's and Anjali's, less polished.

I try to say something back but my mouth won't work. What *is* the matter with me?

"Your sari is beautiful," Janu tells me. His eyes are the same color as mine, almost black. My heart's fluttering like a trapped bird, so when Anjali calls Janu over I can't help feeling relieved. He nods at me and then goes off to help her.

"Told you he likes homespun." Priya raises her eyebrows and dances off.

I'd planned to thank Janu for the paints and the flowers, but every thought left my head the moment I saw him. I feel hot, like I'm about to pass out, so I slide down into the comfy cushions of the sofa to try to pull myself together. An ancient stick-thin man in brown linen trousers and a crisp white shirt eases himself into the seat beside me.

"So you are Bimal's granddaughter. Very pleased to meet you indeed." He holds his hand out to me and shakes it formally. I can feel every delicate bone and vein through his skin. "I was his friend, you know." The old man's voice is dry and cracked. "I met your grandfather when I was Postmaster General of Kolkata. Those days it was top job, you know? Before all this fancy Internet." His eyes are all glazed over with a misty film. I'm not sure how well he can see. "In some ways I was the one who was responsible for him going to England all those years ago. You know, it was me who posted that letter personally to the ship's port with the reference for him to take up medical practice in England." He pauses to take a breath, again scanning my face, searching for Granddad.

I smile. I want him to carry on, because these are the pieces of Granddad's life that I should have asked him about when he was alive.

"He was just a young man in his twenties…handsome, you know, good-looking family, na!" The old man pats my hand and looks up at Prem and Anjali, who are chatting away. He rests his shiny bald head on the back of the sofa, as if he's exhausted himself with the effort of talking. Anjali comes over and gently smooths her hand over the creased skin of his forehead as she speaks to him. He nods with his eyes closed and then she gestures to Janu to come over and he gently lifts the old man out of his seat.

"Strong boy!" says the man, patting Janu's arm. "I too was strong once," he sighs, "but at my age you have to accept weakness. Every time you say good-bye, it may be the last." He turns back to me as Janu steers him away. I feel a weird rush of emotion. All I seem to be doing today is trying not to cry. Normally I'd be really embarrassed about getting so emotional in public, but no one seems to care here…

When Janu comes back into the room he comes straight over to me.

"He's very weak. Ninety-eight years old, you know. But he was so keen to meet you." Janu's looking into my eyes again. I can feel that blush starting to travel up my neck.

"Thanks for lending me the paints," I blurt out.

"It's nothing. You have paper?"

I shake my head, realizing I forgot to buy any at the mall.

"No problem. I can bring some," he says, still gazing into my eyes.

Suddenly Priya springs in between us, and I silently thank her.

"So, what adventures are you planning for us while Mira's here?" she asks Janu.

I hadn't counted on spending any time at all with Janu, but with the paints and now the flowers and the art paper, he already seems to be part of everything.

For the rest of the night all I can think about is how weird Jidé's going to think I am for not having told him that Janu lives with Priya's family. As if I was trying to cover something up, when the truth is I just didn't think about it. After all, Janu's at the refuge more than he's here. But what if Jidé thinks I kept it from him on purpose?

It's late and most of the guests have left now, and Janu has gone up to his balcony room. "Do you mind if I go and lie down for a while?" I ask Anjali. I am so tired all of a sudden.

"No, no. You're probably still jet-lagged! Priya will help me clear up, you go and have some sleep," she says gently, steering me toward the bedroom.

❧ ✦ ☙

Jidé is standing at the end of my bed.

"So you've lost my note," he says.

"It was in my case." I tell him.

"But you'll get it back?" he persists.

"I don't know."

"It's lost then." He sighs, turning and walking away.

The tears are rolling down my cheeks.

122

"But I know all the words off by heart…" I call after him.
He doesn't turn around.

~∞ ✤ ∞~

My pillow's soaked. I look over at Priya's bed, but she's already up. It's a relief she's not here to see me in such a state. I don't think I've ever cried in my sleep before, but that dream about Jidé was so real and horrible, and I've woken up feeling so muddied with guilt, even though I haven't done anything wrong. Except for…how can I start to explain the way I felt the moment I saw Janu, because the truth is I've never felt anything like that for anyone before.

I don't even want to think about yesterday. Even saying Janu's name feels like I'm betraying Jidé.

I've read about this sort of thing a million times in books and seen films, when people meet and there's something instant between them, some sort of pull that they don't understand… supposedly like Cathy and Heathcliff in *Wuthering Heights* (I read it from cover to cover on the plane). But I'm not sure that I believe in "love at first sight"…that being "meant for each other" stuff, Life's not like it is in books and films, is it? You don't actually have to *do* anything about those sorts of feelings, do you? I mean, that's the whole point of being human. We can reason so we don't have to let our emotions take over.

Anyway, you can't betray someone by just *thinking* about

someone else, can you? No one knows me better than he does, and probably no one knows him better than I do. I'm being ridiculous even thinking about Janu, he must think I'm so immature, blushing up bright red and not being able to talk to him! He probably just sees me as Priya's little cousin. And, as soon as I can, I'll tell him all about Jidé. Maybe Priya's already told him?

I go over to the bathroom and blow my nose, staring at the red-eyed me in the mirror. I splash some cold water on my face and try to wash away the smears of guilty tears. When I'm in this sort of mood the only thing to do is escape into my art… just lose myself in colors and shapes. Maybe that's what's wrong with me; my head's so stuffed full of pictures I need to get them out, but I've got nothing to paint on.

I take out my notebook and start scribbling down some words, just stuff that's going round and round in my head. Somehow just playing with words on a page and making them sound right together helps to calm me down. After about a hundred crossings out I only get this far:

World is turning round and round
World is turning upside down
Words are floating out in Space
Little girl
Tapping at the window of my mind
All the colors floating through the windows of time

My stomach rumbles. I put on Priya's robe and go into the living room to find a feast laid out on the table.

Normally I have toast or cereal for breakfast, but here there are curd sweets, mango slices, and doi yogurt, puri, and aloo. As I bite into a piece of mango I notice a note propped up against a vase.

> *Got to dance! See you around lunchtime. Help yourself to*
> *breakfast. Ma's at refuge.*
> *Number by phone. Need anything, call on Manu's wife.*
> *Chill!*
> *Priya x*

It's actually a relief to be on my own after all the busyness of yesterday. I glance at the clock and see that it's already ten. I can't believe I've slept for so long. I help myself to a puri stuffed with aloo, still hot from the warming plate.

There's a gentle knock at the front door of the flat. I get up from the table and walk toward it, but then pause, wondering if I should open it.

"Hello?" I call out.

"It's Janu," comes the low lilting voice from the other side of the door.

My heart's racing again and my face and neck are turning crimson. I will my cheeks to cool before I open the door. Janu's standing with a scroll of paper and a sketchbook under his arms. He's slightly out of breath, as if he's been running.

"I brought you this paper and book from the refuge," he says, pushing his hair away from his face.

I can't think of what to say. I feel like I can't move.

"I'm thinking you might want to do some painting?" he prompts, holding the paper toward me.

"Thanks. It's really kind of you," I say, taking the scroll from him. He must think I'm dim.

"Are you OK?" he asks. "No tears?"

My eyes are still puffy from crying. "Just tired," I lie, finally finding my voice.

"Probably this heat. Sorry, I have to go back now. Today is too much happening. You'll come soon to see. I will show you around so you can meet the staff and children. They are so looking forward to your artistic project!" He smiles.

"Me too." I smile back at him, but it's only half true.

I do want to see the refuge, but it's also been niggling at me since I got here. It was so easy to *say* I'd come up with a project to get time out of school, but now that I'm here I can't even begin to imagine standing in front of a class of children. Compared to the children I've already seen here living on the streets, what have I experienced that would make me qualified to teach them anything?

"Priya tells me you are talented artist," says Janu.

"Not really!" My voice comes out too high-pitched.

Why can't I just be normal with him?

"I also like art, especially working with wood—making things and carving. Anyway, I must go now," he says, looking straight into my eyes, just as he did last night.

"Thanks for these!" I tell him, lifting up the paper scroll and sketch pad.

"Not a problem," he says.

I close the door and breathe out, looking down at myself. I'd completely forgotten I'm still wearing Priya's dressing gown. Janu has probably been up for hours working...I'm not even dressed and I'm telling him *I'm* tired! He must think I'm so lazy.

I walk through to the bedroom and place the handmade paper on the low table beside the bed. It fits perfectly, but it's curled up at the ends and needs something to weigh it down. I run my fingers over the slightly bumpy surface; it's as if it's ingrained with some sort of hair. I've never painted on anything like it before. I walk over to Priya's trophy cupboard with the idea I can use her dance trophies as weights, but then the carved wooden edges of the border give me an idea of how to begin this painting. Working out how to start is always the hardest part. I pick up the paper and take a charcoal rubbing of the carved pattern around the outside of the cupboard. At first I think I'll use it as a border, like a picture frame, but I love the effect so much I decide to make it the background of the whole painting, like a textured wash under everything. It looks a bit like ancient peeling wallpaper.

I think about Granddad's brother, Shudi, who carved this cupboard so long ago, yet there's still something of him here to trace. I plug in my iPod, turn up the volume, and let the music flood my mind. I let a drop of deep red paint splash into the middle of the paper and watch it seep into the texture and spread, like blood through a bandage. Then I take a fine brush and trail blood lines all over the page.

I don't really think about what I'm going to paint. I just sketch in the things and people that pop into my mind…a suitcase floating in space, the old couple kissing at the airport, Dust Boy…"ma'am, ma'am, little money, ma'am…" I can still hear his voice echoing around my head. I draw School Girl in her clean uniform, sitting under her blue tarpaulin; then I add her mother plaiting her daughter's hair. Next comes the great glass dome of the mall, with Manu's Ambassador parked outside, Branded Woman and her baby peering in through the window. I draw Priya and me dancing on her bed, and the sari shop with Anjali holding up a piece of cream silk. Then I sketch a sari cupboard, and in the door I place a little silver key with a heart-shaped end, just as Anjali described it in her letter. I take out all of Shudi's rainbow paints and the finest brush I can find, and brush stroke by brush stroke, line by line, fold by fold, I fill the cupboard with saris and even manage to paint in the detail of some lace-like border patterns in gold and silver.

Priya bounds into the room and I pull out my earphones. I have no idea how long I've been working on this.

"OMG, have you done all that in half a day?!" asks Priya.

"I'm just sketching really," I tell her.

"That's not what *I* call sketching. Wait till Janu sees this! Serious talent! You'll never get away from teaching at the refuge," she says, taking the paintbrush out of my hand and springing a great big cousin hug on me.

Human Garlands

✿✿✿

There's no fan in the yellow cab we've jumped into, and the driver refuses to have the windows open because of the pollution, which is really bad today. After being stuck in here for about half an hour I feel like I'm cooking. Even Priya keeps fanning herself.

As soon as the oven doors of the cab are thrown open I take a deep breath of hot air, scented with the sweet smell of roses and petrol fumes. We stand under the vast metal arches of the Howrah Bridge, where thousands of people and vehicles of every kind are crossing back and forth as if they're taking part in some epic choreographed dance. This place makes the middle of London look like the countryside!

I look down at the water flowing slowly under the bridge. I love the feeling of being this close to the river. It's like in London when you walk along the Thames—the city suddenly feels rooted. The water keeps on flowing, and no matter how important people might think they are, the river was there before them and it will be there after them, flowing on and on through time. I look down at the wide brown river as boats of every size—from great metal tankers to tiny rowing boats with colorful bunting flags—pass along the river. There's so much I don't know about this city. Today I read in my guidebook that the River Hooghly was a tributary of the holy River Ganges. I read about those ghats too—the steps that lead right down to the water's edge, where people are washing their clothes and bathing.

"I wouldn't recommend it!" Priya laughs as we watch a bare-chested man walk into the murky brown water. "But this you've got to see!" She grabs me by the hand and leads me down some steep concrete steps and along a pathway. A smell of roses fills the air, getting stronger and stronger. And then I'm in among a festival of flowers and people.

"How do you like the flower market?" asks Priya.

"I love it!"

"Thought you would!" She smiles, looking pleased with herself that she chose the right place to bring me to.

I take out my sketchbook and try to capture anything that grabs my attention, which is just about everything: a baby peering over her mother's shoulder, wearing a crown of pink and white roses in her hair; ancient hands stringing a garland of marigolds; a young girl in a bright pink salwar-kameez, her bare feet planted among a mountain of yellow flowers; a teenage boy who is smoking a cigarette and blowing smoke rings in our direction.

"Why don't you take photos?" asks Priya, leaning over my shoulder and watching me sketch.

I shrug. I feel a bit strange about taking photos of people I don't know. It's cowardly of me, I know, because I'm happy to snap away through the window of a car, but face to face with people like this is different. But I would like to record it all because I know that I could be inspired to write and paint about all this for ages when I get back home. Just as I think this, a girl about our age walks past us with a basket of marigolds on her head.

"Photo, photo!" she chants, clicking her fingers.

Priya raises her eyebrows to ask me whether she should, and I nod yes. As soon as the picture's taken the girl holds out her hand for some money. Priya drops a few rupees into her palm and she walks on. I suppose I should ask people's permission before I sketch them too, because in a way I think you can take even more from someone when you draw them than when you take a photo. Once, when Jidé and I went to Brighton, I started to sketch a homeless woman and her dog that were sitting by the pier. She got so angry that she chased us up the street, grabbed my sketchbook off me, and ripped out the page. I'll never forget her dog growling and baring its teeth, as if it was standing up for her. When Jidé tried to calm things down by offering the woman some money she just spat in his face and said, "You think just because I'm poor I don't have any." I couldn't get her words out of my head for ages afterward.

We walk between mounds of flowers and smelly gutters, along the dirt path lined with more blue-tarpaulin-roofed shacks. Priya leads me to a raised platform that looks like an empty market stall and sits down.

"You can sketch all you want from up here," she says.

I'd love to sit here and draw all day, but I don't know how much longer I can take this heat. It's hotter than ever today, and the smells and colors of the flowers are so intense, that I feel dizzy with it all. I rub my eyes to check I'm not imagining this…because what I think I'm looking at is a mountain of flowers walking toward me. Now I can just about make out the thin limbs of a man. He's almost completely camouflaged by the garlands of roses and jasmine tumbling like a waterfall over the edges of the basket he's carrying on his head.

"Priya!" a high-pitched voice shouts out from somewhere in among the flowers.

I jump backward in fright. Priya laughs and puts a hand out to steady me. When I look closer I see that in the middle of the basket, swathed in garlands, is the sweet smiling face of a woman wearing an enormous red powdered teep between her eyes and sindoor through her parting. Priya waves toward her as she's lowered carefully to the floor, still in her basket. The man lifts her up as if she weighs nothing at all and places her on the platform beside us. She slowly begins to remove garlands from her neck and childlike body. Underneath her flowers she's wearing a bright blue salwar-kameez. I look down at her feet and see that they're twisted in the wrong direction. I am trying not to stare as Priya holds her hands together in a namaste and introduces me.

"This is Chameli and her husband, Ajoy," she says as we namaste each other and Priya hands Chameli an envelope. "For the flowers yesterday," Priya explains to me.

"*Ki sundor*," I tell Chameli, pointing to the garlands and hoping you can use the same phrase to describe flowers as beautiful as for humans—it's something Granddad used to say to me, and it just slipped out.

Priya smiles at me a bit taken aback. "I think you know more Bengali than you let on!" she says.

"Only a few words," I say as Priya listens to Chameli.

"She says you are very beautiful!" Priya translates, giggling and chatting away to the woman before she turns back to me.

"Chameli predicts that you are sure to meet the boy of your dreams here in India. She says that *I* on the other hand should go to London!"

I smile back and I can't help thinking of Janu, even though I've been trying so hard not to.

Chameli places a garland of marigolds around my neck.

"Have you got a few rupees for me to give her?" I whisper to Priya.

"Not necessary, she'll be insulted," says Priya.

"Would you ask her if she minds me taking a photo?"

Chameli nods and holds out her arms to me. I hand my camera over to Priya and I sit down next to her and her basket of garlands. I can't get over how warm and generous people are here, even strangers.

❧ ✦ ☙

"So what's their story?" I ask as we meander back through the market past the mountains of flowers.

"They came to the refuge when they were still young. Since then they have taught so many children how to make garlands, and sometimes they go with Ajoy and Chameli to stay in their village and help them to farm the flower fields. Janu is trying to build it into a partnership for the refuge kids. Anyway, they're quite famous, you know. Ajoy carries her over the Howrah Bridge in a basket loaded up with garlands maybe three or four times a week. They have to carry as many garlands as they can, so when they sit on the train their faces are sometimes covered by flowers. They've been written about in tourist guides and everything. If they've had a good day, Ajoy says, he only has to carry his

135

'most beautiful flower' back home. Romantic or what!"
Priya laughs.

Now she's tugging me across a sea of bodies, and I'm clinging on to her because I know that if we get separated I won't have a clue how to get back to her flat. I haven't even memorized her address. I should *really* sort my mobile phone out and ask Anjali for one that works. At least then, when Jidé comes back I can text him. I don't know why, but I didn't think we would have as much freedom to travel around Kolkata as I do in London.

At the end of the bridge we're pushed through a bottleneck of human bodies and out onto the road. Within seconds Priya manages to hail a yellow cab. Once we're inside she passes me a bottle of water and I drink greedily. I'm so hot and bothered— my hair is plastered over my skin and my spine's sticking to the plastic seats. I lean back, trying to catch a breeze on my face from the slightly open window.

Priya hands me a wipe. "I forget you're not used to this heat. It builds and builds so you think you can't stand it anymore, and then the sky opens…whoosh! I love it when all this city noise is drowned out by the music of the monsoon rain. They're saying it's coming early this year…I hope maybe before you leave."

Sometimes when Priya talks it's almost as if she's composing a song, trying things out for the way they sound: "drowned out by the music of the monsoon rain…"

When we get back to the flat Priya rushes in, flings on her

dance clothes, and runs out again. "Sorry I've got all these rehearsals," she calls as she disappears down the stairs. "I promise I'll race back."

I pick up my garland and study how the flowers have been woven so skillfully into it. Then I paint a border of jasmine around the edges of my painting. After that I add a scene with Chameli in her basket, her face peering out through the garlands.

"Everything all right, Mira?" calls Anjali as she comes in from work.

"Fine!" I shout back.

"Have you had something to eat?" she asks, wandering into Priya's room and taking a good long look at my painting. "That's really coming on. You met Chameli and Ajoy then?" She smiles, inspecting the basket of garlands I've been painting. For a moment I think she's going to say something else, but then she seems to get lost in the detail of the painting. She looks over to Priya's trophy cupboard in the corner of the room and back at the paper.

I follow her gaze to the section I've worked up of the sari cupboard with the little silver key.

"What's this?" she asks, a thundercloud passing across her face.

I suppose it is the most complete bit of the painting. Strange in a way, because it's more or less the only thing I haven't actually seen with my own eyes. It's just the thing that captured my imagination in her letter. And then I get why she's asking about it…I should have realized the danger of adding the detail of the heart-shaped end to the key.

"Just one of the cupboards in the sari shop," I mumble.

"I didn't see anything like this." Anjali looks straight at me as if demanding an answer. "Or that little key…"

It's strange how she's so kind and calm about things except when I touch on anything to do with what was written in her letters: first the house in Doctor's Lane and now the sari cupboard. It's like she knows I've read them and is waiting for me to admit it. She walks over to the wardrobe and takes out my sari, smoothing her hand over the silk. She turns to me as if she's about to say something, but then she just sighs and places the sari back in the cupboard. Definitely weird.

Anjali takes a deep breath and walks over to the door but just as she's about to leave she turns around and says, as if to apologize, "It's going to be an amazing painting, but I don't want you spending so much time here when you could be experiencing more. I'm sorry Priya's so busy. She was only supposed to have a couple of hours' rehearsals a day—it's why we thought this would be a good time for you to come, despite this heat, but one of the dancers, Paddy—I think you've met her—has hurt her hip, so they need extra practices to rework the dances without her."

"It's OK," I say. Anjali looks really tired, and I don't want her to feel like I'm something extra to worry about. Anyway, the truth is I sort of need a bit of switch-off time.

"No, it's not OK! So I have organized for Ma to take you sightseeing, and tomorrow you can come to the refuge and maybe Janu can show you around."

I don't even hear the rest of what she says because my head is whirling. If I'm going to spend any time with Janu, I'll have to find a way to tell him about Jidé. That will settle everything.

The Refuge

✿✿✿

This continuous heat, the sights zipping past the window of this tram, and, if I'm honest with myself, sitting this close to Janu, is making my head spin. At least I've been able to talk to him today and, now and again, even look him in the eye. I snap away at the street scenes, but I'm not thinking about what I'm seeing. I know it's sad of me, but as well as becoming a bit obsessed with trying to capture everything, this camera is coming in useful to hide behind. I'm still trying to find a moment to tell Janu about Jidé. So far we've sort of had polite conversation; he's asked me how I liked the flower market and now we're on to Priya and her dancing.

"Bharatanatyam," he says, "is Priya's best dance. It is funny, because all the time she's trying to be so…modern, but already she is one of the best young classical dancers in Kolkata."

I've been so fixed on talking to Janu that I've hardly noticed the dust, sweat, and bustle of the rest of the journey to the refuge. Maybe I'm learning, like Manu said, to close my eyes and my ears to the road. And I think he was right, because even in this heat I'm starting to feel more at home.

The tram grinds to a halt and Janu stands up, gesturing for me to follow him.

"This area is called Chowringee," Janu says as we step off the tram.

We walk down a street bustling with traders selling cloth, handbags, children's clothes, sizzling food…Some jalebi are being thrown into sizzling fat, the sweet batter spirals round and round, spitting and spluttering up into coiled sweets. My mouth instantly waters as I inhale the sugary smell. An image of Granddad eating these for breakfast fills my head and makes me smile. Now I know what he meant when he used to talk about "memory food."

"Want to try?" Janu asks, stopping to buy a packet and offering me one. I've had these cold at home, but never fresh from the pan. This hot, syrupy sweet must be just about the most delicious thing I've ever eaten.

"Don't tell Anjali. She thinks eating from the street will make you ill. But it is the best food you can find anywhere. The most delicious is when you don't expect it. It's there in front of you and you just have to try it."

"Do you eat these every day?!" I ask, wiping my mouth.

"No! Only for special occasions"—he smiles at me—"or I would be getting fat!" He taps his flat, muscly stomach.

"How did the refuge start?" I ask, trying to change the subject. I already know some of this but I want to hear it from Janu.

"Anjali and Dinesh opened it about sixteen years ago. It started in one room and now the whole building belongs to them. Your uncle and aunt are good people," says Janu. "Dinesh is campaigning for new businesses to make partnerships, sharing the wealth and paying more for education and health of the poor. This is the only way to move forward."

Janu speaks with the same passion Granddad Bimal used, when he would say that people in Britain don't realize how lucky they are that they have the right to go to a doctor or to school no matter how little money they have.

As we walk through the tall turquoise door of the refuge I stop to look at a plaque and take a photo. A Bengali inscription is written on it, as well as a picture of a basket overflowing with flowers.

"Translation is 'House of Garlands,'" Janu explains. "Anjali wanted to teach the children some trade as well as schooling, so they can sell what they make from here to tourists. The number-one most popular thing tourists buy is garlands of flowers."

"Priya told me that Chameli and Ajoy teach them," I say.

"Not so much now—some of the older children have learned," Janu explains, but he looks a bit taken aback. "Oh yes, I am forgetting that you met them at the flower market." He smiles at me as we walk into a simple, clean reception room. There is a man wearing an orange turban sitting behind the front desk. He immediately stands up and greets Janu warmly. Janu takes me around the building, giving me a guided tour.

"You don't mind if I take photos, do you? I promised my school—"

"Of course!" he says, waving my question away. "Here is where we teach lessons. Basic literacy and mathematics," he says, pointing into a classroom where children are sitting cross-legged on floor mats and reciting times tables in their singsong voices. Some of them smile and wave at Janu and he waves back before indicating that they should turn round and concentrate. Janu seems so at home here that it feels almost as if this place belongs to him.

"Blue rooms are for learning and orange rooms for painting, drawing, garland-making, and carpentry. The green room is for sewing, yellow room for eating," says Janu. We walk along a beautiful corridor, its walls are lined with hundreds of brightly colored floor mats rolled up and neatly tucked into deep wooden shelves. The different colored scrolled ends make the walls look so pretty. Janu notices me looking at them.

"Since I made this I don't understand why everybody loves it so much." Janu shrugs. "I call it my wall of beds."

"Where do the children sleep?" I ask.

"In all the rooms!" We stop at a window that looks down onto a communal courtyard. There are pots of flowers scattered among the water troughs, where children are soaping themselves, washing and playing happily. Janu laughs as a little boy takes a great mouthful of water and spurts it all over his friend, and his friend splashes him back. Janu opens the window and shouts something that makes the boys laugh before they go back to washing.

"What did you say to them?" I ask.

"I told them if they want to play with water there is always washing pots to do in the kitchen!" Janu looks out of the window again. "Don't look so worried! We try to lighten their hearts." I smile nervously, not realizing I'm covering my mouth with my hand, which has been a habit since I started wearing my braces, even though they're not there anymore.

"You should not cover this smile," Janu tells me, taking my hand and leading me along the corridor to another room, where girls and boys are sewing on old-fashioned black and gold machines or by hand. I've noticed people here are much more relaxed about physical contact, so Janu holding my hand probably means nothing at all to him, but my heart is thudding as I feel the rough patches on his palm.

"We offer only basics, but we are always looking for scholarship funds." He says, letting go of my hand and then steering me up a staircase that has a white door at the top.

"White is for medicine. Often our children need medical attention." Janu explains as he taps on the door and then quietly opens it. Inside a doctor is examining the encrusted eyes of a boy who must be about my age. Many other children are in the room too. I can see that most of them have eyes in a similar condition to those of the boy in the doctor's chair.

"OK, Lal?" asks Janu.

"Not really, Janu! I could do with some more help here," replies the young doctor, with a cheery voice. I wasn't expecting that. "If you could bathe their eyes and put in some antibiotic drops that would be great."

Janu walks over to a glass cabinet, takes out some disposable gloves and hands a packet to me. Then he takes out cotton-wool pads and a stack of tiny metal bowls, the size of egg cups, and hands me half of them. Taking one from the top of the stack, he pours into it a tiny amount of boiling water from an urn.

"Watch closely," he says. He sits down on the floor cross-legged and asks me to do the same. The boy gets up out of the doctor's chair and comes over to us. He forces one of his gunked-up eyes to open into a tiny slit so that he can just about make his way to Janu, who takes the boy's hand and eases him to the floor. The boy's head rests on Janu's lap. Janu dips the cotton wool in the warm water before wiping from the inside to the outside of the eye. After each wipe he throws the cotton pad into a plastic bin. He does the same, again and again, until the yellow crust that's gluing the boy's eyes together starts to flake away.

"Clean the eye, then pull the lid up and squeeze three drops. Fresh pad for each wipe, then throw cotton wool away. Put new pair of gloves for each child. OK?" Janu gives me a piercing look as if to ask, "Are you up to this?"

I nod, because I don't want him to know that I've never done anything that matters like this before. Occasionally I'll help Mum look after Laila, and I used to change her nappies, but that's about it.

"Many children go blind because simple infections are not dealt with," Janu tells me. "You know it takes only a few days of a little care to get better, but if not treated…"

A young woman wearing small black-rimmed glasses, a bright yellow kurti, and trainers enters the room in a rush. She nods at the doctor a little shyly and he smiles back before she goes over and talks to Janu. She places a hand on his arm and I notice how delicate her hands are. One of the things that happens to you when you can't really speak a language is that you get better at watching…at reading people's body language and the looks on their faces. So I know even before he tells me that, whatever it is she's asking him, it's something urgent he's got to do.

"I must go. Lal will instruct you," says Janu, getting up and telling the other children in the room in English and then in Bengali to wait nicely to have their eyes cleaned by me. By *me*!

I count at least thirty children waiting to be treated. I take a deep breath and steady my nerves. I clean the boy's other eye and then call the next child over. I can't believe how quiet and patient they all are, even the youngest child. When Laila once had to have drops in her eyes she screamed like she was being murdered, but not even the toddler being held by her big sister, who can't be more than five years old herself, cries when I lift her practically sealed eyelid. It feels so weird to take these strangers' heads onto my knee and wipe the infection out of their eyes. They all have wet hair from bathing outside and smell of the same slightly herbal antiseptic soap and shampoo. I notice that their clothes, a combination of T-shirts and shorts with different logos all over them, all smell of the same washing powder.

Granddad Bimal often used to ask if I wanted to be a doctor, and it seemed so far away from anything I like to do, like art and writing. But now I'm here, helping these children, I can understand why he loved being a doctor so much.

The boy whose eyes we treated first goes to sit next to Lal and, even though he can only half see through his sore eyes, it's clear he's desperate to help.

"This young man is interested in training in medicine!" says Lal when he notices me watching him. The boy looks my way through heavy lids and nods.

"Are you training too?" Lal asks, wiping the sweat from his forehead.

"Oh, no! I'm just visiting, from London. Anjali's my aunt. I'm Mira!"

I can't picture myself choosing a profession. I'm not even sure what I'll do after secondary school—maybe go to art college or university, but then what?…Janu's only two years older than me, but he's already got so much responsibility it seems like he's practically running this place.

"Are you training to be a doctor?" I ask Lal.

"I'm in my third year! I chose to come here for my volunteering job. It's where my family's from." He smiles.

"My granddad too," I tell him.

"The children keep laughing at me for huffing and puffing away in the heat. They think I should be used to this temperature." Lal chatters on as I carefully clean eye after eye.

Finally I treat the last child. I have no idea how long I've been sitting here, but one of my legs has gone to sleep under me.

"Great work!" Lal says. "Want some food?" He goes over to the sink and scrubs his hands, and I do the same.

ᜰᜱᜲ ✿ ᜳ᜴᜵

We sit down at a table in the yellow eating room. There are children scattered over little mats on the floor, eating dhal and rice from bowls. Some I recognize from this morning. They wave and I wave back and they nudge each other and giggle.

"How did you get on?" asks Janu, striding over to us and taking a seat.

"She was a star!" says Lal.

"I knew she would be!" Janu beams at me.

Here it comes again, my ridiculous blush. I'm saved from

speaking as the man who was sitting in Reception enters the room and speaks to Janu.

"Sorry!" says Janu. "A fund-raising company is in today and I must show them around quickly." He looks apologetically at me and then walks out of the room.

I suddenly feel hungry. I take a huge spoon of rice and dhal, but as I watch some of the children ladle food into their mouths I realize that I don't really know what hungry feels like.

I chat to Lal and enjoy the delicious food. I find myself drinking glass after glass of water. The heat today is intense. My clothes are drenched in sweat, but I'm starting to get used to that, and now Janu's walking back toward me, mobile phone in one hand. He pats Lal on the back and asks if I'm ready to leave. I say my good-byes and we stroll back down the "wall of beds" corridor, then through another door, which takes us into a shop that faces out on to the main road.

In the shop there are lots of tourists milling around a huge carved wooden tree in the middle that almost touches the ceiling. Garlands of flowers hang from its branches. That's why it smells so sweet in here. As I get closer I see there are lots of little hollows and shelves carved out of the trunk and the branches, and inside these hollows are things that the children have made, like table napkins and coasters, handmade sandals in every size, little carved animals, and paintings on silk, all on display in this beautiful carved tree. I look at the faces of the people as they move around the trunk, and they all look as enchanted as I am. Every wall of the shop is covered in quilts made of tiny scraps of saris like the one on Priya's bed. Little tags hang off the quilts. *Not for Sale. Commission only* they say, and some of them have *sold—display only*. I've never been into a shop like this before; it's more like an art exhibition. I touch the great leaves of the carved wooden branches.

"Is this the Kadamba tree, the one outside Anjali's house?"

Janu nods.

I can't believe the skill that's gone into making this. People are pointing at the incredible carving and all the different objects in the tree, taking things off shelves and out of hollows to inspect them before buying. Then I see that nestling in the largest hollow in the trunk is a wide-rimmed basket lined with roses and jasmine. I peer into it and there among the flowers is a hand-carved, life-sized sculpture of a newborn baby, legs and arms all curled in on themselves, eyes closed. I take a photo of the tree and the baby, though I don't suppose it will really capture how amazing this is.

"Can I pick it up?" I whisper to Janu.

He smiles and nods.

I lift the baby carefully off its pillow of flowers, because it looks so real it almost feels like I don't want to wake it. A few other people peer over my shoulder to look at it as I cradle it in my arms.

A man with a red face and drips of sweat pouring from his forehead asks Janu how much he wants for the baby carving.

"Sorry! Not for sale," says Janu in a sharp voice I haven't heard him use before. The man shrugs and then walks away grumbling, "It shouldn't be on display then, should it?"

Janu ignores him.

"Is this your work?" I ask, pointing from the tree, that I notice is concreted into the ground, to the lifelike baby I'm holding in my arms.

Janu nods. "Actually the tree is crude—needs more decoration. I'm still working on it, but people are always trying to buy the baby. Once an artist from America offered me three thousand dollars. He said he would put it in his New York gallery. It was so much money I told Anjali to sell it, but she swears she never will. I tell her we should secure it, so no one tries to pick it up, but she says when people hold it in their arms it pulls their hearts out. She's so sentimental!"

I'm running my hands over the smooth wooden surface of the baby's cheeks, but a high-pitched cry punctures the air, almost making me drop it! Janu touches my arm and points to the lank-haired woman who's carrying her tiny baby in a carrier on her front.

"It's not real!" he laughs, taking the carving off me and placing it back on its garland pillow.

On the way back to the flat I close my eyes and rest my head against the worn black leather of the tram seat. Janu places his hand on my arm. I open my eyes and sit up.

"Thanks for helping today." He looks at me with so much kindness in his eyes. I feel—how did he say it?—as if "my heart's being pulled out."

"I enjoyed it," I tell him, very aware of his hand still resting on my arm. "Well, not exactly enjoyed, but…"

"I know, working with the children brings complicated feelings. Now, tell me something of life in London."

So I describe my family and then…Jidé. I tell Janu how I love hanging out with Jidé and that he's clever and funny. As I'm talking Janu pulls his hand away from my arm and moves away from me so that there's space between us on the seat.

"He sounds like a fine boy," Janu says, staring out of the window.

We're quiet together for the rest of the journey, but it's a deafening silence.

The worst thing is, I *should* feel better because I've told him early enough so that neither of us needs to feel embarrassed. This is exactly what I planned; it's the right thing to do, so why is it that I feel so miserable now?

Cat's Eyes

✿✿✿

Bacha's barking wakes me up.

"Mira...Mira!" Someone's whispering, "Shhhhhhh," and giggling.

I kneel on the bed and look through the window. Two huge midnight-blue cat's eyes peer back at me through the darkness, making me gasp with fright.

"Let me in. It's me, Priya!"

I release the catch on the wrought-iron grid and pull back the lace curtains. Now a leg appears through the window, then a graceful arm, and finally through the dark looms Priya's elfin face. "Shh," she whispers, even though *she's* the one making all the noise. She pulls herself through the window and tumbles head first toward the marble floor, finishing her entrance with a forward roll. She's obviously done this before.

I'm still dazed as I stare up at her cat's eyes.

"Funky contacts or what?!" she says, inspecting her reflection in the bathroom mirror. "Well, aren't you going to ask me where I've been?"

I nod, feeling a bit disorientated—Priya was in her bed when I went to sleep, and I have no idea when she sneaked off or where she's been.

"The time has come to introduce you to DJ Prey!" She laughs, drawing her hands into a namaste. She jumps onto my bed and starts to swing her hips and pound her feet in the weirdest mixture of club and Kathak dance.

"DJ Prey is in the house, so you better get ready for some serious sounds!" she announces, holding her hand to her ear as if she's listening in to headphones.

I take out my camera.

"Got video on that thing?" she asks.

I nod and point the camera at her.

"And tonight in the house of DJ Prey,

"I present to you my coz,

"Hot from the club scene in…

"London town.

"Give it up for…

"Miiiiiiiiiiiiiraaaaa!"

She leaps over to her wardrobe and flings open the door.

"Right! No arguments." She grabs my iPod, searching through it and handing me the earphones. "Just choose something and sing!"

"I can't, without rehearsing," I say, laughing.

"Why not? Have you written anything while you're here?"

I go over to my bag and take out my notebook and hand it to Priya.

"Intense! This is great. Got a tune in your head?"

I nod. The fact is I can never write lyrics without thinking up the tune first. They sort of go together.

"Yes, but I haven't practiced it or anything," I hesitate.

"Well here's your chance to become a recording artist," Priya laughs, thrusting a microphone in my face and counting me in. I take a deep breath, doesn't seem like I have much choice...

"World is turning around and around
"World is turning upside down
"Words are floating out in space..."

My voice peters out as I start to giggle. But for once Priya is dead serious. I can't believe it, but she looks as if she's actually quite moved.

"I love the break in your voice. Keep singing, come on, this could be good."

She waits for me to compose myself and start again.

"World is turning around and around
"World is turning upside down

"Words are floating out in Space

"Stolen words

"Stolen glances

"Little girl

"Tapping at the window of my mind

"All the colors floating through the windows of time

"Smell of jasmine haunting all my days and nights

"Secrets floating to me

"Secrets floating from me

"Smell of jasmine floating through the windows of time

"Stolen words

"Stolen glances

"Little girl tapping at the window of my mind

"All the colors floating through the windows of time."

"Not bad! Sing it once more!" Priya orders.

I have two more goes before she's happy.

"Peeeeeerfect! Got that!" Priya listens back to my voice through her earphones. "I always knew with that mad laugh of yours you'd be able to blast it out a bit!" she says, handing me the earphones.

It sounds OK actually. I'm always a bit surprised when I hear my own voice, as if it belongs to someone else.

"What're you going to do with the recording?" I ask Priya.

"Surprise!" she says, cranking up the music to full volume again. Then she jumps back on to her bed and pulls me to my feet. We are both laughing and dancing now.

"Turn that music down!" Anjali appears at the door with a half-annoyed, half-amused look on her face. "It's one o'clock in the morning, for goodness' sake," she tells us in a mock-strict voice, but I can tell that she's trying not to laugh. My mum would go ballistic if I woke her up at this time of night playing music. "I've got tickets for you for Nicco Park, when the gala's over," says Anjali. "You and Mira can go wild then! But for now you two need to get some sleep—and so do I."

In one swift pounce Priya has jumped off the bed and is lifting Anjali off her feet and swinging her round. She's incredibly strong for someone so slight.

"Thanks, Ma! You're the best in the world!" says Priya, planting a kiss on her cheek.

"OK, OK, put me down!" Anjali laughs. "Anyway, what are you doing still dressed? And what have you done to your eyes?"

Priya shrugs.

Anjali sighs. "Never mind, I'm not sure I want to know. Just quickly get washed and into bed." She shakes her head and goes back to her own room.

Priya closes the bedroom door and goes into the bathroom. When she comes back out her eyes are normal again. She flicks off the light and I hear her get changed and into bed.

"What's Nicco Park?" I whisper in the dark.

"It's like Disneyland. Best rides ever. You wait till we do the water chute! It blows your brains!"

"OK! But where *have* you been?"

"With the Pod," Priya says, which doesn't really answer my question.

"Anjali told me Paddy's hurt."

"Doesn't stop her organizing a gig though! That's where we've been, checking out somewhere to *party*! I'm telling you, we'll get this scene buzzing like Mumbai, but first we've got to build it, getting hotter and hotter till we break out big time, like the monsoon…there'll be no stopping us! Top secret, *yaar*! I wish I could have taken you with me but, trust me, the surprise will be worth it!" she whispers. "And don't tell Janu I was out either."

"Why not?"

"He always wants to play the great protector, like his Lord Vishnu. How did you two get on anyway?"

"Fine!" I don't dare say anymore in case I give away my feelings.

"Thought you would! No *stolen glances* then?"

"I wasn't thinking about…"

"Whatever!" Priya grins.

It hadn't occurred to me that Janu might be religious. I suppose I don't really know anything much about him.

"Night, coz!" Priya yawns.

"Night!" I say, trying to wipe the disturbing memory of Priya's midnight blue cat's eyes from my mind.

Kali Force

❁✸❁

Anjali and Priya are arguing in Bengali at a hundred miles an hour. I hear my name at least six times, mostly out of Priya's mouth, so I'm beginning to wonder what I've done to offend her until I hear…

"Gala, gala, gala, all day, all night…gala, gala…"

And then *slam* goes the front door. Priya must make it down the stairs at breakneck speed because Bacha's already barking his greeting at her. I climb on the bed and look out of the window to see Priya batting him off her and stomping up the road with her chin in the air, ignoring Bacha's whine until he finally gives up trailing her. Anjali knocks gently and then comes in to the room. "I'm so sorry, Mira," she says, "I've called the airport every day since you got here, but I'm getting no joy from them at all. I told your ma she'd better think about claiming for your case on the insurance. She was happy to get your email, by the way.

She told me she's fine just to email, if you think it makes you less homesick than Skyping."

"OK. But don't worry about the case," I say. At first I was upset about losing everything in it, all my clothes and the presents for everyone, but now the only thing I really care about, that I know can never be replaced, is Jidé's note.

"Where's Priya today?" asks Manu, looking at Anjali and me sitting on the backseat.

"Rehearsals," answers Anjali as she turns to me. "You probably heard that she was annoyed with me this morning because she wanted to take you out today. Still, you won't mind spending a few hours with your old auntie, will you? It'll be a good chance for us to get to know each other a little better!"

"So that's why she was upset?" I check, relieved that it wasn't something I'd done to offend her.

Anjali nods. "It's hard on her, having all these extra rehearsals while you're here. And maybe hard on you too."

"I'm having a great time," I assure her.

"Good. I'm just so happy that you and Priya are getting on so well."

"Can we go to a bank to change my money?" I ask. So far Anjali's refused to let me pay for a single thing.

"Na, na, not necessary!" She smiles, "You hold on to it. This is all my pleasure," she says, squeezing me to her. "It's just like

161

me and your ma when she came over…" Her voice catches with emotion.

I do love being here, and meeting Priya has been brilliant. The problem is, I feel exactly the same with Anjali as I do about talking to Mum—guilty, guilty, guilty, and sort of annoyed with them both at the same time. I just want to know the truth, why mum and granddad lost touch with their family for so long.

It's starting to drive me crazy thinking about it!

～❀～

"Prudence…Learning…Motherhood!" reads out Anjali, pointing at three enormous sculptures of women inside the gardens of the Victoria Memorial. "That just about covers it! Here it is. What do you think?" she asks as we walk through the manicured formal gardens and the enormous sculpture of Queen Victoria looking mean and moody, towering over everything and everyone on her great stone plinth. I suppose she does what she's supposed to, makes you feel small.

"Granddad used to talk about this statue," I say. "When we were learning about Queen Victoria at school he always said that she needed an enormous gown because under her puffy skirts her legs were straddling continents."

Anjali laughs. "He was right about that!"

We wander up to the great marble dome—the symbol of the

British Raj—up the steps, and into the building. There are classical paintings hanging everywhere.

"I can't get my head around the idea that you can just walk into someone else's country and take over," I say, following a wall of golden-framed grainy black and white photographs of British colonels and officers, all proudly wearing their uniforms and medals.

Anjali smiles. "You do remind me of Uma at your age," she says.

"What was she like?"

"Thoughtful, a bit dreamy, head in the clouds…a real idealist. She was full of big questions…and she would ask and ask and ask until she got an answer."

This *must* be my moment to ask Anjali what happened. By the sounds of it, Mum would have.

"So why did everyone lose touch for so long?"

"That doesn't matter. You're here now." Anjali shrugs and I feel that great heavy door being slammed shut against me again.

"Next stop Kalighat Temple?" asks Manu, peering at us through the mirror.

Anjali just nods and closes her eyes. It's obvious her eyes, and ears, are sealed against any more questions.

～❖ ～

Bright orange marigolds line the paths to the temple. We walk up the stone steps where there are hundreds of pairs of brightly colored sandals patiently waiting for their owners to return. I take a photo because I'd love to do a painting of this sea of shoes. In London if I left my shoes on the steps of St. Paul's I would be worried that someone might steal them, but here, even though there are so many people who don't even have shoes, I don't think anyone would take them.

I place my sandals next to a pair of shiny black shoes. They're exactly like the ones Granddad used to leave sitting neatly in the hallway. I know it's weird, but I keep getting a feeling that he really is traveling with me on this journey, not only in my dreams either.

As we step over the threshold of the temple Anjali covers her head with her chunni and I do the same. Once we get inside I can't believe how much energy and heat can be produced by people walking and chanting. The air smells of incense and sweat. As we wait our turn to approach the Goddess Kali I realize that this is the first time I've felt comfortable to be among the heat and bustle of a crowd. In fact I actually like the feeling of disappearing into this mass of people and just becoming part of something bigger. With chunnis covering all of the women's heads, I stop trying to pick out people's features and instead just walk. The atmosphere of this city sort of seeps into you.

The chanting of the puja settles on me like a trance. Now here we are face to face with the three-eyed Goddess Kali, staring down at us, sticking her tongue out as far as it will go and wearing a garland of skulls around her neck.

"Why does she have three eyes?" I ask Anjali when we move on.

"To see into the past, present, and future—wouldn't that be a gift?—but I'm not sure I would want it!" Anjali sighs.

"And what about the garland of skulls?"

"One for every letter in the Sanskrit alphabet! Each one is a different kind of knowledge," she explains.

"I didn't know there were so many types of knowledge," I say.

"Well, she's the wise mother goddess; she should know!" jokes Anjali.

"I thought she was a bit scary!"

"That's the thing about our Hindu goddesses—like we mothers, they can be soft and cuddly or wild and wicked!" Anjali says, sticking her tongue out at me! "I expect your mum can do both too."

"That's true." I half smile, trying not to imagine what will happen if Mum ever finds out that I stole her letters.

∾ ✿ ∾

When I slip my feet back into my sandals I notice that the shiny black shoes are gone, and I feel strangely sad.

We walk back to the car and I feel a real closeness with Anjali, as if I've known her for much longer than just a few days. Maybe it's because she does remind me a bit of Mum. The truth is that

I keep feeling waves of homesickness washing over me. Anjali catches me watching her and smiles.

"Were you like Priya when you were my age?" I ask.

"I'm afraid so! Don't tell her though! Sometimes we're a bit too alike…Uma said *you'd* had an argument before you left. Is that why you don't want to talk to her?" Anjali asks me gently, taking my hand in hers.

I shrug. My tummy suddenly tightens and I feel all knotted up inside again.

Anjali frowns slightly at my silence. "I argue with Priya all the time, as you've probably heard, but I never stop loving her!"

I'm afraid that if I speak I might burst into tears. The more time goes by since I actually spoke to Mum, the guiltier I feel for stealing her letters, and even though I've emailed her I know that she must know I'm avoiding speaking to her.

Anjali looks concerned but then pats my arm, as if to lift my spirits. "I thought we'd go to the outdoor market," she says. "Priya tells me you want to buy some presents. And I'd still like to buy you a salwar-kameez or sari dress, while Priya's not with us complaining! Maybe I'll treat you to an iced tea at Dolly's Tea Shop. You might want to have a sleep on the way—it's a bit of a journey."

It's weird how fast the time is going. It only feels like yesterday that we were sitting among all those beautiful saris with Sari Man unraveling cloth after cloth, and now I'm nearly halfway through my trip.

⟅ ✤ ⟆

I'm standing in a darkened room. An ancient old lady wearing a white sari is sitting in the middle of a metal bed. Around her neck hangs a garland of skeletons. She beckons me toward her, and as I approach, her three eyes search backward and forward through time—past, present, and future.

⟅ ✤ ⟆

My head hits the back of the seat with a thud.

"Kali statues, Rajasthani wall hangings, jewelry…anything you want to find, it will be there!" Manu chatters on. At first I think he must be talking to Anjali, but then I see that she's also asleep, head lolling against the window. Now I remember Manu was telling me that his wife has a stall in the market and I suppose I must have dozed off for a second without him noticing.

⟅ ✤ ⟆

I walk around the little stalls, wondering how it's possible to have so many beautiful ornate things in one place: papier-mâché candle holders painted in the most delicate colors, handwoven tablecloths, paintings on silk, bags, bedspreads, decorated pots, statues of bronze and silver, little tables, and ornaments inlaid with mother-of-pearl, embroidered Rajasthani wall hangings glinting with a thousand mirrors, (Anjali tells me she bought hers from here), puppets in the shape of every kind of person and animal, a carved family of sandalwood elephants, a tiny

167

stone sculpture of an owl carrying a baby inside its tummy…I could buy something at every stall. Anjali's being so generous, but I wish I had my own money. For Laila I choose the puppet, for Krish the family of elephants, for Dad I get a board game in an engraved wooden box, for Mum one of the mirrored wall hangings, and for Millie I buy the owl. That just leaves Jidé, and it's taking me longer to find anything for him than for everyone else put together. We're also still looking for clothes for me.

"This boyfriend of yours must be a very special person," Anjali says, raising her eyebrows.

"He is," I agree.

I step behind a curtain at the back of a clothes stall and try on the simple block-print salwar-kameez Anjali's picked out. "I believe it's your favorite color!" she says as I inspect myself in the mirror. It's pretty and the orange cotton's cool against my skin and it fits. It's a bit like my other one but I'm not in the mood to keep trying things on. I pull back the curtain.

"You look lovely. Why not keep it on?" says Anjali.

We buy the salwar-kameez and then browse more stalls looking for a present for Jidé.

"Maybe Janu could carve him something?" Anjali suggests. I know she's trying to be helpful, but my stomach clamps. The truth is I can't find anything for Jidé because I keep thinking of Janu and wondering when I'll see him again, and that just feels so wrong. "Come on, let's get some refreshment," says Anjali, taking me by the arm and leading me into a homely open-air cafe, with crates for tables, gingham tablecloths, and rattan chairs. Suddenly my tummy rumbles so loud that the girl sitting next to me giggles.

"Cinnamon and orange, mango and lychee, passion fruit and lime…"

Anjali reads me the list of teas to choose from as we relax in the shade of an umbrella.

"The good thing about shopping here is that everything you have in that bag is made by cooperatives, so the money goes back to the craftspeople instead of into the pockets of the big companies," explains Anjali as I savor every mouthful of my mango and lychee iced tea.

"Like the things that are made and sold at the refuge. You've made the shop so pretty."

"Well, that's all down to Janu," says Anjali, handing me a tiny silk pouch that I didn't notice her buying. There's a miniature Kali goddess inside. Then she lifts her teacup up to mine and we clink our rims together.

"May the Kali force be with you, Mira!"

The House in Doctor's Lane

❁ ❁ ❁

Dappled light filters through the lime-green leaves of the Kadamba tree and creeps in through the shutters. I open the wrought-iron grid and breathe in the hot, heavy air.

I wander over to Priya's wardrobe, put on my plain navy-blue kurti and pick out one of the brightly patterned chunni scarves Priya got me to buy at the mall. I pull on some leggings and think I'll wear my Converse today. I haven't worn them for a few days because actually Anjali's right: *chappals*—the little strappy sandals with the toe loops, or leather flip flops, are the things that keep your feet the coolest, but I think Converse look better with these leggings. I wander through to the bathroom to check my hair. It's gone flat and shiny in the heat so I scruff it up a bit. I think for a moment about putting some eyeliner on, but then I can't be bothered. It's weird how I haven't even thought about wearing make-up since I got here. When I walk through to the front room, Janu's at the table.

❧ ✢ ❧

"Janu, don't you think Mira would look good with short hair?" asks Priya, messing up her own pixie cut.

Janu looks up at me, and I can't help feeling the heat rising from my belly and up toward my face.

"She looks good like she is," says Janu.

"Who do you think you are? A Bollywood hero?!" teases Priya, slapping him on the back.

I wonder if Janu minds Priya's constant jibes and jokes. He doesn't seem to, because he smiles at her good-naturedly.

"Not at the refuge today?" Priya asks him.

"Anjali's asked me to take Mira sightseeing," Janu says, without looking at me.

Priya takes her spoon and slams it back into her bowl, making the yogurt splash on the tablecloth.

"Great! So *you* get to take my cousin out, while I have to rehearse! I can't wait till this gala's over!" She sighs and stomps off to her bedroom.

I feel I should go after her. It's really not fair that she keeps missing out on us spending time together. But before I can, Janu's walking out onto the communal landing. "Shall we go?" he asks.

I follow him and he waits for me to lace up my trainers and then offers me a hand.

He notices me hesitate.

"Friends," he says heartily, clasping his hand in mine, "what places do you wish to see?"

"I would really like to find my grandfather's old house in Doctor's Lane," I tell him.

He smiles and says, "Of course. I understand."

~ ✥ ~

Janu runs into the road, sticks his hand out, and a yellow taxi comes to a halt in front of him. Within minutes he's chatting away to the oily-haired taxi driver. Janu is probably the sort of person who could talk to anyone. He's got a quiet confidence. Maybe it comes from being so good-looking, but there's nothing showy or vain about him. I catch my own reflection in the car window. I wish I could be so careless about the way I look. I'm glad Janu's talking to the driver because otherwise I don't know what I'd say, sitting so close to him like this. What I notice is that Janu smells faintly of jasmine.

The taxi driver inspects me in his mirror. "English, yaar? London, Big Ben, Trafalgar Square." He lists the landmarks in his singsong voice. "How you think, of our new road, new airport, flyover, fly-under, metro too?" He spreads his hands out proudly, letting go of the steering wheel. "See very brilliant

172

India Museum, many, many treasures there, although British Museum should be returning many more, but that is other story! Also, please to look left. Park Street...sari shopping..." He points to the store Anjali took us to on my first day here. "Right side New Market, also very beautiful hotels...Oberoi Grand...hotel fit for kings...but these old roads I will not take, one time cows kicked my car. Even if sacred, I'm not going there anymore!"

Janu laughs, hands over the fare, and then opens the door, offering me his hand.

"Better hold on to each other or you may be swallowed by crowd," says the driver, grinning from me to Janu before driving off.

The streets are packed full of people and we are funneled and shunted into the maze of narrow lanes.

I get out my camera and start snapping away.

"So, this is New Market...built by British railway architects," Janu tells me, pointing up to the red brick arches that remind me of the ones at St. Pancras Station in London. It's so strange to think that on different sides of the world the same architects were busy making this place into a "home from home." I suppose they were trying to make it feel familiar.

"Imagine, this market was built only for the British, so that they wouldn't have to brush shoulders with Indians," says Janu, shaking his head in disbelief. "In those days you and I would not be walking here together!"

"Well, with a British Jewish dad and a half-English, half-Indian mum, I probably wouldn't be walking here with myself!" I tell him.

Janu looks at me and laughs as if he wasn't expecting that. "True! But some people think you and me should not be walking together in modern India."

I'm not really sure what he means, so I just shrug and say, "I can't really get my head around all that race/class/caste stuff. What I think is that no one should be able to tell anyone else who they can or can't walk with." The words just slip out of my mouth. Janu looks at me for a moment and I think he's pleased I feel that way—maybe he wasn't expecting me to? I know it's vain of me, but I'm glad that he doesn't think that I'm just a silly little girl.

"Good job for all of us the world is changing," says Janu as he steers me into the market.

I remember once someone calling my mum a "half caste" and I asked her what it meant, because I'd never heard that term before. She told me it's the description people used for "mixed-heritage" people when she was a little girl. I think "half-caste" is a horrible way to describe someone; it sounds like some sort of reject pottery. Mum says it never bothered her because Granddad Bimal and Nana Kath always made her feel like she had double the world, not half! Anyway, I suppose the fact is that me, just being me and walking here in New Market with Janu, means that things are always moving on.

I stop to take a photo of the pyramid-mountains of spice: oranges, cinnamon brown, reds, turmeric yellows, pistachio, even shocking pink. As soon as I pause, the curly moustached trader starts shoving tea bag size envelopes of spices under my nose, but Janu shakes his head and walks on. Next we pass through a larger hall and the smell changes to something cloying and warm. Hanging on giant metal hooks are whole sheep carcasses, skinned and bloody. Below them chickens scrambling in nets are being bartered for and carried away clucking on bicycles. I look down and see a gutter of blood, blackened by flies, streaming and buzzing millimeters away from my feet. The contents of my stomach heaves into my mouth and just in time I swallow it back down again.

"Careful for your pretty shoes!" Janu says, pulling me away. "Maybe not for vegetarian eyes!" We walk through the market hall and out onto the narrow back lanes.

I immediately notice that the sounds of the street are different here, quieter. These roads belong to people, carts and rickshaws, not cars—people carrying impossibly high piles of boxes on their heads or loads of rubbish on their backs, barefoot children screeching as they play their "which coconut shell is it under?" game, families soaping themselves at water troughs by the roadside. It all feels weirdly like walking into the past, and I can't imagine that this place has altered very much from how it was when Granddad lived here. A rickshaw boy is shrieking at me to get out of the way and pointing to an enormous wheel, which is careering toward me. Janu grabs my arm and I turn to see the skeleton-thin rickshaw boy, not much taller than me, desperately trying to balance his wobbly vehicle on its remaining three wheels. And all this effort is for a giant man sitting motionless on his enormous behind, smoking a fat cigar. I feel like I should do something right now about the unfairness of this little boy carrying the weight of an overfed man. But not knowing *what* to do makes me feel like screaming.

"I thought you didn't have human rickshaws," I say to Janu as we walk away.

"Everywhere else in India it is banned, but unfortunately not in Kolkata." He uses the same resigned tone that I've heard in Priya's voice, and even though I've seen real poverty and homelessness in London, it's not on the same scale. When you see it in pictures you don't appreciate how extreme the differences can be between the rich and poor, living side by side. I feel a heaviness in my gut that I can't shake off. Every day here someone's tapping on my conscience and saying to me, "Mira Levenson, this is not fair. What are you going to do about it?" and just like everything else that's happening to me here, the truth is I don't know. What can I do to change anything? All I know is that I want to do something worthwhile for the art project at the refuge—if only I can find an idea soon. The very least I can do is to *try* to find a way to—how did Janu put it?— to "lighten the children's hearts."

Janu squeezes my hand. I'm sure he's only doing this because we're about to cross a busy road, but I still have a pang of guilt for thinking how good it feels.

"Now!" he shouts, walking straight into a road where a red and yellow bus spilling people from doors and windows is heading straight toward us, horn blaring. I can't believe that this is supposed to be the *safe* moment to cross, until the policeman blows his whistle and signals for the traffic to move off again. That's the strangest thing about the traffic in Kolkata—when you're in a car it feels like you're at a standstill all the time, but when you're on foot it feels as if the traffic never stops. Safely on the other side now, Janu drops my hand and leads us down the narrowest lanes we've walked through yet, where the dust seems to settle and the pace slows. A shocking pink dome of a mosque towers above us, brightening the sky.

"I very much like this place," says Janu, looking up at the old Victorian shuttered houses that, even in their crumbling state, still manage to look grand. "My wish is that they would… how do you say?" I can almost see Janu's mind hunting for the right word. "Make better these old buildings, not only starting new ones."

"Renovate."

"Acha! Renovate! Repair."

I'm taking hundreds of photos, because everywhere I look here I see something I would like to paint: cotton saris being hung out to dry on a rooftop, a shopkeeper sitting on top of his counter; behind him are hundreds and hundreds of bottles of medicines of every kind.

"Ayurvedic—natural medicine," explains Janu, pointing in the direction of the street-side pharmacy.

A few paces up the road we come across a stall stacked full of Indian sweets of every color and flavor: pistachio, orange, carrot halwa, sonpapri (Granddad's favorite), creamy rasamalai (my favorite), syrupy rosogolla, and curds, all protected from the flies and the heat behind sparkling-clean glass. Janu notices me looking.

"Sweet tooth, na?" he jokes.

I nod. "I'm afraid so." I hope I don't look too greedy.

"Why afraid?" asks Janu. "Sweet tooth, sweet heart!" He smiles, sweeping his hand to his chest.

"You made that up!" I laugh.

The boy behind the counter greets Janu and hands him a pistachio sweet, which he passes on to me. They both smile at the appreciative noise I make as I taste it. The boy makes up a box, and when Janu goes to pay he won't accept it.

"We helped some of his family once at the refuge," explains

Janu as we walk away. He stops for a moment to watch a group of children scrabbling in the rubbish, separating bottles, cans, and papers from every other kind of human and animal waste. I watch his face turn from a smile to a scowl.

"You should take a photo of that," he says as I lower my camera. "This is the shame of our country, what children have to do to survive."

One of the boys is dragging his naked little sister alongside him like a rag doll; she can't be more than two years old. He plonks her down on the rubbish heap while he sorts through it, and she tries to copy him and starts to rummage too.

Janu yells to the boy, pointing toward his baby sister. The boy throws his arms in the air as if to say, "What do you want me to do about it?"

"I'm telling him he should put some clothes on his sister," explains Janu.

Just at that moment the naked little girl looks up at me and smiles the sweetest of smiles, like she has nothing in the world to bother her. I take off my cotton chunni, walk over to her and wrap it around her little body. She's so tiny that my scarf looks like a sari on her.

Janu doesn't say anything, but when we walk on, six or seven more children trail behind us with outstretched hands.

"You are a sweet, soft-hearted person. Problem is, no easy fix!" Janu says, shooing away the group of children swarming around us. Anjali's letter echoes back to me. Isn't that what she said to my mum? "*There's no easy fix.*" I feel a bit silly for giving it to her now. The truth is I'm out of my depth in so many ways as I walk in silence with Janu along this dirt road.

Janu points up to a sign half hidden by hanging electricity wires.

31 Doctor's Lane Kolkata 700014

The house is more broken down than I'd imagined. Whole parts of it are covered in blue tarpaulin, the brickwork is crumbling, the pillars are cracked, wooden slats are rotting in the shutters, and wires hang everywhere, fighting for space with vines that creep through the walls. A washing line with a pair of trousers and a shirt hanging on it is strung among the rubble on a high balcony. Only the door is how I imagined it. Two cracked sandstone pillars, two carved panels with orange flowers and green vines and, just as Anjali wrote in her letter, it's as "*heavy as a tree.*"

Perhaps it's because I know that Anjali really doesn't want me to come here that my heart's beating so fast.

"This was the house of your grandfather and your great-grandparents," says Janu. "I come here sometimes to look at the carving on the door. The finest example in this area. I study it and try to make my own carving beautiful like this."

180

The tears well up with no warning. To be standing outside the house where Granddad used to live is the weirdest sensation. A bit of me is happy that he never saw the house in this state, so he could keep his memories just as they were. But, for me, this crumbling house is still holding on to the stories that once happened inside it—like the building is guarding the secrets of the past.

"Can we go inside?" I whisper to Janu.

At first he looks unsure, but then he takes my hand and leads me toward a tall shuttered window to the right of the door. He looks around to see if anyone's watching, but the narrow street is quiet, except for a cow meandering along. Janu pulls the shutter toward him and it opens easily. He levers himself up onto the rusting wrought-iron balcony, then offers to help me. I shake my head and place my hands on the railings to hoist myself up and over. We both step through the window.

The house smells of age and rot and, now that Janu's standing by my side…jasmine. It's dark except for a soft orange light that creeps in through the slatted windows and shutters. Dust plays in each light shaft, so that it feels as if this empty house is dancing with life.

"Be careful where you place your feet," warns Janu. "There is rotten wood."

The hairs stand up on the back of my neck as those words echo back to me from my dream, when Granddad called me to climb up to the top of the house. I walk through to the room that, from the description in Anjali's letter, must once have been Great-Granddad's surgery, and after that Shudi's studio. Janu wanders around, inspecting the remaining pieces of broken furniture. Then I see him pause and pick something up off one of the shelves. He turns to face me.

"You're like a painting in this light," he says quietly.

I realize that I'm holding my breath. Everything is silent and still, except for the dust pouring slowly through the cracks in the floor above us like sifting sand. I look up through the missing floorboards, searching into the gloom, and when I look back at Janu he is still staring at me. I don't know how much time passes or how much dust falls as I stare back. Time stands still.

I nearly jump out of my skin as somewhere above my head there is a huge clatter, like something falling through rotten wood. I glance up. Two huge eyes are peering down at me. I scream, and Janu steps close in beside me, looking upward, but the eyes are gone.

"There was a b-boy, up there," I stutter, my whole body shaking with shock. Acid rises up into my throat, so that I think I'm going to puke. Janu sinks to the ground, pulling me with him, and wraps his arms around me firmly until my breathing goes back to normal and my stomach settles. I feel better, but I don't want to speak because…no matter how much I want to deny it…being held this close by Janu is so good. Anjali said in

182

her letter that "*the dark shrinks the whole city into one room.*" And, in this moment, that's exactly how it feels. "Probably this boy lives here in this house, better than living in the streets," explains Janu. "We must go now. This place is not safe. Soon they will come to knock it down, and next time you visit it will be all new glass and concrete."

"That's why I need to see the rest of it, before it disappears." I hear the wobble in my voice and will myself not to cry.

Janu shakes his head firmly and we both stand up. For a moment I think he's going to kiss me, but then he takes my hand and leads me back through the shuttered window. This time I let him help me through.

The heat and brightness of the sun are blinding after the dimness inside, and my eyes are blurred by a film of sun fire. I stare up through the orange light and the heat haze, toward the top of the house, where Anjali described her grandmother sitting on her bed. My eyes are still dancing with too much light after darkness. As my vision shimmers I watch a boy on the top balcony of the house take the shirt from the washing line, put it on and button it up. When he sees me looking at him he stuffs food into his mouth, leans over the balcony and waves.

"Hah! Cheeky boy!" Janu laughs, following my gaze. "He's stealing our sweets! Janu looks at the grand door. "Do you want me to take a photo of you here?" he asks, holding his hand out for my camera.

I've been so caught up in being here I'd completely forgotten to capture it.

When he's taken the picture, Janu hands back my camera and shows me the photo. "Maybe better not to mention to Anjali we went inside." He looks a bit guilty.

I nod in agreement—this is definitely our secret.

As we walk down the street I try to push away my own guilt and the strange feeling I can't throw off that Janu and I have always been wandering around Kolkata together. I look down at my feet and I love the idea that my shoes are walking the same streets that Granddad walked when he was growing up.

"What did you take from the house?" I ask as we enter a park and the road turns to grass. After the dust-filled streets, the ancient trees are like a great breathing lung in the heart of the city. Janu stops, feels around in his pocket and pulls out a tiny piece of carved wood, painted in faded orange, green, and golden colors.

"It's for you. I was thinking you might want something from your grandfather's house," he says, laying the wood onto my palm. "It's a miracle the house still stands. But someone should at least save the carving; it's the work of a master carpenter."

"Thank you," is all I can say, running my fingers over the fine leaf pattern. Now I know where I've seen this design before! Janu probably has no idea how much this means to me. If I never go back to that house again, at least I have this tiny piece of wood to hold on to forever.

We walk on in silence, past an arbor cascading with roses. A couple are sitting inside. They have covered their heads and bodies with the woman's bright green shawl to stop prying eyes, but the strange thing is it only makes you want to look more. It's a bit like me with Janu—the more I try not to think about him, the more he fills my mind. The couple are facing each other and you can just see the tops of their heads above the border pattern of the shawl. Underneath their bodies sway as they kiss.

Without saying a word Janu holds out his hand for me to take. There are no busy roads to cross here. I glance down at the map of scratches and cuts that score his skin. There is still space between us—a safe, friendly space I know he'll never cross unless...I reach for his hand and we walk through the park, together.

Under My Pillow

✿✿✿

It's only early evening when I get back to the flat, but Priya's already asleep. Janu says the only time she really rests is before a gala, like she's storing up her energy. I creep into the bedroom, take the wooden carving out of my pocket, and walk over to Priya's trophy cabinet. I knew it! I trace my hands along the edge where the carving's broken away and slot the piece into place. It feels so good to see the frame complete. I would have loved to see how this once looked when it stood in the house in Doctor's Lane.

If I gave this piece to Janu he could probably mend the frame, but I can't risk Anjali knowing I've been inside the old house, so I tuck the piece of wood inside my pillowcase. I eat dinner with Anjali and then quietly slip into bed. The air is full of heat and dust and guilt as I keep going over the moment when I stood in that stream of orange light with Janu and the rest of the world seemed to melt away to nothing.

Priya hasn't even moved for the last hour. I switch on the tiny lamp. I rummage in my bag and take out Mum's letter album. I go through everything again, trying desperately to read between the lines. This is exactly how it feels, like…"*The paint is flaking away, leaving the old brickwork peeping through as though a layer of skin has been grazed off…*" and I'm only just starting to get a glimpse of what's underneath. I imagined seeing the house would settle something inside me once and for all, but now all I want to do is go back and explore deeper.

After everything that's happened there is no way I can sleep. The heat seems to grow more intense every day, and the days are running away so fast, but I don't ever want this to end. It feels as if I'm wrapped in a kind of heat spell and if the weather breaks I'm afraid that the spell will be broken too.

I move the lamp over to the table and open up the box of paints. The canvas is starting to fill up, but what's missing, what I would really like to paint into the picture, is Janu and me, caught in a dust haze in the house in Doctor's Lane. Instead I draw the red arches of New Market and two figures holding hands rushing across a road strewn with taxis, a rickshaw with a stray wheel, tuk-tuks, and bikes. The figures I've drawn *could* be anyone…

Priya's Wig

❀❀❀

I'm not in bed.

My arms are splayed out over a hard surface and something is sticking into the side of my chin. My back aches. Without moving I half open my eyes and see that I'm slumped over my painting. Then I remember. The letters. What did I do with the letters?

I hear Anjali and Priya whispering, but the words spewing out of them are glinting and sharp, like blades cutting through the air. I sit up and yawn, trying to look as innocent as I can. It takes me a while to work out who it is sitting on the bed opposite me, but of course it's Priya. She's wearing a short blouse and a rich emerald and gold silk sari skirt, which has fan pleats at the front. She is literally draped in jewelry and her long black plait is trailing almost to the floor.

She sees me wake up and switches to English, as if she wants me to take her side. "I'm *not* wearing it!" she shouts, tearing off the wig to reveal her flattened crop.

Anjali shouts back, "This is the *dress* rehearsal and you've been told to dress in the standard costume; your hair is not standard! Anyway, you know that was the condition of having it cut."

"Well, I've changed my mind," yells Priya, throwing the long black wig at the wall. "In what ancient Sanskrit rule book does it say that you can't have short hair to dance Kathak?"

"One day you'll learn to have respect for the past!" says Anjali, but she's looking at me now, not Priya. I glance down at her lap and see Mum's letter album. I feel like running away, but there's nowhere for me to go.

"*You* are in so much trouble," Priya mouths behind Anjali's back.

Anjali leafs through the letters, takes one out, and starts to read it silently. Then she looks down at my painting again.

She sighs. "So you *have* read these," she says.

I nod. I feel awful that I've lied to her after everything she's done to make me feel at home.

"Where did you get them?" she asks in a tiny voice, tracing her fingers over the surface of the album.

"Mum doesn't know I took them," I tell her, a sick feeling rising up in me.

"You stole them then?"

Steal seems like too strong a word for what I meant to do, but I suppose she's right. I did steal them.

"I was going to put them back," I say feebly.

Anjali stands up with the letter album tucked under her arm and walks out of the room. She closes the door behind her quietly with a final determined click, as if she would rather not set eyes on me or Priya for a very long time.

Priya sits down next to me, where I'm still slumped over the table. The tears are pouring out of me onto my painting. She lifts my head up gently.

"Careful you'll smudge it! My plan was to be the decoy duck! Make her angry with me so she'd be less upset with you. Guess it didn't work."

"Do you think she'll tell my mum?"

Priya shrugs. "Hard to tell, but I'm sorry to say it's not a good sign when she goes off in one of her silent moods."

Howrah Bridge

✿ ✿ ✿

"Let me take a photo of the two of you," says Manu, as Lila envelopes me in the warmest of hugs. "Lila has brought you to best view. No tourist guide will tell you how to get to this ghat," Manu smiles, looking up at the bridge. From this angle its great metal web almost looks like it's been spun by a giant spider.

Lila walks down the steep steps and sits down slowly on the second to last one before you reach the water. She stares up at the underbelly of the bridge and starts to talk again as Manu translates.

"No connectors…not a single nut or bolt, much stronger this way," he says, as Lila continues to give me her personalized tour. Poor Manu's voice is actually getting hoarse from talking all day, but he doesn't seem to mind.

I can't believe that Lila's in her late sixties. She's got so much energy. I remember Nana Kath telling me how Lila had insisted on buying a pair of walking boots in the Lake District, and Nana Kath had been worried that she would be too cold and wouldn't cope with the weather, but apparently Lila had walked through the driving wind and rain all day, scrambling up and down crags and she'd actually been the first to reach the top of the fell! Apparently, when Lila came back to India, Nana Kath told Granddad off:

"All these years have passed, and Lila and I could have been best friends. It must have been so hard for her, losing her husband so young. We should have visited Kolkata every year if we could, but we were working so hard and then I always seemed to be pregnant or nursing a little one. Still, you always did your best to support her."

And I think Nana Kath was right, because all morning Lila's been asking me so many questions about Nana Kath. She even told me that when they first met they'd talked about running an import—export business together. She speaks about Nana Kath with such fondness. Manu paused a long time before he found the right translation for what Lila called Nana Kath—"my fair sister" is what he came up with.

If Nana Kath wanted to go back to Kolkata so much, especially to see Lila, it makes everything even more confusing. Even though Granddad was busy, they still had holidays. Why would Granddad stay away for so long? Whatever the reason, I'm sure it has something to do with mum and Anjali. Maybe even Nana Kath doesn't know the truth?

I thought I had an idea of what Lila was like, but after today I realize I didn't really know her at all. This morning when Anjali left the curt note on the table saying that Lila would be coming to take me out, I wasn't expecting her to be so into all the modern buildings in Kolkata, including her flat. I couldn't believe it when she took me back there for lunch. Her flat's part of a new complex, with a swimming pool and everything. She even showed me the gym she uses. So far today she's taken me to two contemporary art galleries and the planetarium and she even got Manu to wait for us by the Howrah Bridge while we went on the underground—I mean, the metro—just for the experience.

Lila takes off her sandals, walks down the last step and beckons me to follow. I place my hot achy feet into the cool brown water of the river. Lila wiggles her toes and starts gently paddling them this way and that.

"Anjali's angry with me," I tell her.

"Acha." She nods slowly as we watch the sun sinking through the sky. I think she understands quite a lot of English; she's just not confident about speaking. I know how she feels, because I'm starting to understand much more in Bengali, but I feel self-conscious about speaking even the smallest phrase.

After a while of staring up at the bridge and the sky Lila starts speaking slowly and deliberately to give Manu more time to translate properly.

"You see, no language between us, and we hardly know each other, but we are like Howrah—no matter what happens, strong standing family. Bimal, your granddad, built the bridge, now it's up to the next generations to cross from one side to the other. After I visited Bimal and Kath in the mountains they were planning to come back. Bimal was even saying he would like to bring you with him. But maybe he is here in spirit." Manu pauses as Lila wipes away her tears. She coughs to clear her throat and gather her emotions together. "I'm happy we had this time together, because you know in a few days I'm traveling with Prem to New York. Elen is having a baby soon, and I must go to help with my grandchildren. Have you ever been to New York?"

"No, I would like to though!" I say to Manu, and then turn to Lila. It's weird having a translator!

"So, now you have met Prem you can go. Perhaps you and Priya will go there together one day. Such a fun city, but I don't get chance to go often. This is why I am a big fan of this Facebook. Distance is not so final now. Every day I am emailing or Skyping Prem and Elen, and my little grandbabies. I am not missing birthdays or anything. Anjou is even putting her dancing videos, her spinning on her head, on YouTube. So distance doesn't have to make you strangers. After Bimal's passing I am always telling Priya to Facebook you. So, the way I see it, you and Priya are the new bridge." Manu translates as Lila cups my

194

chin in her hands and hugs me to her. "Now I have to leave it up to you to make the connections."

"Thank you for bringing us together," I say.

Manu is about to translate but Lila raises her hand and he walks silently back up to the top of the steps and sits down, as if he doesn't want to intrude.

I would like to ask Lila what happened between mum and Anjali, what is hidden in those letters, but the only way I could do that is through Manu translating, and that would be wrong. And, I suppose, if Lila wanted to tell me she would have done it by now.

A family—a mum, a dad, a little boy, and an even younger girl—are bathing in the river and washing their clothes. The little girl is splashing water in her brother's face. The way he leaps and prances around reminds me of Krish.

"Bimal...bring me here...when small, small." Lila indicates with her hand, smiling as she watches the girl play in the river with her brother.

Something about Lila's words makes me understand why Anjali's so angry with me. Like the day Jidé told me about his sister dying in Rwanda, wrapped only in his precious piece of orange cloth; that memory belongs only to me and him, no matter what happens between us. Just like Lila's memory of Granddad standing on this ghat with her when she was just four years old belongs only to her.

195

We're both lost in thought for a while watching the fading light dancing on the water. I think about trying to capture this amazing sunset on camera, but then I change my mind. I notice that as the days go by I'm taking fewer photos; it's sometimes better to see things just as they are. We watch the sun turn from yellow to orange to almost red and then disappear from the sky completely. Lila's holding my hand and I'm glad that I don't have to talk to her, because this feels like sitting with Granddad used to. Sometimes we wouldn't talk at all, but no matter what was happening to me, I would always feel better from just being with him.

The family bathing in the river have darkened into silhouettes. And I suppose when they look at us, that's all they see too…Suddenly I feel smaller and less important than I've ever felt before. I'm just a tiny speck among millions and millions of people.

Street Wishes

❀❀❀

"Your mum's avoiding me, isn't she?"

"She'll take a couple of days to cool off. She always brings Didima in for emergency backup when she doesn't know how to cope! Anyway, she's got meetings all day so you won't have to bump into her. Don't look so worried," Priya says, throwing an arm around my shoulder. "Ma said you're working at the refuge with Janu today. I'll be back later. I can't believe it's my last rehearsal! After tomorrow, I'm all yours!"

I sigh. I actually really do want to do some work at the refuge and start the art project, but Janu will be there and I feel weird about seeing him. I wish I could see more of Priya. What I love about her is she's so straight down the line and she's sort of the opposite to me, so light and airy. I really need that side of her so I don't just sink down into myself. Priya mistakes my frown as me being upset with her. "I'll make it up to you, promise!" She smiles. "You won't believe the rides at Nicco Park, and I've got my own surprise for you! After tomorrow you won't know what's hit you!" She laughs as she runs out of the door and slides down the banisters.

I get dressed in a pale-green-cotton kurti and white leggings. I'm going to wear sandals today (I don't care how they look—I can't stand my feet sweating in Converse all day long).

When I walk out into the living room Janu's already sitting at the table eating dhal. "Hungry?" he asks, picking up a spoon to ladle some into a bowl for me.

"No, thank you," I say, feeling my stomach tense.

"We have planned today for your art project. Everyone is very excited."

I should have prepared all of this before I even arrived. I can't believe I've been so caught up in myself that I haven't thought it all through properly yet.

～ ✤ ～

As we ride the tram I start to remember all the children that I've seen living on the streets since I got here, especially the little naked girl sitting among the rubbish. The other thing that keeps coming back to me is Janu's beautiful carved Kadamba…a wishing tree.

"You're very quiet," says Janu as the tram comes to a stop near the refuge.

198

"I'm just thinking about the project."

"Make it a surprise!" he says luckily.

⚜

As we walk through the door into the reception area some men and women in smart suits are waiting for Janu. They shake hands with him formally. He seems so much older when he comes here. As he takes the visitors through to the refuge he catches my eye.

"I am so looking forward to seeing your project. Nili will show you where everything is," he tells me, nodding toward the young woman with glasses I saw when I was last here. She must be about twenty. Today she's wearing jeans and trainers and a pretty pale blue kurti that has green and white beads decorating the ties at the neck. Her hair is pulled back in a businesslike ponytail. She smiles politely and shows me through to one of the orange rooms.

"Janu tells me you're an artist." She has a sweet, soft voice. Maybe it's just her glasses, but she reminds me of my friend Millie. They've both got that way of looking at you that makes you know straight away that they're figuring you out. I'm not sure she's happy about having to help me.

"I'm learning," I tell her, feeling completely out of my depth, and then an idea for the art project pops into my head!

"Acha. So, everything we have is here." She walks me over to a whole wall of wooden drawers, the kind you see in old chemist shops, each one filled with something different—tiny scraps of material, beads, mirrors, feathers, paints, paper, string, glue, sticky tape, scissors—everything I need except for rubbish. So I explain to Nili my idea, to make street wishes: to collect cartons, cans, things obviously found on the street, and then to wash them, decorate them and get the children to write their wishes on them.

"Then I thought we could hang the wishes on Janu's tree in the shop. He said it needs more decoration!" I say.

Nili nods but looks a bit unsure about the idea. "We will see," she says. "If these wishes sell, I will be able to carry on this project after you've gone."

I suddenly feel so naive. I never even thought about having to make sure their work sells. All the art I do is just for myself. Sometimes it works out and sometimes it doesn't, but I guess that everything these children make, even artwork, has got to contribute toward their survival. I wish I'd taken more time to think this through.

Nili walks into the next-door classroom and asks some of the older children to go and look for rubbish.

I hear one boy complaining bitterly. As he talks he looks up at me through the doorway and says something about "English tourist" and spits on the ground. Nili raises her voice at him sharply and reluctantly he follows the rest of the children out.

"What did he say?" I ask Nili.

"Don't worry about it!"

"No, really, what did he say?" I insist.

"He said, 'Why doesn't she collect her own rubbish?'" Nili sighs. "You can understand—some of these children are full of anger."

I nod as if I do understand, but the truth is of course I don't. How can I, coming from my life, know what it's like to have to rummage in rubbish just to get by. I suppose these children come to the refuge to get away from that life, and I've sent them back out there. This isn't a great start.

"How much do you think people will pay for these wishes?" asks Nili, breaking into my thoughts.

"Hopefully enough to make them come true!" I say, smiling at her. I would like Nili to be my friend, but I can feel that she's standing back from me, as if she's waiting to decide whether she likes me or not.

"But you know some of these children have very big wishes!" she says.

Since the idea of making a tree of "street wishes" has been growing in my mind I've been feeling quietly confident about it. But it's only taken Spitting Boy and Nili's very reasonable questions to make all my confidence drain away.

"How old will the children be?" I ask Nili.

"All ages. Whoever's around," she says, looking at me as if it's a stupid question. "I have many tasks to do. You want to wait in the restaurant till the children get back?"

"Maybe I can go and help Lal in medical," I suggest. I can't stand the thought of sitting on my own getting more and more nervous.

Nili nods and smiles at me warmly for the first time. For some reason it matters to me that Nili thinks I'm OK, just like it matters that Janu does too. I don't want them to think I'm some clueless English girl who's afraid of hard work.

I walk up the staircase to the white room.

"Ah! My eye specialist!" Lal greets me as I make my way toward him through the crowded room. It's oddly comforting to hear his Birmingham accent.

There's a little girl of about four years old sitting in his reclining chair, which looks as if it might once have belonged to a dentist. Lal is telling her a story and she's smiling up at him even though he has a pair of enormous tweezers in his hand and is tugging at her front tooth. She makes a little yelp, and the tooth is out. Lal carefully washes it, wraps it in a piece of cloth and hands it to her. As she climbs down off the chair she says something to me and grins, sticking her tongue in the bloody gap.

I can't help but smile because I think I know what she said.

"She says now the fairies will make all her wishes come true! I was telling her about the tooth fairy," explains Lal.

Somehow that little girl's hopeful grin makes me feel a bit better, as if my idea isn't completely useless. I know what I'm expecting to do in this room, but soon I'm going to be standing in front of a class of children, including Spitting Boy. My stomach tightens. I'll probably stumble over my words as Nili translates everything I say, watching me with her quiet, piercing eyes.

I collect the little stainless-steel bowls from the cupboard and pour water from the kettle as Lal hands me the antibiotic eye drops. Some of the children smile and chatter away to me as I bathe their eyes, removing the yellow gunk. Even though I don't understand most of what they say, I nod and smile back.

"Could you do the last treatment for Sunil, my brilliant assistant?" Lal indicates a boy who has just walked in the room, the boy I treated first when I was here before.

Sunil lays his head on my knee and closes his eyes while I wipe away the little bit of infection that's still there. Then I lift the lid, so that his eye rolls back, and drip in the antibiotic drops. When I'm done he looks up at me and blinks away the bleariness. It's not until now that I notice his eyes are a hazel-green color. Suddenly he twists around and starts shouting something excitedly, pointing at me and holding my hand tightly. The other children in the queue jump up and surround me as if watching some kind of sideshow.

Lal is telling them to move aside as he pushes through. He crouches down next to Sunil and talks to him gently. Sunil lets go of my hand but he's still talking to Lal in an animated way, like he's telling a story, and all the other children are gathered around listening intently.

"Acha, acha, acha!" calms Lal.

And when Sunil finally stops talking Lal turns to me, takes a deep breath, and explains.

"He says he knows you. He says he knows your eyes."

As Lal translates Sunil keeps interrupting.

"He says he knows your granddad...He says he's seen you in the house."

"What house?" I ask Lal.

"Doctor Lane, Doctor Lane!" shouts Sunil.

My head tilts and I feel like I'm going to pass out. Sunil's eyes...were the eyes peering through the floorboards. Now I know for sure that I'm being pulled back toward the old house where Granddad grew up.

"Sorry, sorry!" Sunil jumps up and goes over to the water cylinder. He comes running back with a glass of cold water for me. I take tiny sips as I stare at him.

Sunil starts talking again and Lal explains his words to me. "He says your grandfather is teaching him medicine in the house."

I feel a cold chill run up the length of my spine. "My

granddad's dead," I tell Lal in a tiny voice I hardly recognize as my own. Lal places a firm hand on Sunil's arm as if to say, "Stop now! That's enough!"

Sunil keeps talking, less frantically now, but Lal ignores him and practically has to lift me up because my legs have gone to jelly under me. He leads me out of the medical room and into the canteen. He calls over to a man behind the counter for some tea and helps me to a chair.

"You'll feel OK in a minute once you've had some sweet tea. I'm sorry Sunil frightened you. I've been working with him for weeks now. I would never have expected that from him. Strangely, he does know a surprising amount about medicine. I was examining one child and I couldn't believe Sunil knew stuff about the human eye I didn't learn until I started university. He says he's got his own textbooks and a tutor. He told me his parents had an Ayurvedic stall, so he probably learned from them."

"What happened to them?" I ask, taking a calming sip of chai.

"There was a fire in their roadside business and they were killed. Sunil tried to save them. He was badly hurt in the fire— he had extensive burns, he showed me his scars—but he told me that he treated his wounds himself using the medicine he saved from their stall. Poor boy, you know he's probably still traumatized and pretending to know your granddad may be a cry for help, a way to impress you." Lal sighs and pats me on the arm, "I'd better get back to work."

⚜

I sit at the table and finish my chai, wondering how on earth I'm going to be able to teach anyone anything feeling this shaky. I was nervous enough already.

Janu walks into the room and sits next to me. "I haven't missed your project, have I? Some possible funders from one of Kolkata's multinational digital companies are looking around today. We're hoping they're going to set up a computer room. You don't mind if they pop in?"

I shake my head. I can't exactly refuse, can I? "I'm about to start," I tell him, trying to steady my voice.

"Ah! There you are!" says Nili, popping her head around the door. "The rubbish is all washed! We're ready for you."

"Sounds interesting!" Janu smiles encouragingly as we all walk toward the art room together. The noise coming from the room is deafening. My legs are still wobbly and I feel as if my every move is being followed by Nili and Janu and all these expectant faces. I can't believe how many children have turned up—maybe fifty, ranging from about two to fourteen. How am I ever going to explain this project? What if they hate it? What if they all feel like Spitting Boy and think the whole idea is a waste of time?

The children are all sitting on mats on the floor, each holding on to a piece of cleaned street rubbish. There are two chairs at the front of the room. Nili sits on one, and gestures for me to sit down next to her. I notice that someone has set up a row of chairs by the door. I suppose those must be for the funders. Please, please, please, I beg Notsurewho Notsurewhat, don't let them have time to come in here. How bad would I feel if I messed this up and it made them think twice about funding the computer room? You couldn't get more low-tech than what I'm planning to do, so I don't see how any of this is going to impress them.

"You want me to take a video?" asks Janu. I reluctantly pass him my camera. I suppose I did promise my school that I'd document the project, but to be honest, it's the last thing I need right now.

Janu walks to the back of the classroom, chatting to some of the children as he goes. Some of them hang on to his legs and others high-five him. He leans against the wall, and switches on the camera. Janu takes a few photos of the children around the room, and then I see him flick the switch to video. The red light blinks at me.

Nili raises both hands in the air and gradually the children nudge each other and look our way. There is silence in the room now and I don't know how to start. My heart is beating hard and I suddenly feel sorry for my teachers.

"Over to you!" whispers Nili, just as the smart-looking funders file in and sit down on the waiting seats.

My whole body is shaking with nerves. I take a deep breath and hope that my voice isn't going to shake too.

"Hi! *Amar naam* Mira," I say. I *really* wish I'd planned this better. I've seen teachers' lesson plans on the table that look like military operations; now I know why.

A few children giggle at my accent. Tooth-Fairy Girl jumps up in excitement, saying my name over and over, and that sets all the other children off laughing.

"She's excited because her name's Mira too!" Nili explains.

I look at this little girl with her eyes full of hope and the bloody gap between her teeth, and my mind goes completely blank. Spitting Boy scowls at me, and there's a general level of children shuffling around and starting up conversations again. I know I have to say something else quickly before I lose them completely. I look out at all the faces and see that Janu has lowered the camera. I can't read the expression in his eyes, but the lines on his forehead are set in deep furrows. He's probably regretting asking me to work with the children in the first place, especially in front of these VIPs. The thought of letting him down makes me feel sick.

Nili touches me on my arm as if to remind me where I am.

"Would you like *me* to explain the project?" Nili whispers, glancing over toward the funders and looking a bit concerned.

I touch Nana Josie's artichoke-heart charm, twisting it around and around, and I start speaking. "I got the idea for this project when Janu and I were walking in the streets and I saw children collecting rubbish, scrabbling among the dirt…and I started to think about how different the life of those children is to, say, my little sister's life in London." I take another deep breath as the children start to hush and face forward again.

Nili looks a bit surprised, but then she starts to translate. I hear some of the children muttering, "Janu Dada," and looking back at him as they hear his name.

He smiles and gestures for them to turn around and listen to me. Talk from the heart, I tell myself as I try to steady my voice.

"I think children everywhere have 'tender loving hearts,'" I say, twisting the charm on my wrist as I remember Nana Josie's words. "And they should be looked after and protected, not treated like rubbish on the street."

It's good to have the time to work out what I'm going to say next as Nili translates.

"I saw a little girl with no clothes on sorting through rubbish, and I wondered what she wished for…what her dreams for her life were."

I glance up at Janu and he's pointing the camera back at me. I look away from him before I lose my nerve. As I wait for Nili to repeat my words I look around the room at the reactions of the children, and they are definitely listening now. I dare to glance over at the funders out of the corner of my eye. One of the young slick-looking suited women is smiling with real emotion in her eyes. As Nili finishes, the children's attention turns from her to me.

"I love painting and drawing, so I thought if this rubbish could be made into something beautiful with the dreams and wishes of the child—artists written on each piece, then people might be touched and pay some money toward each wish coming true."

Nili looks over to me as if she's expecting me to say something else, but that's all I can think of at the moment. She must be asking the children if they have any questions because Spitting Boy's hand shoots up. I feel my heart racing as he stands up to talk. We must be about the same age, and he probably resents me just for being me, and having the life I have, which I don't blame him for. I glance up at Janu as the boy talks and he is nodding as if he agrees with whatever the boy's saying. When he's finished speaking Spitting Boy sits back down as the children start to clap. I notice Janu claps too, and the scowl on the boy's face softens.

Nili translates, and as she does I make myself look the boy straight in the eye.

"This is Kal. He says, 'I thought your idea was rubbish at first. I have had enough of collecting rubbish and being treated like rubbish. I've been collecting since I could walk. But now I think your idea is good because it should make people feel guilty to treat children like rubbish. Some of these tourists who buy from the shop will have children of their own and it will make them think…that we are not rubbish…that we have wishes and dreams too. All of these children have ambitions. I want to wear a smart suit and work in one of the big new computer companies, like these people,'" Nili finishes, pointing to the funders.

I look at Kal and he stares back. There is an understanding between us that wasn't there an hour ago. I want him to know that I care. Janu stands up, walks to the front, and pats Kal on the back in a brotherly gesture. Then he turns to me and smiles.

"If I have time, I might make a street wish of my own," says Janu, handing me my camera, then walking out with the funders.

I'm so relieved it went well and that Kal isn't angry with me anymore. It feels like the best way to start the project is to make my own street wish. I take a plastic Coke bottle and walk over to the wall of drawers. I decide to decorate the bottle with sequins. Then I make a paper scroll that I'll attach to the lid, so when someone opens it they can pull out my message in a bottle. Some of the older children gather around as I work. They start talking, sounding excited—I suppose they're bouncing ideas off each other—and soon they take a few of the younger children off and help them to make a start. I've never thought about this before, but there is something really lovely about people of different ages working together, helping each other out. No one being the boss. Kal stands over me, watching me work, and asks Nili a question.

"He wants to know what your wish is," she says.

I unravel the little scroll I've made to fit inside the bottle. I write:

I wish I could make your wishes come true.

Nili reads my wish and Kal smiles at me. "What's your wish?" I ask him.

"I wish I could *write* a wish!" He sighs and wanders off.

I hadn't even thought of that. Of course, some of these children are too young to write, but some of them, like Kal, just haven't had the opportunity to learn. I should have thought about that.

I wander around the room to see what everyone else is making and to take some photos. Little hands that are normally scrabbling in rubbish are now painting, drawing, and sticking on sequins. The room is full of children laughing and chatting. I feel so ridiculously happy: that an idea that's come from me,

Mira Levenson, could actually bring some happiness to these children who have such hard lives. Nili walks around with me and writes down the wishes for the children who can't write. She translates every wish into English too—"for the tourists," she tells me.

I wish I could surf the World Wide Web! (Bankim, aged 15)

I wish I could live in a proper flat (Rani, aged 14)

I wish I could have a mother and father (Anima, aged 8)

I wish I could work in the mall (Shoma, aged 15)

I wish I could be a Bollywood star (Indrani, aged 5)

I wish I could never feel hungry (Hem, aged 6)

I wish I could not collect rubbish (Tarun, aged 10)

I wish I could go to Disneyland in Florida (Kamini, aged 8)

I wish I could fly on an airplane (Lolita, aged 5)

I wish I could never beg again (Debesh, aged 13)

I wish I could play cricket for India (Gopal, aged 3)

We walk down the rows of glittering street wishes. I bend down to little Mira, who is just finishing hers off. She has spent over two hours decorating a matchbox with feathers. She opens the outer box and inside is a smaller one completely covered in pink sequins. She hands it to me to open. Sitting on a little soft cushion of cloth is her newly extracted rotten tooth!

Nili asks what her wish is, but before she can answer I jump in.

"Her wish is that the tooth fairy will come—am I right?" Nili translates, and the little girl nods and giggles.

⤞ ✦ ⤝

"Come on, let's take a break." Nili's smiling.

I nod. I'm tired, but it's a good tiredness, as if I've done something worth sweating for. I think of what Jidé says about "girls glowing, not sweating" and smile. Because I actually do feel like I'm glowing with happiness inside. I'm glad this has been caught on video now, so that I can show Jidé. He would love this place.

We leave the street wishes to dry and go through to the canteen, where some of the children are already eating. I sit with Nili and we tuck into more simple rice and dhal. Lal and Sunil walk in and my stomach tenses.

"I told Janu what happened with Sunil. He's spoken to him and Sunil wants to say he's sorry, that he didn't mean to frighten you," says Lal. Sunil is talking urgently, but Lal doesn't translate; instead he keeps shaking his head as if to say, "I'm not telling her that." Nili looks from Sunil to me as if she doesn't understand what's going on. She says something to Sunil in her soft, firm voice and he stands up and leaves.

"What did he want you to tell me?" I ask Lal quietly.

"He said to ask you how many hands it takes to clap. He kept saying, 'Tell her...she knows...It takes two hands to clap!'"

My whole body shudders. "My granddad used to say that whenever my brother and me had fights."

"We always tell this to children when they argue." Nili shrugs. "It takes two to make an argument. Two hands to clap. One hand only is silence! Talking of hands…we could do with some help to carry the street wishes to the shop."

Nili, Lal, and I carefully carry the children's artwork through and start to hang all the wishes on the carved tree. When we've finished we step back to admire it. Janu walks into the shop with a look of sadness on his face.

"Oh. So we didn't get funding for computers." Nili's voice has gone flat.

Janu looks down at the floor without answering, but then looks up again with an enormous grin on his face.

"Yes, we did!" he shouts, lifting Nili in the air and dislodging her glasses so they shoot across the room. I've never seen this exuberant Janu before!

Lal picks up Nili's glasses and hands them back to her.

"We're calling it the Mirakal Suite!" Janu announces triumphantly. "It's already agreed!"

"You definitely live up to your name. So prosperous!" She laughs, still jumping up and down in excitement.

Have I, Mira Levenson, actually done something to help the refuge? None of this feels real…I have never felt this happy before. I can't help the smile spreading across my face. Standing

215

in front of that classroom was unbelievably terrifying, but it was also one of the best things I've ever done, and now that it's over, I want to do it again! But better next time.

"No matter how many good arguments you have, you've got to get them here!" Janu taps his chest. "And between you and Kal," he says, looking at me, "you pulled their hearts out. Thirty top-class computers are coming our way, with training sessions too. I love this place when it goes like this." He laughs, stretching out his arms wide as if to encompass the whole refuge.

And now we're all laughing together because it is just magical to be a part of this moment.

"Has Nili shown you her work yet?" asks Janu, walking over to the walls and running his hands over the beautiful sari quilts. "This is another of our business ventures."

"These are yours?" I say. So *she's* the girl who made the quilt on Priya's bed. Nili nods a bit shyly. I step closer to the quilts. I'm in awe at the detail of this sewing. I can't believe how patient she must be to sew all these hundreds of pieces of silk and cotton together, and work out what the most beautiful combinations of patterns and colors will be. And over the material there are so many different styles of stitching. It reminds me of what Sari Man said in his shop. I wonder what thoughts and feelings went into all her tiny stitches.

"How long does it take you to make one of these?" I ask her, turning over the corner of a quilt. The one that Priya has in her bedroom has a plain dark-gold silk backing, but this one's double-sided; it's beautiful on both sides.

"Depending on the size, two to six months, hours and hours of stitching a day," Nili says. "Kantha stitching looks quite simple, mostly running stitch, but it is so time-consuming. That's why my eyes are so bad; I've been doing it since I was eight years old! Now I'm working here full time, I don't have so many opportunities to sew, but we are setting up our own cooperative workshop, with proper lighting and everything," she adds, smiling at Lal.

I think of the two hundred pounds in my bag that Anjali won't even let me change into rupees.

"I would like to buy one," I tell Nili.

"You can't have this one," interrupts Lal, walking over to the most enormous double bedspread that's covering half the wall. "Look!" He points to the tiny brown tag on the corner. "It's got my name on it!"

Nili smiles at Lal and nods. "Which one do you like?" she asks me. I point to the smallest one, hoping I can afford it.

"You can have it." She smiles.

I'm touched, but I shake my head. "No," I insist, "I really want to pay for it."

"OK," she says, "Thank you. I accept. Do you mind if we leave it here till you go back home? I'll attach a tag with your name on. It doesn't look so nice to have an empty space, and the more people see the sold stickers, the more they want them! We already have enough orders for two hundred lep."

Looking around the shop at all these beautiful crafts I wonder how we are going to put a price on the street wishes.

"How much should we charge for them?" asks Janu.

"I've been thinking," I say. "Is the best thing for us to appeal to people's consciences and say 'Pay what you wish'?"

"Great idea!" agrees Janu.

"Let me take a picture of you and Janu standing in front of the tree," suggests Nili.

Janu steps closer and wraps his arm around my shoulder and leans his head in toward mine. But as soon as the photo's taken Janu steps away from me.

"Here, Lal, I think you should buy this one!" I say, opening the feathered matchbox to show him the tooth.

"Guess I'm the tooth fairy then!" He laughs. "I'd better go and get some money!"

"I need to get on as well!" says Nili. "It was lovely to work with another artist, Mira. I'm so pleased you like my work too." She places a hand on my arm as she leaves.

"Nili," I call after her, "thank you."

She raises her arm in the air without turning around, as if to say, "It was nothing."

Kumartuli

✿✿✿

I suddenly feel self-conscious standing here alone with Janu, so I rearrange some of the wishes to spread them evenly among the branches. Hanging altogether on Janu's beautiful carved tree, the street wishes form an amazing display of color and texture, and I think the real charm of them is, without even reading the wish, you can tell the age of the artist by the level of skill. I go over to the sari quilt I've bought from Nili.

"Did Nili come to the refuge as a child?" I ask Janu.

"Yes. I think I met her for the first time when she was ten years old. She's very talented, isn't she?" Janu inspects the quilt with me. "Like you! Thank you for your work today." He turns to face me. "But where's your wish?"

I point to the Coke bottle. He carefully examines the decorated sides, takes off the lid and pulls out the scroll.

"We have a very long way to go before that will happen," he sighs. "But the Mirakal Suite might help!"

꙳ ⊕ ꙳

"Do you want to see what I work on with the older children, when I get the time?"

"I'd like that."

We walk back into the refuge and enter a room stacked full of wood and large pieces of half-finished furniture. If he lugs pieces of wood that size around, I can see why he's so strong.

"I'm working on this table, with five or six children... teaching carpentry. These are skills they can be paid for."

As Janu talks I walk around the workshop, stopping at an intricately carved bench.

"Try! I promise it won't break!" Janu comes over and stands next to me.

"Ki sundor," I say, running my hands along the ornate carving.

"Ki sundor," Janu echoes, smiling straight at me.

I can't help the butterflies trapped inside my rib cage. Perhaps my wish should have been not to feel this way about Janu...I sit on the bench, thankful for the rest.

"You're tired. We'll take a taxi home," he says, offering me his arm. It's so old-fashioned and funny of him to do this, but I can't pretend I don't like it. What would Nana Josie say if she could hear me thinking thoughts like that...I can just imagine it: "*Mira, don't let anyone con you into thinking that you need to be looked after. We can fend for ourselves as well as any man can.*" And that's true, I know I can, but that doesn't mean I don't want to hold Janu's arm...

It's starting to get dark when we step outside and hail a cab.

"Why didn't you tell me what happened with Sunil?" Janu asks me as we step into the car.

"I didn't want to make a big thing about it," I say.

To be honest I just want to forget what Sunil said and I don't want to make things more difficult for him.

Once we're sitting in the back of the yellow cab I practically collapse. I keep my eyes closed, but even then there's no relief from my mind's whirring. A whole gallery of eyes is staring at me: Jidé's eyes, Mum's and Anjali's accusing eyes, Priya's cat's eyes, Branded Woman's eyes, Sunil's, Dust Boy's, Kali's three enormous eyes, and now, as I open my lids, I meet Janu's eyes.

"OK?" he asks.

"Fine, thanks. It's just that this heat gets too much for me sometimes."

It's true, the heat is overwhelming, especially when you're working in it, but that's not what's making me feel like this. I can't blame the heat for taking Mum's letters, or for how much I want to go back to the house in Doctor's Lane, or for how I feel about Janu.

"Lal thinks Sunil is suffering trauma. Many of the children

221

need some sort of help like this. In London there is a college where you study how to work with emotion, using art and craft."

"I think there's a place like that near where I live," I say. "Is that something you want to do?"

"When I grow up?" jokes Janu.

I laugh and nod.

"I think they call it art therapy. I want to do the course. I think it's what I'm made for. I would also like to maybe have my own gallery-workshop one day, for carving and handmade work like Nili's, because as you see, many times people are asking us for commissions. What about you? What do you want to do?"

"I don't know yet—maybe something with art too." I tell him, but what I'm thinking now is how much I enjoyed teaching today.

"You really inspired the children." Janu smiles at me, a sincere, warm smile that makes my heart race. "You're a natural teacher!" Not for the first time I feel as if he can read my mind.

"You want to see something special? It's more beautiful to go there in the dark," says Janu, his eyes lighting up. He leans forward to speak to the driver, then turns back to me. "It will take a little time in this traffic, but worth it! If you're tired, you can sleep on the way if you wish."

Whether I wish it or not, it's not long till the din of the road fades out.

My head is resting against his shoulder.

"Jidé?" I say, sitting up.

Janu shakes his head. I can't help noticing a hurt look cross his face, but he quickly smiles to hide it. "You woke just in time…Look!" I peer out of the window down a narrow lane packed with artists' workshops.

"Want to see Potter's Town?" asks Janu, opening the cab door and holding out his hand to me.

The workshops are all floodlit, like mini theatre stages. In each shop an artist is working on figures of idols—gods and goddesses, with their multiple arms outstretched. Some of the artists are dwarfed by the giant limbs of clay. One tiny man, smaller than Priya, is standing on a stepladder to finish the trunk of the elephant god Ganesha. Another artist holds a fine brush in his hand as he paints a kohl line sweeping up over the statue's eyelids. It's ages since I've worn any make-up. At home I never go out without my eyeliner. The artist turns to me and grins before speaking to Janu.

Janu smiles and says something back, then translates: "This artist says you have the eyes of a goddess."

"And what did you say to him?" I ask curiously. Maybe it's because I'm still half asleep, but suddenly, standing here with Janu, holding his hand in this strange floodlit place of gods and goddesses, I feel a seriousness settle between us.

He looks at me with his dark intense eyes and says, "I agreed."

We are both silent for a few seconds until Janu breaks the spell. "Kumartuli is my favorite place in all Kolkata. Artists making magic!" he says. "Like your wishes."

"What would you wish?" I ask him.

"No need to ask. You told me already—my wish cannot be." He sighs, letting go of my hand.

Priya's Gala

❁ ✸ ❁

I'm getting ready to leave for Priya's gala when Anjali comes into my room with a pile of clean clothes. She didn't mention the letters at all last night. She smiles when she sees that I'm wearing the salwar-kameez she bought me from the market, but then her smile fades.

"That's the door of the old house, isn't it?" she asks, staring at my painting. "I must have described it very well in my letters. You are talented," she speaks with a sharp, knowing edge to her voice. I get a sinking feeling. What if she knows I've been inside the house?

I wish I could tell her about going to the house, so I could give her the piece of carving Janu found and she could mend the cupboard. But Priya's right—whenever you mention the house Anjali raises a wall of silence around her. Whatever memories she has locked away, she's not going to share them with me, so there's no way I can ask her all the burning questions I have, whirring in my mind.

❧ ✛ ☙

Manu must feel the tension between Anjali and me because he doesn't attempt to make conversation like he usually does.

"Did you read *everything* in the album?" she finally asks.

"Yes," I answer, the guilt flooding through me again.

She sighs deeply and looks out of the window. "You see, some things that happened in the past should stay in the past."

I can't understand how that can be true. How can it ever be good to bury something in the past as if it never happened? That's like in the documentary Dad and I watched about people who try to deny that horrific things that happened in history—like the Holocaust or the genocide in Rwanda—actually took place. Dad said the only reason people try to hide the truth is to get away with evil and never having to face up to what they've done. How can people learn anything from the past if it's hidden?

"I don't understand," I tell Anjali.

She just raises her eyebrows as if to say, "Exactly."

I feel a surge of frustration again, but I take a deep breath and look out of my own window. It takes me ages to pluck up the courage to ask the question that's been playing on my mind and, when I finally do, it comes out as a cowardly whisper.

"Are you going to tell my mum?"

"I haven't made my mind up yet."

꙾ ✧ ꙾

I think it's a relief, for both of us, to get out of Manu's car. Anjali immediately strides off. A little lump forms in my throat. I know it's a bit pathetic, but I feel really close to Anjali, even though we've only just met. I hate the fact that she's angry with me and upset, but I don't know how to make things better.

There are hundreds of cars parked up in a field. In the middle is a huge white marquee. Women in every color of silken sari are strutting across the field, like peacocks fanning their feathers. When I was little I always found it hard to believe that the pretty show-off peacocks that preen themselves are the males.

Inside the tent it smells like the flower market: sweet roses and jasmine—that smell is starting to follow me around.

It takes me a few minutes to recognize that it's the twins, Chand and Charbak from the mall, wearing identical gold cotton kurta pajamas, who are warming up on the sitar and tabla at the front on the stage. I can't remember which one plays which instrument, and they're too far away for me to spot an earring.

I love the sound of instruments tuning up. I think the bit before a show begins is the most magical of all, when no one sends a signal to begin but everyone just somehow knows when to settle. Just as I think that moment's approaching a large

227

woman comes bustling toward the two empty seats next to me. It's not until she sits down that I see the girl limping behind her.

"Mira!" Paddy calls out, hobbling over. "At least I get to sit with you!" She grins and raises her eyes toward the large woman who must be her mum. Her wild hair is parted down the middle and seems to be smeared to her head with some sort of oil. "Ma made me straighten it! She's always trying to tame me!" she says, touching her hair self-consciously.

We chat for a while. Then Paddy leans forward and concentrates on watching Chand and Charbak.

"Isn't he brilliant?" whispers Paddy, nodding toward the twin playing the tabla.

Now I remember that it was Charbak who plays the rhythm.

There's a pause and the silence sizzles with expectation.

A short, strong-looking man walks on stage and blows into a conch. The sound is hollow and haunting as if it could carry across mountain ranges. The music begins, slowly at first, and then builds into a frenzied rhythm.

Te, tak a Te, te, tak a Te, te tak a Te te te… Charbak holds the beat as he plays.

Dancers in glittering emerald-and-gold saris enter the stage as if summoned. I pick out Priya straight away. She dances in the middle, her ankle bells jangling. She's positioned slightly forward from the others, but even if she was right at the back of the stage she would stand out, and not only because of her short hair (looks like she got her way then!). She's the one you're drawn to, because of her grace and energy, and the fact that every movement she makes is so precise and perfect. Her eyes light up as she dances. Everything about her is alive. Watching her move around the stage I feel so proud of her. I see for the first time that all her energy, which sometimes feels too big for real life, is meant to be here, crackling and lighting up this stage.

"What do you think?" asks Paddy.

I shake my head in disbelief. Now I understand why she's been rehearsing so hard.

There's nothing to say when you see someone as talented as Priya. You just have to watch and feel and let her spirit carry you away so that you almost feel like it's you dancing.

Anjali turns to me with tears in her eyes. She wraps an arm around my shoulder and squeezes me to her. No words pass between us, but I think she's beginning to thaw.

"Sorry you couldn't dance, Paddy," says Anjali kindly.

"Better it was me who was injured than Priya," Paddy says, her hands following the movements of the dancers. It must be awful for her to have to sit and watch after all that training.

When it's time for the interval, I feel breathless, as if *I* had been dancing along with the performers. I turn to Anjali, and see that she's beaming with pride. I wonder what it would feel like to be able to tell a story with your body, to learn the exact phrases dancers have been using for centuries. It's like they're tracing their bodies back through time, movement after movement, into the distant past. If Anjali understands this, why can't she understand why I took Mum's letters?

"Do you need the toilet?" asks Anjali, breaking into my thoughts. I shake my head.

"Give me five minutes," she says. "You'll keep her company, won't you, Paddy?"

"I'm not going anywhere in a hurry!" Paddy laughs.

The marquee's almost empty now; only Chand and Charbak sit on the front of the stage, chatting and joking with each other.

"Charb!" calls Paddy.

Charbak squints into the audience and then sprints up the steps toward her, taking them in threes. Chand lopes along behind his brother.

Now Charbak's sitting next to Paddy. He has flung an arm round her shoulder and they're chatting away.

"Hello!" says Chand, awkwardly leaning on the edge of the seat next to mine.

"Your sitar playing was brilliant," I say, feeling slightly embarrassed.

"Have you heard others on sitar?"

"Um…no, not live," I admit.

"Well, how do you know it was good then?"

Chand has this unnerving way of saying exactly what he's thinking.

Paddy and Charbak are deep in conversation, and I'm not sure how long I can keep this going with Chand, so I make an excuse about needing the toilet after all.

Outside there are crowds of people talking, drinking, and eating picnic food. Families are sitting on blankets on the ground, but I can't see Anjali anywhere among them. I look out toward the middle of the field and catch sight of the mustard and deep plum colors of Anjali's sari. About twenty or thirty women are slowly turning in a circle. They stand close together, chatting and laughing. I watch the group move around, and every few minutes a different silken-robed figure disappears and reappears. I imagine that each of them gets their own turn to dance in the middle. Maybe all these women were dancers once, like Anjali. As the circle breaks up they all scatter in different directions I wonder what it feels like when your body's been as free as a bird, like Priya's, and then you start to get older. Maybe that's why these women come out to the field to do their own dance.

~～ ✿ ～~

In the marquee Chand and Charbak start tuning up again, and slowly people pack up their blankets and make their way back inside. There's that sound again, of people gathering, voices fusing together and bubbling up into a state of expectation. Charbak strikes his tabla three times, and on the third beat the dancers enter, this time dressed in red silk sari skirts, choli, and long garlands of white flowers draped around their necks. Priya is not among them; instead another girl is standing forward from the rest.

"I thought Priya was dancing in this," I whisper to Paddy.

She shrugs and concentrates on the stage. I turn to Anjali to ask her, but she's sitting way forward on her seat with her face cupped in both hands, and I don't want to disturb her, so I just lean back in my seat and try to take it all in.

This time the music is poignant and gentle, a bit like ballet. I can see why Priya would prefer Kathak—it's like her: so fast, strong, and bright. This lead dancer, starting with her eyes and hands, begins to hypnotize the audience, drawing us into every single tiny movement she makes. Her limbs are long and flowing, as if a river is running through her body. Granddad told me once about this ancient temple dance. He said that when Lila used to perform it, it moved him to tears. I suppose Lila must have taught Anjali to dance, and now here's Priya on stage. When I get back to London I'm going to see if I can find a class. Maybe Millie will come with me.

I don't know how long it goes on for—it could be hours, it could be minutes—and for a time I forget where I am or that there is anyone else around me. I'm only brought back to reality by the loud applause. Now people are standing up cheering and clapping and calling out to the dancers. The star dancer steps forward and there's a roar of approval as she takes her bow.

Paddy's on her feet making loud whooping noises. The dancer puts her hand to her head, pulls at her hair and lets her long black plait fall to the ground. She smiles up at us and ruffles her short red hair. I should have guessed, but from this far away I couldn't really see her face.

There is a general gasp, but then the women around Anjali laugh and make comments to her. Paddy's mum in her gold sari is laughing so hard that her three thick tummy rolls are set in motion. She catches me watching her.

"Acha, you are the London cousin Priya and my Padma never stop talking about. London this, London that! *Tomar naam ki?*"

"Mira," I tell her.

"Gita," says Padma's mum as I shake her plump hand. I notice her tiny wrists, jangling with bright gold bangles.

"Gita and I used to dance together once!" Anjali tells me.

"Like tonight, in the field," I say.

The two women exchange a look and burst out laughing.

"That was more of a dance of nature!" Gita whispers in my ear. "The toilets are not smelling well on such occasions!"

I go bright red, feeling like a complete idiot.

"Anyway, we don't dance anymore!" Gita grabs hold of a roll of her tummy fat and wobbles it in my direction. "Too old and fat!"

"Speak for yourself!" says Anjali.

"Your aunty never stops working—that's how she keeps her shape! But what a shame you never got to see my Padma dance." Gita smiles proudly, putting a protective arm around Paddy.

"Oh, Ma! Do you have to?" Paddy protests, trying to squirm away.

We keep clapping as the dancers leave the stage. As Priya waves good-bye, the audience claps a little louder. She takes a final bow and exits, leaving her long black plait coiled on the stage, as if a snake has shed its skin.

Tendrils of Jasmine

✹✹✹

"Come on, let's get some air!" Priya says, grabbing my arm and pulling me on to the outside landing and up the flight of stairs toward the roof terrace.

When we get to the top Priya stands still, pokes her nose in the air and breathes in the sweet scent of jasmine.

"Janu says jasmine calms the nerves. It's probably why he's always so chilled."

I stand breathing in the smell of the tiny white star-shaped flowers with the faintest touch of pink on the petals. They grow in lacy clusters on every piece of trellis up here. Even the slatted wooden roof is intertwined with vines, so that when you look up through the jasmine you see the sky.

It feels wrong to come up here, to Janu's room, uninvited, but I can't help wanting to find out more about him. I follow Priya through the arbor of jasmine to the flaking paint of a turquoise door, the same color as the one at the refuge. Priya opens it and walks down a stone step into a cool room with earthy, copper-colored walls. I stand on the outside of the door.

"Is it OK to be here?" I ask Priya.

Priya rolls her eyes at me. "Janu doesn't mind, he knows he's got the coolest room in the house. Stop hovering."

Inside there's a small wooden bed and a desk covered with tools, like files and tweezers and what look like pens with blades instead of nibs. Above the desk is a shuttered window through which tendrils of jasmine trail.

On a high shelf above the window is a collection of intricately carved wooden objects. I think of the carved piece of wood Janu found in the house on Doctor's Lane. Maybe Janu did know how much it meant to me because, by the look of this collection, it's the sort of thing he would like to have kept.

"I don't know why Janu bothers copying all those old patterns," Priya sighs, slumping back on the bed, stretching out her limbs and beckoning me to sit down beside her.

"Maybe it's for the same reason that you love to dance" I say.

"Are you defending him?" Priya asks mischievously.

I feel my face flush so I get up and walk around the tiny room. There are a few books on the high shelf too, mostly English language books and a few hardbacks that look, from their covers, as if they might be about carpentry. There's also a copy of the *Mahabharata* and the *Ramayana* and a collection of poems by Tagore.

"You should read Tagore's poetry, Mira," I hear Granddad's voice in my head. "Our monsoon poet. If you study Shakespeare, then you must study Tagore also."

When I was young, just starting to read, Granddad bought us an edition of the *Ramayana* epic, written in Bengali, and I used to love looking through the pictures whilst Granddad read them to me. My favorite was the one where the king of the monkeys, Hanuman, led an army against the demon king Ravana. But the bit I really didn't get was when Sita, after everything she'd been through, had to step into the fire to prove her innocence.

At the end of the bed, in a hollow in the wall, is a tiny shrine. Inside is a carved figure of a god; in front of it is a little copper bowl with a candle in it and a scattering of jasmine flowers.

Priya follows my eyes. "He carved that Lord Vishnu himself," she says, placing the statue in my hands. Now I remember Rama the hero was really Lord Vishnu in human form. This carving is so intricate it must have taken him years. I don't think anyone would make such a thing if they didn't believe in all this. I put it back carefully. Priya takes some matches from Janu's desk and lights the candle. Then she picks up a single jasmine flower from the bowl.

"Did you know that jasmine is the flower of luuurve?" she says, turning to face me.

"Really?" I pretend to be serious for a moment before we both dissolve into giggles. Then Priya switches track, as if she's hearing music in her head. She raises her arms in the air and starts rapping.

"Give it up for Vishnu
"Off-er-ings for Vishnu
"Light a candle for the
"Sun god
"Give a little
"Jas-mine
"Give a little
"Jas man
"Give a little
"Jazz to the sun god
"De-vine
"Hope
"Pre—ser-ver.
"As ever
"Give a little jas-mine
"Give a little jazz man!"

If the music that's in her head was blaring out, Priya could set any stage alight. She probably will one day soon. She's one of those tiny people who become a giant when she performs.

"Give it up for DJ Prey!" She dives onto the bed and collapses with laughter. "Phew! Even for me this heat's too much."

"Shall we go?"

"No hurry, let's chill here for a bit longer." She lies back down on the bed.

All I can think of is how embarrassing it would be if Janu came back to find me in his room. I'd feel like a magpie stealing into his nest. I stand up and walk back toward the shrine. The candle casts an amber glow over the walls, and the memory of Janu and me locked in each other's gaze in the crumbling house fills my mind. I watch the flame flicker and my thoughts turn to Jidé. I don't want to hurt him, I don't want to hurt him, I don't want to hurt him, I say over and over in my mind as I blow out the candle.

"It's the jasmine."

I almost jump out of my skin at the sound of Janu's voice. I turn to the doorway, feeling slightly panicked. But Janu is smiling and doesn't seem angry at all. Somehow he looks different with his hair loose. He's leaning against the doorframe, holding a freshly picked vine of the white flowers. He steps into the room and nods toward Priya, who has fallen asleep.

"Jasmine," he repeats. "It can make you sleepy. It's why I come here sometimes after work, to relax."

I try to smile casually and hope that I'm hiding my thudding heartbeat. It feels like anything I say at this moment will be wrong, so I stay silent.

Janu goes over to Priya. He places his arms under her, lifts her off his bed, and carries her back down the wooden steps to our room. I follow behind him.

Once he's laid her on the bed, he turns to me. "Here!" He hands me the tendril of jasmine. "Priya doesn't need it."

"Thank you," is all I can say. I look down at my feet, and when I look up again Janu has closed the door quietly behind him.

Under Jasmine Skies

✿❀✿

I watch Priya's face as she sleeps. It's strange to see someone so animated sleeping because she looks so peaceful now. It's as if all the energy she harnessed for the gala has drained out of her.

I turn on the lamp next to the bed, tiptoe over to the desk, and find the paper and envelopes I've spotted tucked away in her drawer. The packet hasn't even been opened. It's like Priya said: "Who writes letters these days anyway?"

I sit down at her desk and write Jidé's address on the envelope, because that's the easy bit. There is nothing Jidé and I don't know about each other, and I can't start lying to him now. So, even though this is a million miles away from the love letter he joked I should send him, I have to find a way of telling him the truth.

Dear Jidé,

This place has shaken me up so much that I don't even know if I've got the words to tell you what's been happening.

As I write a leaden lump is forming in the back of my throat.

You said that the thing about us you love the most is that we would always tell each other the truth. Well, I'm trying. You were right about Mum's letters—I shouldn't have taken them, but it's too late now. I feel so guilty, but once I had them I couldn't stop myself from reading them and now I know more than I should, but there's still more to learn. I've lit a fuse and it's burning along, whether I like it or not, but it's gone too far to try to put it out. I need to find out the truth. Whatever it is or however bad it is, I just have to know what went on between Mum and Anjali.

I was so upset when I first lost my suitcase, but now the only thing I really want back is your note. I should never have brought it. You've got to know how much I care about you, and the last thing I want is to hurt you…

The smell of jasmine wafts through the window, as if to goad me into feeling even guiltier than I already do. It's no use. I can't say this to him in a letter. Words are too brutal, too final. Now I've made up my mind not to send this I feel more settled, because I know that this letter will never be sent, and that frees me up to write whatever I want, just to get it all out. I realize how much I've missed talking to Jidé, telling him everything, sharing every silly thought that passes through my head, like I usually do. The way I clam up around Janu is the total opposite of who I am with Jidé. I don't know how Jidé will feel when I get home and talk to him, but maybe if he met someone and felt about them the way I do about Janu, he would know that what we really are is the best friends ever. I carry on writing, trying to find a way to make sense of everything and calm myself down.

What I've discovered is that letters are full of secrets, but now I know I'll never send this. I'm going to have to find another way to tell you how I feel about Janu and how it's changed the way I feel about us—I don't know what will happen when I do, but I will be praying to Notsurewho Notsurewhat—or to good karma or anything that could help me—that after I've told you, you will still be my best friend. According to the Goddess Kali there are loads of different kinds of knowledge and maybe there are loads of different kinds of love too.

Because I do love you in my own way, Jidé Jackson.

Mira x

Suddenly I understand why Mum and Anjali are so angry with me for reading their letters. This letter is definitely "private property," and the thought of anyone reading it makes me feel sick. I fold the letter up, put it in the envelope, and seal it closed. I go over to my bed and tuck it inside my pillowcase, with the little wooden carving. Then I lie down and let the tears pour out of me until I think they are never going to stop. I keep remembering all the kind things Jidé has ever done for me, all the fun times we've shared together, the feeling that we would always be Mira and Jidé.

I cry at the thought of having to tell him about how I feel about Janu, I cry imagining the hurt look on his face, I cry thinking what it will be like between me and him at school from now on, but mostly I cry because I know now, no matter how much I fight it, the way it was between us is over. Something's going to happen between me and Janu, and no matter how bad I feel, I don't think I want to stop it anymore.

I walk into the little bathroom, turn on the light and look in the mirror. My eyes are puffy from so much crying and my skin is burning with salt tears. I splatter cold water over my face and then dab myself dry with a towel.

I walk silently past sleeping Priya and then up the stairs to Janu's balcony.

"Janu?" I whisper.

He's still awake, sitting outside reading a book under his lamp. He turns at the sound of his name.

"You are crying?" He speaks so gently and looks so worried that I can't help sobbing again. Why is it that when you're really upset and you've just managed to pull yourself together, someone being nice to you just sets it all off again? He gets up and comes over to me and goes to wipe away my tears, but I stop him.

He frowns, then goes into his room and returns with his bedspread.

"When I have a problem, I stay outside," he says, lying down on the soft cloth with his hands behind his head. "You try!"

I sink onto the bedspread a little away from him and look up through the tiny jasmine flowers, to the twinkling stars beyond.

Janu breathes in deeply. "The smell is calming, na?"

And I do feel calm. I think I'm finally all cried out, but I'm grateful that he's looking up at the sky and not at me. I have no idea what I expected him to do or say to me. I just knew I wanted to be near him.

"So why did you come here?" he whispers.

I shake my head, but I can't talk. How can I explain that there's something about him that makes me feel more like me than with anyone else I've ever met? He's so different to me. It doesn't make any sense.

"OK! Maybe it is time to stop hiding your feelings. I will

trust you; then you must trust me." Janu turns to face me and I look back at him.

"You know the meaning of *Chameli* is jasmine?"

"Chameli?"

"You met my ma at the flower market." He smiles, but with a certain sadness. "A young girl who can't walk, with a baby in a basket, makes a good beggar." It takes me a moment to realize that Janu is telling me his own story. "She was very young, only thirteen…and, you have seen, she cannot walk."

"They were married at thirteen?"

"No…it wasn't this way. She was not married to Ajoy at this time."

"So Ajoy's not your dad?"

"No. Let me tell. She was left by her family as soon as they knew she would not walk. Then the begging ring got hold of her." He shrugs off the thought in disgust.

"Girls like this have not much choice. Ma says the plan was to make her pregnant and carry her around with the baby—that way she would earn more money. But Ajoy and Ma made a plan to escape together, and so he carried us to Anjali's refuge a short while after I was born."

"You're the carved baby in the basket, aren't you?"

Janu nods and I see his eyes glisten. "I think we were the first family to arrive. They were allowed to stay till they were sixteen because they were only children themselves. They even married at the refuge…my ma gave it the name 'House of Garlands' because Ma was the first one teaching children how to make them."

"So you lived with Anjali from when you were three?"

"Chameli wanted me to be educated…you know. She thought I would have more prospects if I lived in the city and stayed with Anjali. Ajoy found work picking flowers and it was hard enough for them to feed themselves. But Anjali has always taken me to the flower market or the village to see them. When I was little sometimes three times a week, and after Priya was born a little less. So you can say I am lucky: I have two families."

Janu stares at the sky, as if he's still trying to make sense of his own story.

"Now time for *you* to trust me!" he says softly. "What is the problem?"

"I don't have any real problems…except for you."

He looks me straight in the eyes, just as he did the very first day I met him, and he listens as I tell him about the letter I've just tried to write to Jidé and how I know I have to tell him how I feel, but I'll do it when I get home. After I finish talking Janu is silent for a long time. I'm so drained of all emotion, I let out a huge yawn. Janu sighs, puts his arm under my head and pulls me closer to him. And even though I feel guilty, being in Janu's arms feels like the most natural thing in the world.

"You know I have never cared for any girl before meeting you," Janu says, looking up at the stars.

❧ ✧ ☙

Everything I was before, all the forever-things, are slipping away from me here under jasmine skies.

Burn Out

❋❋❋

As soon as I see Priya's flushed face I know something's wrong. I walk over to her and touch her head. She's burning up. I go to find Anjali, who comes and sits beside Priya, smoothing her hair over to one side and feeding her water from a teaspoon.

"Can we go to Nicco Park if I feel better later?" asks Priya quietly through parched lips.

"I'm afraid that's not happening today, Priya," says Anjali firmly. Priya groans. "Sorry, Mira!"

"It's OK!" I say but I do feel disappointed, as much for Priya as for me because I know how much she's been looking forward to taking me there.

"This bright candle burns itself out from time to time!" Anjali sighs. "I'll call Lal and ask if he can pop in on his way from the refuge. I promised him a meal anyway."

I get the feeling that Anjali might actually enjoy looking after

Priya, who's not exactly the sort of person who would ordinarily let you take care of her.

Anjali kisses her on the forehead and we go through to eat breakfast.

Janu wanders in wearing a cream silk kurta, the same one he wore the first day I met him. His hair is still wet from the shower.

"Amazing news about the funders!" Anjali smiles, holding Janu in a tight hug.

"Mira had a big part to play!" Janu says, grinning at me.

"Not really!" I mumble.

"Yes! Really!" he insists.

"We'll have to have a change of plan today because Priya's not well," Anjali says as she pours glasses of iced mint tea.

Janu goes through to the bedroom, and I hear him and Priya talking.

He's soon back. "She'll be fine. She's mostly upset about missing Nicco Park!" He raises his eyes to the sky, sits down at the table, and takes a pot of yogurt, which he eats slowly… thoughtfully. "I've been thinking—if she's not going to Nicco Park—to take Mira home," he says, lowering his eyes as if he's nervous of Anjali's reaction. "To meet Chameli and Ajoy properly."

Anjali looks from Janu to me with a question in her eyes.

"OK…" she says cautiously. "This heat is becoming so unbearable. It might be good for her to have a break from the city." And then she chats on and on to Janu in Bengali. It sounds as if she's giving him a list of dos and don'ts.

Butterflies are dancing in my belly. It's strange how I thought that all the great adventures I would have would be with Priya. Anjali was right all those years ago in her letter; nothing is quite as I pictured it.

Haunting Eyes

✿✹✿

"Now you need to stay close!" Janu tells me, wrapping one arm around my waist and taking my hand as we walk under the metal grid that is the roof of Howrah train station. It seems as if a whole world is living inside these red brick arches. It's like someone has turned up the volume on all my senses: a woman's voice is blaring train times over a loudspeaker; a little girl with an infected-looking sore on her mouth is shadowing us: "Babu, babu, babu…" she pleads, hand outstretched; now a family is settling down to rest, spreading out thin cloths on the concrete floor, one for each child to lay their heads, right in the middle of all of this mayhem.

There are little kiosks and traders selling chai and hot samosas, seemingly plonked right in the middle of the station. Weaving our way through all of this we finally find our way to a queue of shouting people clamoring for tickets. In front of us a blond teenage girl wearing a rucksack and a tall, thin boy in a grubby "Make Chai, not War!" T-shirt are holding up the queue as they try to work out which train they should be catching. They're heading for Darjeeling. Behind us, people are stepping out of line to shout at them to hurry up. Janu turns to the boy and asks if he would like some help. The boy's worried expression twists into a grin, and for a moment I think he might hug Janu, who is calmly talking to the ticket man on their behalf.

"Thanks, man. I've never been so stressed!" He clutches his tickets as if they're gold dust. His girlfriend looks at me.

"Cheers!" she smiles, wiping the sweat away from her brow. "Namaste!"

I find myself joining my hands together in response. She must think that I'm from Kolkata. Janu looks from me to the girl in amusement.

"*Cholo!*" He laughs, taking my hand and waving to the grateful couple.

"That was the easy part!" He glances up at the departure boards above our heads that clackety-click into place every few seconds. I wonder how it's possible that from one station you can get to so many destinations. Peering up at all the place names I've never heard of, I get the feeling that this is somewhere I'm going to come back to again and again because I want to visit everywhere.

Finally our platform comes up on the board and we're off

again, weaving our way through bodies and backpacks. Around the train there are a hundred different wires connecting the power, and between these lines tiny monkeys leap and play, looking down on the mass of ant-like humans. Now I see why Anjali was so fascinated by these monkeys when she was a little girl. They have crazily human faces—some look bored, some look cheeky, one looks as if it's brokenhearted. Janu checks the tickets once more and then climbs up the steep metal steps of the slightly rusty blue and white train. He offers me his hand and pulls me aboard.

There is not a single spare seat all through the first carriage: there are mothers, fathers, babies, a tall man in a turban holding a briefcase, and children playing a board game; the carriage is bursting at the seams with people.

We walk on through the train until we come to some old-fashioned carriages with faded dusty curtains at the door. A woman is sitting on a brown leather bench with three children. As she sees us peering in she moves a skinny boy of about six or seven onto her knee. She tells an older girl to put her toddler sister on to her lap and gestures for us to take the two spare seats. Janu thanks her.

It would be hard for anyone not to stare at this family, because if you saw them on a train in London, the children would probably be signed up by some modeling agency and make a fortune, with their gray-green eyes and their beautiful skin. But the whole family are dressed in frayed clothing and their eyes and thin limbs speak of how hungry they are. The woman catches me looking from one child to another and she sits up straighter, holding her son to her proudly. She glances from Janu to me. I think she's trying to work out who we are to each other.

As we pull out of the station I start to feel the mass of the city fall away from us. The windows in our little carriage are open, and as the train picks up speed the breeze cools us slightly. Something about the atmosphere has lifted, as if, as the fields open out, the air becomes less confined too. Janu leans back on his seat and sighs happily.

"I always love going home."

The woman and children look up at us with new interest at the sound of Janu speaking in English.

"Isn't Kolkata your home?" I ask.

"It is…but a piece of me always stays in the village. Look!"

The train slows to a stop as a small herd of cows wander across the track ahead of us. "This is why we are calling this the cow-belt!" explains Janu.

I look across a vast earth field and watch a man pulling a plough through the dusty soil. You can see in the sinewy muscles of his legs how much strength it takes for him to pull the heavy cart along each furrow. As the train speeds up again he disappears into a golden haze, whipped up by a gust of wind blowing across the loose, dry earth. I've seen so many tiny moments of people's lives since I've been here, moments that I don't think I'll ever forget. I will always be wondering what happened to School Girl and Dust Boy, and Sunil and Kal, just like Granddad always wondered what happened to that orphan baby boy he carried out of Howrah station all those years ago. "What would you like to think he grew up as?" I once asked Granddad. "A doctor of course!" laughed Granddad, clapping his hands together.

I'm looking out of the window but I can't help glancing at the family sitting with us. The girl about my age has long, perfectly curled eyelashes, and when she lifts her head I try my hardest not to stare at her eyes. They are also an amazing gray-green, like those of the rest of her family, but she has an "I will not be defeated" look, which reminds me so much of my Nana Josie. I know it's nothing more than an expression, but it's as if she's challenging me not to look away, to *really* see who she is. Those eyes could haunt you.

The little girl starts to moan and her mother picks up a metal tiffin tin and begins to unpack the tower of bowls, handing a layer of watery dhal, a tiny portion of rice, and a quarter of a chapatti to each child. They eat slowly, savoring every mouthful. The woman is just about to take a bite of her chapatti when she changes her mind, placing it back in the tiffin tin and offering it to Janu and me instead. Janu smiles at her and shakes his head. She shrugs before biting into the flatbread hungrily. I can't believe that she can be this generous when she has so little for her own family.

When the little girl has finished eating she jumps off her sister's knee as if this tiny bit of fuel has got her going again. She leans on Janu's legs to stay upright as the train jerks along, and he gets her giggling by taking a coin from his pocket and making it appear and disappear in his palm. She squeals every time he makes it reappear. Everyone in the family laughs except the girl my age, whose haunting eyes follow my every move. I wonder if she's thinking the same as me—what makes *me* lucky enough to be born into *my* life? If that is hatred in her eyes, I wouldn't blame her.

Janu has handed over the coin and now the little girl is tugging at my charm bracelet…she's taking the artichoke heart and rubbing the silver metal against her gums. She must be teething. Her sister pulls her back to stop her, but she clings on to the charm in her mouth. My arm is outstretched halfway across the carriage now as her sister tries to prize the bracelet from the child's mouth. My little sister Laila once put this charm in her mouth and wouldn't spit it out. It's like tiny children know how precious it is. I figure the easiest way to end this tug of war, without the little girl choking on it, is to take the bracelet off and let her sister deal with it. She nods at me as if she's understood my plan and starts to tickle the little girl under her arm. As she falls about laughing, she opens her mouth and out pops my charm.

The older girl glances down at the charm for a moment and

then hands it back to me before staring out of the window. I follow her gaze along the meandering path of the river. Great storks are nesting in the trees, and a family is washing and drying great lengths of sari cloth on giant rocks.

"Come on, Mira!" Janu says, suddenly standing up.

Just as I'm about to leave the carriage the girl reaches toward me and squeezes my hand tightly. I look deeply into her eyes and try to understand what she is saying to me. I feel I have to look at her, that it would be cowardly to look away. I'm still holding Nana Josie's charm. I wonder if she thinks that my charm can bring her luck. I drop my bracelet and my precious artichoke-heart charm into her hands because I have everything and she has nothing. As I stand on the platform, the girl pushes her face up to the window and mouths the words "thank you," her haunting eyes seem to soften.

The girl is waving to me as the train moves off. She opens her hand and my charm glints, catching Janu's eye. He starts to run toward the carriage door, but the train is already going too fast. She smiles. Forget all the models you see in magazines. I think she might be the most beautiful girl in the whole world.

"Pickpockets! You have to be careful—of course they have to find whatever they can." Janu shrugs. "Was it valuable?"

"Not in money. It belonged to my grandmother. But the girl didn't steal it. I knew she wanted it, so I just sort of *gave* it to her," I explain, still trying to make sense of what I've done as a sudden heaviness enters my chest.

Janu stares at me as if I've lost my mind. Maybe I have.

"I think she needed it more than me. And it just felt like the right thing to do!"

He shakes his head and frowns at me. "Her ma will find it, and she will sell it. You don't understand the way things work here. You think your silver charm is going to change her life?" His anger gives a hard, cold edge to his voice.

Janu strides on, still shaking his head. I can hardly keep up with him as he goes toward a cluster of straw-roofed, earth-covered buildings with pads of cow dung drying on their sides. I feel sick. Of course he's right. What was I thinking? How could I have given away Nana Josie's charm?! What good could it possibly do? Janu must think I'm an idiot, a silly girl who thinks she can make things better. I'll never see my charm again. I slump down on a large boulder at the side of the road and stare and stare at my empty wrist. I have never felt so far away from home.

Janu's walking back toward me and holding out his hand. I try to cover up my face as the tears spill over. He must think I'm always crying, which is funny because I usually make sure I keep my tears locked safely behind my bedroom door.

Janu perches on the stone next to me and takes my wrist gently in his hands. "I'm sorry," he says.

But he's right. I should never have given the bracelet away. I feel naked without it.

Jasmine Fields

✿❀✿

Chameli sits under the shade of something that looks a bit like a bandstand. She's stringing garlands of marigolds together. When she sees Janu she opens her arms wide and he runs toward her. She places a bright orange garland around his neck and then turns to me and places one around mine too.

"You have already met Chameli, my ma," says Janu, as she hugs him and starts speaking quickly.

I nod and smile, and she smiles back. The same gentle smile as Janu's—the same eyes. Now that I see them together they are so obviously mother and son.

Women seem to appear out of nowhere with bowls of food and before long there is a feast for us to eat and drink.

"Visitor is like god at table!" one old man says in English, smiling and handing me yet more matar paneer and a small clay cup of sweet lassi.

Janu's treated like a king here. All the mothers of the village keep filling his plate with food. He thanks them and smiles at me from time to time. I think he's a bit embarrassed by all the attention they give him.

A sound strikes the air, as sweet and pure as birdsong. The tune starts slowly at first, like the note of a sitar meandering around before it settles into a groove, but there are no instruments being played, only Chameli's voice. After a while everyone joins in.

Janu turns to me. "She has a beautiful voice, na?" he says, not even attempting to hide his emotion. "The song says…'Though I give you up, my heart will never let you go…Where and how far you travel, your heart will always be home with me.'" He smiles as he speaks, holding my gaze.

Chameli puts her arm around her son and kisses his cheek. She takes my hands too and holds my empty wrist in her soft palms.

"My ma thinks she can tell fortunes." Janu smiles at Chameli. "She wants to know if you remember what she said at the flower market." I nod and Chameli lifts her hand to my face and strokes my cheek.

❖

We walk through the village, followed by a little gathering of children, who giggle at Janu and pull on his kurta top. Janu stops and hands out some pens (he has a pocket full!) and then he kindly shoos them away. He takes my hand and we walk for a while longer. As soon as we leave the earth huts behind I know where we're heading, because I can smell the fields of flowers before I see them. The land dips down to a place where the river widens to almost a lake, and all along the bank, in a long, thin snaking row, are fields of roses, marigolds, and jasmine.

"You should come here after the rains; the air is so full you can taste it. Pick some flowers…" he tells me. "Anything you want but the stems must be long."

I pick jasmine.

We sit down on the riverbank under the shade of a mango tree and Janu takes the flowers from my hands.

I can't believe how fast he weaves and plaits the stems in and out of each other, using the jasmine vine to bind it all together…

"Maybe one day I will come to live here," he says, looking across the river to the fields beyond. He lifts off my marigold garland and replaces it with the jasmine one he's woven for me.

"Thank you," I say, inhaling the scent and savoring all the colors, smells, and beauty around us. We sit in silence for a while, one of those silences that feels comfortable, not awkward. I want Janu to know how much I appreciate his bringing me here and confiding in me. I get the feeling it's not a story he shares with many people.

"Doesn't it make you angry—what happened to Chameli?" I ask him.

"There's no point to be angry," he answers quietly. "Now I perform my *dharma*—my duty—and I will progress. This is part of my samsara—this life is many times, around in cycles."

"How can you think that what happened to Chameli and Ajoy was *meant* to be? You can't accept that. Otherwise, how's anything ever going to change?"

Now I'm the angry one. I know why I gave my charm away. It's because I can't let myself believe that it's just fate that decides everything—why one girl's eyes should look so empty when mine are so full.

"Your turn to be cross," he says. "I saw this fire when you were teaching at the refuge. I think you are a very strong-minded person, na?"

I've never thought of myself as "fiery" before. Janu is smiling and obviously trying to lighten the mood but I still don't feel like backing down or agreeing with him, so I don't.

"Look…" Janu holds out his palms. "This is my left hand. Here is written my story." He traces his fingers along the lines of his palm. "On my other hand is what I *make* of my story…"

"And what if Ajoy and Chameli had never escaped? What would have happened to you if…"

"But they did. That is what they made of their life." He sighs. "It will take me much longer time to explain how I feel about these things…what I believe." I feel my anger melt away—after all, I don't even know what I believe in.

"We have only little time left," he says, looking at his watch, "so let us not argue."

He stands up and pulls a mango from a branch, which is being weighed down by the heavy fruit. He takes out a penknife, peels away the skin and then offers it to me. I bite into the soft, sweet flesh of the most delicious piece of fruit that I have ever eaten.

"Shhh!" Janu whispers, holding his finger to his lips and pointing with his other hand toward the river.

A jewel-bright kingfisher lands on a piece of gnarled driftwood, its turquoise feathers and amber breast are the most stunning combination of colors I have ever seen in nature. I remember Granddad Bimal pointing one out to me on a river in the Lake District once. "Like a messenger from home," he said with a faraway look in his eyes.

There's something about seeing this plump little bird out here in the wild that fits perfectly against this sky...It's not the same color as an English blue sky, more a sort of hazy turquoise-gray.

The kingfisher looks straight at us with its dark, piercing eyes. As it turns its head this way and that, from us to the river; now peering into the water; now diving for a tiny silver fish, it has a fierce intelligence about it, as if it knows what we are saying and thinking. Of course I don't tell Janu any of this, because I've just declared that I don't believe in fate or that things are "meant."

"It was my Granddad's favorite bird—the kingfisher," I

whisper, taking my camera out of my pocket slowly, not wanting to disturb it, but as soon as I have it in view it shakes its wings, revealing the full glory of its markings, and flies away.

"Did you catch it?" asks Janu, looking over my shoulder, but the little screen shows nothing but a blur of color.

"Some pictures belong only to the memory," he says. I nod and delete the picture.

"So, what are you believing about you and me?" Janu smiles, looking straight at me with those great liquid eyes of his. "Is *this* not fate?"

I feel my heart beating fast and I daren't answer him. I suppose I'm still trying to work out what I believe, but if I'm honest, despite what my head tells me, in my heart I feel like fate's been bombarding me since I landed in India...and sitting here with Janu definitely feels like it was meant to be. It's so peaceful here. So right. I watch the silhouettes of the wide winged storks glide over the river as the sun sinks through the sky, casting an amber wash over everything.

Janu walks down to the water's edge and I follow him.

As I approach his side he bends down and lifts my foot so that I have to lean on his back to keep my balance. He removes my sandals and neatly lays them on the river bank, slipping his own off too. He takes my hand and we step into the cool water of the earth-brown river.

"This is my wish," he says with a smile. "Is it yours too?

"Yes." All my butterflies have flown away and I have never been more certain of anything. I close my eyes and feel the softness of his lips, the smoothness of his skin against mine, the coolness of my feet, the perfume of jasmine and roses, and the taste of mango on our tongues. We stand in the river, gently swaying backward and forward, and I wish, I wish, I wish I could stay here, in this perfect moment, forever.

⚘

The horn-blast of a train approaching pulls us apart.

"We'd better go. Mosquitoes are biting," Janu sighs, swishing his arm above our heads.

We slip our wet feet into our sandals. He takes my hand and we walk back toward the station together.

My Lips Are Sealed

✿✺✿

"Interesting day?" Anjali asks, popping her head around the bedroom door.

I smile and yawn all at the same time.

"You look exhausted! Have you eaten?"

"We ate loads of food in Janu's village. How's Priya?"

"She slept most of the day. Lal says it's most probably exhaustion. He thinks she'll be fine by tomorrow, but I've moved her in with me so she's not tempted to get up and party! Sleep well, Mira." Anjali smiles at me and then gently closes the door.

I'm glad I'm alone in here tonight because I can't help going over and over what happened today, and I keep picturing Janu upstairs on his balcony, lying looking up at the sky. I wonder if he's thinking of me too.

It's 5 a.m.

At least at this time of the day you can feel a tiny trace of a breeze on your skin. The bedroom door opens, letting in a chink of light.

"I didn't expect to find you awake at this time," says Priya, tiptoeing into the room.

"Feeling better?" I ask.

She nods and wiggles her shoulders as if to ask her body the question. "Yep, all well again. There's only a certain amount of catching up on sleep a girl can do!" She springs onto my bed and stares out of the window.

"I love this time of the morning, when everything's waking up! I'm telling you, the monsoon is definitely near." She smiles and blows a flattened spike of hair free from her forehead. "I can always tell. I've got a radar. Ma says it's because *I'm* like the monsoon, always building up to some-thing and then breaking."

Priya's tummy rumbles loud and long, making us both laugh.

"Told you!"

She lies next to me on the bed, her hands tucked underneath her head, elbows wide.

"It's not long till you go home," she sighs. "Have you seen everything you wanted? If you could go anywhere in Kolkata, where would it be?" she asks.

"The old house in Doctor's Lane," I answer without a second's hesitation.

"Thought so!" Priya grins and leaps back up. She wanders into the front room and returns with a plate of sweets, fish chops, chutneys, and naan bread.

"Dawn fridge feast," she grins, offering me the plate. I take a sweet.

"Well? What did I miss?" she asks through a mouth stuffed full of curd.

"Can you keep a secret?" I whisper.

"Didn't you know I'm one big secret?"

"Me and Janu…we kissed yesterday."

For one moment she stops chewing long enough to let out a low whistle, but then she shakes her head as if she doesn't quite believe me.

I nod to insist that it's true.

Priya pulls an exaggerated "I don't believe you" face and then snuggles down next to me and pulls Nili's sari quilt up over our heads, making a cozy tent. Her eyes are shining brightly in the dark.

"I knew it!" she says. "The moment I saw you two together, there was something electric going on! I've got a nose for it. I told Paddy that Charbak liked her ages ago, and she just laughed at me and now look at them!"

"I just feel so guilty," I groan.

Priya gives me a sympathetic look, "Well, I suppose you can't fight it. Are you going to tell Jidé?"

I pour out everything—how I'm going to tell him when I get home, how I'm scared I'll lose his friendship forever…how my feelings for Janu have made me realize that I will never feel like that about Jidé, even though I love him so much, and we know each other so well, and I hardly know Janu at all. It's all such a mess!

When I can't talk anymore she pulls back the quilt and we sit up. "Wow! You'd better not say anything to Ma. I don't know how she would take it," Priya warns me.

"What do you mean?"

"Well, she might think Janu's taken advantage of the situation…being older and everything," she explains.

"But you know him. He wouldn't. I *wanted* to kiss him," I admit.

"But Ma might not see it like that. Anyway, you know *my* lips are sealed! Now back to sleep," she orders, dancing over to her wardrobe and plugging herself into her headphones. I think about telling her about the girl with the haunting eyes, but she'd probably think I'm crazy.

I look down at my wrist and wonder where Nana Josie's charm is tonight.

I'm sitting on the train with Janu. We have the whole compartment to ourselves. Then the door's pulled open and standing in front of me is a young Nana Josie. She looks so pretty! She smiles and walks over to us. She picks up my wrist to find it bare.

"You gave away my good-luck charm," sighs the young girl Nana Josie sadly.

Janu looks up at her. "She doesn't believe in luck," he tells her.

"Still…" Nana smiles. "It was a good instinct to give the girl my charm. Anyway, I've always wanted to travel around India." She shrugs, sits down, and looks out of the window.

After a bit she glances back at me. "Guess what?" she asks. "It does!"

"Does what?" I say.

"It brings her luck!"

The Clear Light of Day

✿✿✿

"I had a call from Uma last night," Anjali tells me at breakfast. "They're missing you too much." I feel bad because I haven't even emailed them for three days. "They want to Skype you. I arranged it for eleven o'clock this morning. Will that be good?"

I feel as though I don't have much choice in the matter, so I nod and force a smile on to my face. I'm so tired from waking up all through the night.

I drink some water but can't stomach anything else. When Janu walks in and sits down beside me, Priya kicks me under the table and I joke-glare at her. My head is teeming with questions. Just being in this room with everyone, and the thought of having to Skype home, makes me feel like I'm drowning in all this emotion. I think Janu can tell I'm distracted because he chats to Priya and Anjali about all the jobs he's got to do at the refuge today, only occasionally glancing my way. I don't meet his eye but I'm aware of him watching me as he talks, eats, and drinks. He pours water from a bottle, and when he sees that my glass is empty he takes it and fills it without even asking me. He turns and smiles, but I can't bring myself to meet his gaze as he says his good-byes and leaves for the refuge.

"Why don't you two freshen up and get dressed before you Skype London?" suggests Anjali as she heads for the door. I follow her out onto the landing.

"Have you told Mum about the letters?" I ask.

"I'm leaving that up to you," she answers, giving me a purposeful look before turning and walking down the stairs. My heart sinks.

⚬ ✦ ⚬

"No one gets dressed up to Skype!" says Priya.

But I do. I want Mum and Dad to know I'm doing fine without them. As a kind of peace offering to Mum I wear the orange salwar-kameez—the one I've worn a lot since I've been here, the one I told Mum I'd never wear. Last of all I put on Mum's earrings.

Priya slings on her jeans and a bright red T-shirt.

I sit at the computer and Priya dials "Uma." I think how weird it will be for Mum to see me sitting here, where Anjali and Priya usually sit. Priya leans on the arm of the chair, peering over my shoulder.

The image jumps slightly, but the first person I see is Laila, with her bright face squished right up close to the screen.

"Mimi, are you in there?" she asks, holding her little hand out, as if she wants to grab hold of me through the screen. I can't help it—the hard lump sitting in my throat has suddenly dislodged itself and I'm in floods of tears. I've really missed Laila.

"Why is Mimi crying? Take her out of India," Laila orders, scratching at the screen.

"She's probably just feeling a bit homesick," explains Mum, pulling Laila's podgy hands away and blowing me a kiss.

"You look lovely. The earrings suit you."

"Thanks, Mum."

"Sorry! I know you didn't want to do this, but we were all missing you so much, even Krish, we just wanted to catch a glimpse of you out there."

Dad's face suddenly peers at me through the screen. "Hi, Mira. Look at you—so cool."

"No one says *cool*!" I hear Krish moan in the background, and then his face appears around the side of Dad's.

"I meant she looks fresh and cool, like the heat's not getting to her!" Dad tells Krish.

"Hi, Mira, don't come back soon. I've moved into your room!" Krish pulls a face at me.

"Ha ha! Very funny!" I hate to admit it, but I've missed him too, though I'd never tell him.

"Like the hair, Priya!" He grins and then disappears.

"Thanks, Krish." Priya giggles.

"Anjali's been telling me that you've been all over Kolkata, and you've been a great help at the refuge," says Mum.

"We're so proud of you. See you very soon," I hear Dad shout from somewhere in the background. He hates using Skype.

"Bye, Dad!" I call out, but he's already gone. I look back at Mum. "I've done a lot of sightseeing and I've been busy with my art project the last few days. Sorry I haven't emailed—I've been so busy…"

"You've been busy." Mum's voice echoes my own words back to me. "Is it unbearably hot?" she goes on, our words fusing into each other's. I can never get used to the time delay. "What was that?" she asks.

"Sightseeing. I've been to the flower market and Victoria Memorial, Howrah Bridge and the Burla Planetarium with Lila and to a village and Priya's dance gala…"

"Ah, sightseeing with Lila. Send her my love. Shame about your case—I've put a claim in. But never mind, they're only *things.* You look tired, Mira."

"It's hard to sleep in the heat. Mum, I've got something I have to tell you…"

"I love you. No need to say anything—it's all forgotten. Here's someone who hasn't had much sleep recently either. I'll leave you two to it." Mum smiles mysteriously, and before I know what's happening Jidé's face is grinning at me.

Priya makes a little whistling noise under her breath.

"Hi, Jidé! This is Priya," I gush out the words, pointing to Priya and feeling the heat shoot up my neck and over my face.

"Hi, Priya!" Jidé says, but he's looking at me.

"Heavy." Priya whispers, placing a comforting hand on my shoulder. She slides off her chair and leaves the room.

"Kissy kissy, I love you, I miss you so much." I hear Krish in the background. Even though he's only two years younger than me, he's such a baby sometimes.

"For goodness' sake, Krish, give Jidé and Mira a moment *on their own*," Mum shouts, shooing him out. I hear the door slam.

"So you're back from the trip?" I say.

"Looks like it."

"How was it? The mountains?"

"You know! Tough! Manly stuff, but I made it through!" he jokes. "I've missed you," he says. Then a fuzz appears on the screen and everything starts to jump about. I hope it's happening at his end too so that he can't read my expression.

"I thought there'd be a ton of your texts waiting for me when I got home!" I hear him say, even though the image is still jumbled at this end.

"I would have but my phone's not working!"

"You don't exactly look happy to see me."

"Of course I am!" I protest, "It's just a surprise, that's all!"

"OK, let's email then from now on. So, what's it like out there?"

"It's too hard to explain. There's been so much going on…I've taken loads of photos, and video too."

The image on screen settles and I can see by the way he's looking at me, even across the slight delay, he's not really listening.

"I wish you were coming back today." He smiles the biggest, loveliest smile. Then he frowns slightly. "You're being very quiet," he says, and then leans forward. "Did you write me that letter?"

I shake my head. "Jidé? I…"

"Mira…"

Our voices overlap, then the screen crackles and his face cuts out. My head is aching with the tension of having to face Jidé like this.

"I'm coming to meet you at the airport" is the last thing I hear him say.

⁂

"Well, that was awkward! Did you tell him?" asks Priya.

"No, I have to talk to him face to face, not when he's at my mum and dad's."

I feel completely drained. I just want to be by myself.

277

"I'm sorry to leave you again, but I've got to go and see Paddy," says Priya. "I'd bring you with me, but it would spoil the surprise! Tonight, you and me are sneaking out, and no arguments!"

I have no idea what Priya's got planned, but I'll need to do something to stop my mind endlessly replaying that conversation.

"Are you sure you're going to be OK?" Priya calls out to me from the stairs.

"Fine," I shout back.

I listen to my iPod for a while and check my Facebook, but nothing I do can erase Jidé's face from my mind, or the twisted feeling in my gut. I head to the kitchen and pick at some food but, even though I haven't eaten breakfast, I'm still not hungry.

I kneel down at the little wooden table that's become my easel. I start to remember all the clothes that were packed in my case: my favorite little blue cardigan and my peace T-shirt, one of the ones Jidé gave me. I start sketching a crowd of people, some wearing my lost clothes. I like the idea that instead of my things being abandoned somewhere in a lost property office, someone like Dust Boy has got hold of it all, and handed the stuff out to his family. There could be someone walking around Kolkata in my T-shirt right at this moment. I think maybe when that case was lost, with Jidé's note inside it, a bit of me was lost too, the bit that said, "This is who I am…this is who I belong to." I don't know how people can actually belong to each other.

In a few days' time, me and Janu will be thousands of miles

apart. Jidé will be waiting for me at the airport and I will have to tell him, and it will change everything.

I take the silver paint and trace a thin line around a girl's wrist and add a tiny charm to it. The girl has her head turned toward me, her gray-green eyes sparkling out from the canvas.

I open the wardrobe to decide what to wear tonight and spot the shoebox with Priya's new white Converse inside.

I'd completely forgotten I said I would personalize them for her. She's been so kind and friendly, I'd like to give something back to her. It's not like she's had the best of times, what with all her rehearsals and being ill. I open the box and inside I find a packet of twenty felt-tip pens especially for drawing on fabric. She's thought of everything! I sit on the bed and start to doodle anything that comes into my mind when I think of Priya. Headphones, CDs, the sitar, the tabla, I manage to draw a tiny doll-like outline of her dancing Kathak with her punky red hair; I draw a pair of her red Converse, a yellow taxi, a basket of flowers, jasmine, her midnight-blue eyes, Bacha…I just keep on going and going until every available piece of white on both shoes is covered in pictures and swirls. By the time I've finished my head feels like I'm floating through a bank of clouds. I love the way I can lose myself in art. I place the shoes at the end of Priya's bed and lie down, a wave of tiredness washing over me.

House Party

✹ ✹ ✹

I open my eyes to the shocking blue of Priya's contact lenses staring back at me. She's sitting on her bed carefully studying her Converse. Her eyelids are lined with a dramatic thick black signature of kohl, sweeping upward beyond the end of her lashes. It's the same stage makeup that she wore on the day of her gala. As if that's not over the top enough she's also wearing an enormous glittery silver bindi that glints at me through the darkened room, like Kali's third eye.

"These are amazing!" she hugs me to her and holds the shoes closer to the lamp. "You could make a living out of doing these! This is the best present ever!"

"You like them?" I smile.

"I *love* them."

"Good! But what time is it?" I ask sleepily. I have no idea how long I've been asleep.

"Only eleven," she says, raising her finger to her lips and pointing toward the door. I can hear Anjali chatting away on the phone in the front room. After a few moments there's a knock and Priya turns off the lamp and springs back onto her mattress.

"Pretend you're asleep!" she whispers.

The door creaks open slightly and Anjali says something, but Priya groans as if she doesn't want to be disturbed and keeps the covers pulled over her face.

Anjali says good night and closes the door again.

Priya doesn't move for a while, until she hears Anjali's bedroom door click shut. Then she throws back the covers and flicks the light back on.

"Come on, get dressed," she says, flashing me a wicked grin and handing me my own Converse that she must have picked up off the landing.

What I'm thinking, as I do up my laces, is that the Mira Levenson stepping into these shoes and getting ready to sneak out in the middle of the night, is a different person than the one who left London.

"Is Janu coming?" I ask in the most casual tone I can muster.

"Why? Do you want him to?" Priya smiles at me mischievously.

I shrug, trying not to be too obvious. The truth is it suddenly feels like my time here is draining away so fast, and I've hardly got to know Janu yet. I want more days like yesterday...

"Janu doesn't know anything about this. And if he did, he would probably bust the whole thing," Priya says. "And believe me—what I've got planned is something you'll want to do just as much as kissing Janu!"

She puts her fingers to her lips, levers herself up by the arms and climbs out of the window. I try to do the same, but I quickly realize how much stronger Priya is than me, probably from all her dancing. She holds her arms out for me to cling on to and yanks me through the window. Halfway in and half way out I get the giggles!

"Too many ladoos!" I laugh.

This sets Priya off too, but with one last tug she hauls me clear. I tiptoe along the metal gridded balcony, past the outstretched branches of the Kadamba tree and around to the main stairwell. At the bottom Bacha barks a greeting at us.

"Shhhh!" Priya scolds.

I have never seen the road so deserted. The tram pulls up, and we take a seat in the women's section, which is empty apart from us. Some men turn and stare. I don't like the way they're looking at us.

"Pretend we're tourists!" says Priya quietly.

"Isn't this a bit dangerous?" I feel a sudden panic.

"Not if we keep our wits about us. Anyway, I chose tonight because of all the weddings! No one's going to notice us."

"Why are they all on the same night?" I ask, looking out of

the window at all the floodlit street side wedding venues, lavishly bedecked in garlands of colorful flowers.

"It's why Chameli and Ajoy have been so busy lately. This is one of the auspicious days, when all the planets are lined up to bring happiness," explain Priya.

"You believe that?"

"Why not?"

I'm leaning my head against the tram window and remembering standing by the river, Janu placing the garland over my head, holding me in his arms and his lips touching mine...

"Look!" Priya points as the tram stops just outside a hall where a bride swathed in red and gold silk is being lifted in the air on a plank of wood.

"It's part of the ceremony," says Priya. "Her feet must not touch the ground."

～ ✛ ～

The two men get off the tram first, looking behind them a couple of times to see which direction we're walking in. I'm probably being paranoid, but I'm worried they're planning to follow us. Priya takes my arm and stands a little way behind a policeman, who is busy directing traffic. "We'll just stay here for a while," she tells me. The two men loiter for a moment and then one of them shrugs and they walk off. Priya grabs my hand

and we head in the other direction, through the narrow streets I walked with Janu.

These side roads are sleepy now, and people are sitting outside in the hope of catching a cool nighttime breeze, but if anything the air feels heavier tonight than usual. Even the cows are taking a rest. We walk past one cow dozing under an old film poster of Marilyn Monroe. I can't resist taking a photo.

"Know where we are now?" Priya looks so excited.

We are standing outside the carved wooden door in Doctor's Lane.

"Thank you for bringing me here," I say, thankful to be here again.

"That's OK. I know how much you wanted to see it."

I hear Janu's voice echo through my head: "*It's not safe, I should not have brought you here.*" I think about telling Priya that I've been here already, but it feels like it would spoil her surprise, and, well…that memory belongs only to Janu and me. Priya's already climbing onto the little balcony and through the shuttered windows, as if she's done this a hundred times. Before I even get inside I hear the music start up, a heavy, pulsing bass.

The rooms are lit with battery lanterns, and flowers have been hung around the doorways and beams. The place looks so beautiful in this half-light. The exposed rafters make me feel as if I'm in the hull of an ancient ship. I peer up the staircase where garlands are wrapped round and round the banisters. Music is pumping through the ceiling and it sounds as if there are hundreds of people upstairs. Paddy and Priti's faces appear over the rail, shouting and waving at us, but the music's too loud to hear what they're saying.

I tread carefully, looking out for rotten wood.

"Don't worry! We've fixed it all up for you," says Priya, pulling me up the staircase. I was desperate to see around the house the day Janu brought me here, but now there are so many people dancing in this room I can't get a good look around. We follow Paddy through a sea of bodies. Occasionally Priya stops to chat to friends in the crowd. Among them I recognize some of the dancers from the gala. At the far end of the huge room someone has built a stage with a mixing desk and speakers on it. Chand and Charbak are sitting on this platform with their sitar and tabla.

"What do you think?" asks Priya, buzzing with excitement.

I just stare into the crowded room. I can't believe what I've walked into, what Priya and her friends have created here.

"Get this on video!" she laughs, before walking over to her decks. She puts on a piece of ambient dance music that seems to calm the mood. Priti and some of the other dancers come up to the stage area and gradually people turn toward them, as if they're expecting something to happen. Now Priya plays a more upbeat track...Charbak starts to pick up the rhythm on the tabla, improvising around it, and I watch Priya's feet pound out the beat, just like she danced Kathak at the gala.

"This is DJ Prey in the house," Priya calls out, her voice booming through the microphone.

Her friends raise their arms and start to chant: DJ Prey…DJ Prey…DJ Prey…!

Priya takes a low, graceful bow and comes back up to flash her brightest grin at the crowd.

"This one's for Mira." She winks and points straight at me.

Everyone looks in my direction, and Priya cranks up the music even louder. I can feel the bass traveling through my body. Another chant starts up.

"Prey, dance…Prey, dance…Prey, dance…!"

Priya laughs and the music fades to silence. She nods at Chand and he starts to play the sitar. I recognize the tune straight away. After a few seconds a different track starts playing. It takes me a few seconds to realize that the voice is my own. Priya must have done some serious technical stuff to make it sound that smooth.

> *World is turning round and round*
> *World is turning upside down*
> *Words are floating out in Space…*

So this is why she wanted me to record it for her. Priya begins stretching her body into graceful statuesque shapes, then Charbak ups the tempo on the tabla and Priya's slow moves change to something more unpredictable as the track transforms into something heavier. At exactly the moment she's timed the drop into dubstep, at the end of my lyric, Priya leaps in the air. She must have rehearsed that over and over to get it so perfect. The crowd go wild, leaping and dancing around. I whistle and cheer along with everyone else, feeling so proud that this daring, talented girl is my cousin.

"This is the next big voice!" shouts Priya, pulling me on to the stage. "My cousin, Mira Levenson, from London! You heard her here first!" Priya laughs as she gets swept into the throng of dancing bodies.

I look up at the ceiling, where the boards have all rotted away, and wonder if Sunil could be hiding somewhere, watching all of this. It's strange to think that Anjali once danced, and my mum sang, for Priya's and my great-grandmother here. Priya's gone to so much effort for this party, but right now I wish that it was quiet for a few minutes so I could just go walking through the rooms of this house alone. I'm sure no one will miss me if I have a look around on my own.

I go back into the hallway and pick up one of the lamps. Someone has stuck a red and white tape barrier across the bottom of the staircase that leads to the next landing. I hesitate for a second, but then I place my foot on the first stair and it feels secure enough. I just need to be careful. When I reach the next landing I see that the brickwork of the walls has crumbled away and ivy is curling in through gaps wide enough for me to put my hand through. It's actually quite spooky up here, and my heart is starting to pound. I look into a room, which has a sink and a few old metal pans strewn over the floor—this must have been the kitchen. I take a step in and the floorboard cracks under my weight.

"You should go back, Mira, go back down," I tell myself, but my feet are carrying me up the next flight of stairs, up and up as I hear Anjali's voice…

I will paint a picture of Dida, your thakurma…

I pick my way up the staircase, in one place having to stretch over three rotten boards to climb onward. The air suddenly feels cooler. Once I get to the top there's another small landing and the way is blocked by a tree that's fallen right through the roof, exposing the gray, bulging sky. That must be what's left of the fruit trees on the roof terrace…"*I always think the branches growing above the top balcony make the house look alive.*" I bend down to get a closer look at the tree and find that lemons are growing on its branches. It must have fallen recently. I pick one off and put it in my pocket.

Walking the rooms of this house is like reading a book, only instead of reading it, I'm in it. I know that something happened in this house, something that pulled Mum and Anjali apart. Something that kept Granddad Bimal away after Great-Grandma's funeral. And if I look hard enough, perhaps I'll find the truth. I shudder as hundreds and hundreds of black moths flurry up between the branches of the lemon tree, buffeting against me as I squirm to get away from them. I step over a branch and enter what must once have been my great-grandmother's bedroom. My heart is beating so hard I put my hand on my chest as if that could calm it. I look into the room and find that all that's left from Anjali's description is a wrought-iron bedstead with an old mattress. I don't know what else I expected to find. I walk around the bed and shine the lantern against the wall. The faded flaking blue paint is lighter in one patch, where a tall piece of furniture might once have gone. This must be the place where the sari cupboard stood. I was so longing to see it and now there's nothing here I feel so flat.

To the right of the bed is a window that looks down onto the street below. My great-grandma must have had the best viewing point in the house. I trip over something heavy. I shine the torch and find a stack of books. I open the cover of one and read the name Bimal Chatterjee. I feel breathless. I open the next, and the next, and in each one Granddad's name is written. I flick through the books and see diagrams of hearts and lungs and skeletons. As I pick up another book I hear something under the bed, maybe a rat, I think, as something scuttles over my hand. I jump backward, but a hand reaches out and grasps mine. I am frozen to the spot as Sunil's eyes shine out of the gloom.

He's talking on and on excitedly. "Doctor Sunil, Doctor

Chatterjee…" he chants over and over again, grabbing the books out of my hands and hugging them to his chest. Then he opens my palm and places a small rag of green cloth in it. My heart is thudding so hard against my rib cage that I feel as if I'm about to split open as I back out toward the door. I can't understand what Sunil is saying. All I know is that I need to get back downstairs to Priya. I turn away from Sunil and walk toward the door.

Crack!
Lemons fall from the tree
Branches breaking
Dust pours into hair, skin
Tree is falling
Feet dance
Dubstep
Color flashes
Through time
Orange
Through space
Green
Tumbling over and over
Turquoise
Dancing
Through crumbling brick

Loud music
Pounding
Silk threads
Breaking
Red and gold
Through skin
Loud music
Thudding into wood
Arm snapping
Wrist twisting ·
Head throbbing
Crack!

A tiny ancient woman with a thin white plait is sitting next to me humming the tune to my song…but she makes it sound different, somehow old-fashioned. She's wearing a white sari with golden edging and she looks so frail it feels as if, with one breath, I could blow her away, like the seeds of a dandelion clock. She unwraps the piece of green rag and takes out a small silver key with a heart-shaped end. She peers out of the window to the busy street below, where people are wearing the brightest of saris, as if they're going to a wedding. It seems as though she's searching for something and then a sad look crosses her face as she raises her tiny arm to point. I look through the window to see a woman in a shabby red-and-gold wedding sari walking down the street, trailing the ends through the mud. As she follows my gaze the old woman begins to talk. I think she's telling me a story; she talks on and on. I watch as tears stream down her face. Then she turns away from the window and holds my hands in hers, pressing the little silver key into my palm. I breathe too hard and the old lady disintegrates into tiny feathery flecks…

> Dust falling
> Dust through light,
> Dancing glitter

Someone's pouring water on me, like I'm a fire they want to put out. Hands pummeling my chest, moving over my waist, pulling at me, turning me on my side, taking something from me…

> "Mira! Mira!"
> People running
> Screaming
> Calling my name
> "Mira! Mira!"
> Drowned out by the music of the monsoon rain
> Silence
> Fading light
> Darkness

"Didn't I tell you to be careful where you place your feet? Monsoon has come early. Not to worry, I will sit with you." Granddad Bimal smooths his hand over my brow. "Sunil is a good boy; he will find help, you know. I am teaching him medicine."

Dust in my eyes, falling through past, present, future...

"Don't sleep, Mira, listen to Granddad's voice."

Listen
Silence
Darkness
The darkness shrinks the city into my room.

"Mira! Mira!"
Rain pouring on my head.
Black moths rising.
Ash-filled mouth.
Bitter taste.
Hands on shoulders.
"Mira! This is Nayan—can you hear me?
Remember me, from the airport? Bimal's friend?"

A low moan escapes from my mouth.

Janu's voice and jasmine
Janu and Mira
Wading through water…
Kingfisher watching

Monsoon Memory

✵✵✵

The rain beats a constant rhythm in my head, drowning everything out. A strong-smelling chemical is dabbed onto my face. My head is held in a tightening clamp.

My hand is tugged this way and that. Strangers come and go, and sometimes the voice of someone I know enters my head. I don't know who. But Granddad never leaves my side. Not for a second.

"Soon I must go," he tells me.

"Please don't go, Granddad," I beg

"It is time now…Shhhhhhhh," he sighs, stroking my forehead.

Painting Arm

✤✤✤

"It's your painting arm, isn't it?" Priya says, as she takes a pen and writes "DJ Prey" in stylish block letters on my cast. I try to forget that this broken wrist is the one where my charm used to sit.

"Ma's gone crazy! It was bad enough when we told her about the party, but when she got the call from your mum to say that you were with the old couple in the hospital I've never seen her go so quiet. What are the chances of that? You having Nayan's card, and Sunil running to his address. It must have been the weight of all those people in the house that made the place collapse. You were lucky to get out of there alive. We all were, Mira—I didn't realize how dangerous it was. When I found out that you were still in there I felt sick…I'm so sorry!"

My head's still so foggy that I can't take in half of what Priya's saying.

"It's not your fault. I shouldn't have climbed the stairs…"

Priya and I are quiet for a moment; I think we both know we've had a lucky escape.

"By the way," says Priya, "Ma changed your bed sheets and found the carving. Why didn't you tell me you'd already been to the house?"

I can hear the hurt in her voice, but panic seeps into my chest. I sit up and feel under my pillow. The little block of carving isn't there any more, or my garland, or my letter to Jidé.

"My letter?!" I ask desperately.

"Ma posted it! I told her not to, especially when I saw who it was to, but she wouldn't listen to me. She said *I* had no right to give her advice about anything. She kept going on and on about how *she* would never read other people's letters. She's angry at Janu for taking you to the house in the first place, and I think she knows something's going on between you two—it was pretty obvious who gave you the jasmine garland. But I think she's most upset about some of the things you were saying in your sleep."

I try to take everything in: the letter to Jidé, Janu…

"What sort of things?" I ask.

"I don't know—stuff about Boro-Dida being in the house with you, and your Granddad Bimal, and weird random stuff like moths flying and blowing dandelion seeds. Nayan says you were concussed, but it really got to her. She just sat by your side and refused to sleep. All she did was her puja, day and night. I've never seen her pray like that. She said that if you lost your memory it would be all her fault. She kept going on about history repeating itself. I don't understand any of it. I only know that Janu and I are in big trouble…"

All I can think of is the jumble of words I wrote to Jidé, words that were never meant to be read.

"When did she post the letter? How long will it take to get to London?" I ask.

"Not sure. There's a slim chance it could arrive before you, but maybe not."

I hope Jidé never has to read that letter. I so wanted to handle this in my own way, but it seems like fate, bad karma, or whatever—Notsurewho Notsurewhat—had other plans.

"How long was I in hospital for?"

"Four whole days. I was so worried about you. I'm so, so sorry! If I hadn't taken you there…"

"It's not your fault," I insist, grimacing. My head is throbbing.

Priya stands up on the bed and holds her hands out of the window, catching the rain in her palms. I climb up beside her slowly as I feel so dizzy. She takes my hand to steady me and wraps her arm around my shoulders.

"You know that Jidé's been emailing me every day to see how you are, so I've emailed back. Hope that's OK?" says Priya gently. I nod. I don't know what to think about anything any more.

I have never seen rain like this in all my life. The road below has turned into a river. Water pours from the gutters as though someone's emptying buckets from the sky. Even though my head aches, I like the racket that the rain makes. It stops me having to think too much, and that's a relief, because my thoughts are all tangled up like twisted vines. Janu was right— when the rain comes the smell of jasmine's even stronger.

"Look!" Priya grins as she points through the branches of the Kadamba tree to Bacha swimming along the road, his sharp little nose stuck up above the water. She laughs and I smile, but even that is painful.

"Can you pass me my camera?" I ask Priya.

A look of pity crosses her face.

"Sorry, Mira. It must be somewhere among the rubble of the old house, you didn't have it on you when you were pulled out. I'm afraid you'll just have to store it up here," she sighs, tapping her head.

All those hundreds of pictures I've taken. I can't believe that I'm going home without a single photo to show anyone, or to remind me…Priya takes my good hand and eases me back down to the bed. She pulls Nili's sari quilt over our heads.

"And you don't remember anything about the police?"

I shake my head. "You have to tell me what happened."

Priya needs no encouragement. I get the feeling that despite everything a bit of her is caught up in the drama.

"The police must have heard the music, and they came to chase us all out. I couldn't find you anywhere. I was screaming for them to let me go back in to get you, but the monsoon broke and the streets were flooding so fast. They wouldn't let me past, so I called Janu. But then Dr. Sen arrived and an ambulance. We thought…well, we thought—"

"Did they find a key?" I interrupt her.

"What kind of key?"

"A little silver one wrapped in green cloth?"

"No! No key. You've been talking about all sorts of strange things though. You probably imagined it."

I nod, searching through the fog of my mind trying to work out which bits were flashes of memory and which were just dreams…it all felt so real.

"Weird that you had a lemon, of all things, in your pocket!" says Priya, handing it to me.

Facing Up

✿✿✿

Anjali seems on the verge of crying all the time. Apparently she's only speaking "because I have to" words to Priya and Janu. Mostly she's been having endless conversations on the phone with Priya's dad, Nayan, and my mum and dad.

"Happy birthday, Ma," says Priya in a quiet voice, but Anjali ignores her.

So today is Mum's birthday too. Priya says when Mum got the call she was so worried about me that she was going to fly out. But Nayan convinced her it wasn't necessary. I don't think I could have been any better looked after. Anjali's had poor Lal coming around to see me every day since I left the hospital. Part of me's glad Mum's not here, fussing over me, but another part wants to see her more than anyone else in the world.

Now Anjali's getting ready for me to Skype Mum and Dad. She's pacing around the flat nervously, sorting out things that don't really need sorting. I catch sight of my face in the living-room mirror. The egg-shaped bruise on my forehead is turning an attractive purple color, and my eyes are still swollen and infected from the dust. There's a cut under my chin with two stitches holding it together. I know it's vain of me, but the worst thing is that they had to shave a bit of my hair to stitch up another cut, on the left side of my head. Priya says it looks "street," but I know it looks awful. Mum's going to freak out when she sees me.

Anjali takes a soft brush and smooths it through my hair, being careful not to go anywhere near the shaved patch above my ear. I feel so guilty. She's done everything for me, and now she's blaming herself for this. I don't even ask her about the letter to Jidé because, in a way, I feel like I deserved that. Stealing Mum's letters was what set all this in motion, and there's only one person to blame for that. I just hope I get to talk to Jidé before that letter arrives.

"That's better," Anjali sighs, stroking my hair, then she checks her watch. She looks so tired and stressed.

"I'm really sorry, Anjali…about everything. It's not Priya's fault and it's not Janu's either. It's just mine."

Anjali shakes her head but doesn't answer me. She walks over to the computer and clicks on Dial. The call is picked up in an instant and Mum and Dad's faces flicker onto the screen.

"Happy birthday, Mum," I try to smile but it's still too painful. I'm determined not to cry.

Mum puts her hand over her mouth, as if that can hide the expression of horror on her face. Dad pats her shoulder reassuringly but his calm expression doesn't look reassured. He has his fake "cheery" face on, but his deep worry lines are giving him away.

"Hi, Mira! Been getting yourself…into some scrapes then? Can't wait to have you back." Dad smiles and blows me a kiss, squeezes Mum's shoulder and then disappears from the screen.

"Oh, Mira!"

"I'm all right, Mum, really."

"You don't look all right."

"I am. I promise."

"Will you be OK to travel? We can still delay the flight and I can come out there and travel back with you…"

"I'll be fine, Mum. Nayan and Iris will look after me."

"OK to fly?"

"Yes, fine to fly."

This conversation is missing at every turn, and it's making me feel even farther away from home than ever.

"Honestly, I'm OK, Mum."

"And Dr. Sen…Nayan. Isn't it strange him finding you? We'll have to think of a way to repay him…and his wife. How's your arm?"

I can always tell when Mum's nervous, because usually she's a good listener but now she's just firing question after question at me and not even waiting for the answers.

"Fine," I say, lifting it up to show her the cast. "Fine" will just about do for the answer to everything.

"Mum, about the letters…I'll explain everything when I get home, I'm so sorry."

Krish's head appears around Mum's and he whistles as he takes in the bruised mess of my face and head.

"Wow! I thought you were faking it!" He looks impressed and snuggles up next to Mum to get a better look at me.

"The only thing I care about is that you're safe," Mum says, wrapping her arms around herself for comfort.

"Wait till Jidé sees you!" butts in Krish. "He'll probably dump you."

"Thanks, Krish." I sigh. I'm in no mood for his jokes.

"Miss you, Mimi," he says, suddenly turning serious as he peers at me with his huge forget-me-not blue eyes. He only ever uses his baby name for me when he really means something. The tears are rolling down my cheeks and I see his eyes well up too. Mum is obviously fighting back her own tears.

"Get everyone to sign the cast!" he says, then runs out of the room.

"Jidé sends his love; he's been calling every day to see how you are," says Mum. I thank Notsurewho Notsurewhat that I don't have to speak to him right now. "Oh! And you'll never guess what arrived here today! Your case! It's sitting on your bed waiting for you!"

I just nod. The idea of seeing that case again, after everything that's happened makes me feel all wrung out.

"Can't wait to have you home. Love you."

"Love you too," I say to Mum for the first time in ages, and my words wobble into a strange weak wail.

Anjali puts her arm around me and I stand up and walk away because I don't want to upset Mum by crying anymore. I go into the bedroom, where Priya's listening to something with a miserable look on her face. She takes off her earphones when I walk in.

"How was it?"

"Awful."

"Not much of a birthday for your mum or mine." She sighs.

I leave the door slightly open so that I can hear Anjali making arrangements for the flight home, but she's plugged the headset in so I can't hear Mum's side of the conversation any more.

"Dr. Sen—Nayan—and his wife...Iris. I know. Extraordinary coincidence. Don't worry, they'll look after her. Lovely people... your ma remembers them?"

Anjali is quiet for a long time. She must be just listening to Mum talk.

"It's because of the letters. She needed to find out what happened between us."

I wish I could hear what Mum's saying right now.

"Me too. I overreacted, you know, and took them off her. It must have made her even more curious. Isn't it incredible that something can feel so raw after so much time. We were only their age, we didn't know what we were doing, but I suppose that's about the time when life starts to get complicated...You know, I don't remember feeling regret until then..."

There's silence while Anjali listens.

"I know, I know." I can hear the tears in her voice.

Another silence.

"No, no, I should never have kept it all to myself."

Long pause.

"OK, I'm coming for a craft exhibition in December. Yes! I'll bring Priya too—she'll be so excited, and we will talk and talk."

"Hear that!" whispers Priya, grinning. But I can't help wondering when I'll see Janu again.

"And I'm so looking forward to seeing you too. After so long. I'm just so sorry Mira got hurt. But Nayan says the stitches will dissolve and there should be no scars, which is a relief."

Pause.

"And to you too. It's definitely one to remember! Bye for now."

I watch Anjali through the crack in the door. She rests her

elbows on the table and her head in her hands and she stays like that for ages without moving a muscle. Then she sits up straight as if she's decided on something. She takes some paper and begins writing. Occasionally she pauses as if working out what to say before she starts again, but I count that she uses at least five sheets of paper.

There's a knock at the door and Anjali gets up from her desk and shows Lal through to my room. She leaves the door open and calls Priya through into the living room.

"How's my patient?" He smiles.

"I feel a bit better," I tell him.

"That's good, because you look terrible!" he jokes, lifting my eyelid and dropping in the antibiotics. "Strange, me ending up having to do this for you." He smiles as he moves my head gently to one side and examines the stitches. "These are all superficial wounds. They'll heal in time. Oh! I almost forgot. Nili sent you her quilt," he says, laying a neat-looking package wrapped in brown paper on the bed.

Dear Miru,

I wish you well. I wish one day to see you again. Here's the quilt you wanted. Pay whatever you think it's worth.

Love from your friend Nili x

"She says that you should give Anjali the money, because it's all going toward building the new sewing workshop."

I nod, feeling happy inside that Nili thinks of me as a friend.

"Sunil sends you his good wishes too."

"What's going to happen to him? Will he live at the refuge now?"

"I promised Dr. Sen I'd let him tell you that story!" Lal smiles. "I'm flying back home soon," he says. "Anjali has my details so we can keep in touch. Oh, and Nili's coming over to London in December—she's been invited by a Designers Guild to show her work, so I'll be coming to the exhibition. Maybe we can all get together?"

The Sari Cupboard

✿✹✿

"I would like to talk to Mira on her own," says Anjali solemnly.

Priya doesn't argue; she just stands up and walks out of the bedroom.

Anjali places her hand on my good wrist as she sits down next to me on the bed.

"Poor Uma," she sighs. "What a shock it must have been to see your pretty face like this. It was supposed to be such a relaxing holiday for you two girls. She notices the brown paper package on my bed. "What's this?" she asks.

"Will you open it for me?" I ask.

She carefully peels off the tape and unravels Nili's beautiful quilt. I get up so that she can lay it out on Priya's bed and we both admire it. The colors are soft and subtle and the stitching is so detailed. The combination reminds me a bit of Nili!

"A present from Nili?" asks Anjali.

"No, I bought it." I tell her, walking over to my bag and taking out the money.

"I can't take this," she says, pushing it back toward me.

"It's for Nili's workshop," I say firmly.

Anjali pauses for a moment and smooths her hands over the beautiful sewing. Then she turns over the end of my new quilt and compares it to Priya's.

"Priya's was the first one Nili ever made. She was only ten years old!" Anjali smiles as she traces her fingers over the stitches. "Look how her work has advanced since then! Such talent! It makes me really happy that you appreciate the work that's gone into it. Come and rest," she says, patting the place on Nili's sari quilt beside her. "You want to know why the letters stopped?" She almost whispers it.

I nod. Despite nearly killing myself I still want to know the truth; otherwise it will just keep eating away at me.

Anjali stands back and walks over to the wardrobe—she gently lifts my sari out and comes back to the bed. Then she does the strangest thing. She sits next to me and throws it over us so that the long piece of silk unravels.

"It seems like ever since you arrived you've been drawn to all the pieces of the past that have lain hidden for so long. Maybe, like Janu says, all this was fate—you coming back here and blowing away the cobwebs. Out of all the saris you could have chosen…you had to pick an old one, like the ones that used to live in that cabinet over there." Anjali points to Priya's trophy cupboard. Then she takes the little piece of carving Janu found for me out of her pocket and hands it back. I should have realized that this is the sari cupboard that I have been searching the rooms of the old house for. And it was here in front of me all the time.

"My Uncle Shudi, your granddad's brother, made it, and it was once the most beautiful piece of furniture I have ever seen." Anjali is quiet again for a moment, remembering. "Your mum said something lovely just now, and maybe it's true—you and Janu finding that missing piece could be a message from Boro-Dida—Old Grandmother—to all of us…"

"I don't understand," I say, but my spine tingles with the memory of the frail old woman handing me the key.

"I know, and I'm sorry." She strokes my hair, just like she did Priya's when she was ill.

Only Saris

✿✿✿

"You can come in now, Priya!" Anjali calls, as Priya practically falls through the door. "Oh! And pass me my bag," she adds.

Priya picks up a cloth bag that's hanging over the door handle, hands it to Anjali, and settles herself on the bed with her legs outstretched. Anjali takes the sari and covers Priya with it too. Then she pulls Mum's letter album out of the bag, undoes it, and takes out a blank envelope and a letter I haven't seen before. She hands me the envelope.

"Now you must take this letter album back to Uma," she says. "I'm sorry about your camera, Mira. Here are a few photos I've taken for you to share with your ma. I open the envelope and there's a photo of Lila, Priya, and me at the party, one of me and Priya after the dance gala, and a few of Anjali and me shopping in the market, and that's about it. I thank Anjali and tuck them in the album.

"The letter is for Uma. It's the only way I could work out how to tell this story. Maybe if I had written this a very long time ago, everything would have been different." She sighs as she begins to read the words she's written.

Dear Uma,

I am reading this first to our daughters, on our birthday, so that we can put the past behind us and look forward to sharing many more birthdays to come. I was thinking how you should come here to celebrate our birthdays next year. Our great mistake has been thinking we could go forward without sorting out the mess we made so long ago. So, if what's happened is anyone's fault, it's probably ours.

Anjali looks at me and faintly smiles.

So, how to begin? We were cousins born on the same day. Forty-five years ago today, to be exact. One living in Kolkata, one living in London. From the beginning our parents celebrated this day, our shared birthday. It felt as if fate had brought our two families a blessing to keep them bonded together over space and time. As soon as we learned to write we would send each other little cards and pictures, drawings, and birthday wishes. From when I was very young I had a wild imagination.

As Anjali reads this she smiles at Priya and scruffs up her pixie hair.

In my cards and letters I told you that I had a house filled with pet monkeys and as the years went on we loved to make up stories for each other, so that after a while it was difficult to know what was real and what was pretend. When I was a little girl what I hated most about home was that, except for Ma missing Baba, our family seemed to have all we needed. But there were other people, living side by side with us, who had nothing.

Whenever I would pass people in the street who had no food, no clothes, no fresh water, people living in the gutter, I'd feel ashamed. So over the years, as I wrote to you, Uma, I invented a different reality for our family. You can do that in letters. I told you that we ran a refuge for the poor and that we lived in a house with no servants. It's taken me a lifetime to make that a reality. Anyway, you and I got to know each other through the pictures we painted in our letters and when we were fourteen years old, as our daughters are now, you flew to India for the first time. For you it was a real culture shock. But I was so happy to meet you. We were like long-lost sisters, weren't we? But you kept asking questions about people who lived in the streets or servants who worked in the house or where the refuge was…and I came to feel like such a fraud.

Remember how every day we used to climb the stairs, right to the top of the house, to visit Dida? I had never seen her so happy as when we danced and sang together on her balcony of fruit trees. It was such a beautiful house.

By that time grandmother was very weak, but she loved to take her saris out of the cupboard and share stories of when she'd worn each one, telling us what occasion it was, or who she had inherited it from. Her mind was so sharp. Sometimes we would take a sari out and she would remember three or four new tales about a day when she wore it. She would even let us dress up in them and dance; we just thought it was good fun. This much you probably remember.

She stops reading and reaches out to the table where my painting sits.

"It's a shame you won't be able to finish this before you leave," she says, running her eyes across the scenes I've painted and glancing down at my broken arm. "But then maybe nothing's ever finished."

"Maaaaaa!" Priya groans. "You can't stop there!"

"OK, OK." Anjali takes a deep breath as if she's trying to find new strength to read this part of her letter to us.

This is how I remember it. It was Christmas Day and we were already feeling sad at the idea of being apart again soon. As we watched the servants patiently folding away the saris we decided that it wasn't fair that grandmother had so many beautiful expensive saris while so many of the people on the street below had practically nothing to wear. So when she slept we took the saris out of the cupboard, wrapped them up as presents and distributed them to people on the street. Remember their faces? Some of them couldn't believe that we were giving them away. They thought it was a trick, and the police would be waiting to arrest them!

"And you say *I'm* crazy!" laughs Priya.

"In the letter you said it was Mum's idea," I blurt out.

"We encouraged each other. We were *both* responsible, I was just angry with your mum, because she could go away and *I* had to stay and face the consequences…"

"But, Ma, it wasn't that big a deal. They were only saris," says Priya.

"Not to Dida they weren't. We didn't know it at the time, but what we did was steal her memories." Anjali turns back to the letter.

We should have known it, Uma. We should have thought it through, but we were so young and how could we have known how it would end? Dida could hardly move her body, but whenever she took out one of those saris her mind was alive with stories full of color and texture and detail. They were the way she mapped out her life. They were her ma's wedding day, her own wedding day, the days her children were born and married, the day she went to Ma's first dance gala. You know how it is, Uma—we understand now what we never did then, that sometimes old people find it easier to remember the distant past than what happened yesterday. They were her memories, her past, and we took them from her and gave them away. Imagine what it must have been like for her seeing some woman in the street walking in her wedding sari. Dida couldn't understand why we would hurt her like this.

Her words get all choked up as the tears roll down her face.

"Don't cry, Ma!" says Priya, sitting up and wrapping her arms round Anjali.

And the next days, after you went home, were the most painful. I resented you because I was left behind to watch Dida slipping away from us. Every day I would go up to see her and she would just stare and stare at her empty sari cupboard, not talking, not laughing, not telling stories anymore. Ma would ask me to dance for her and she wouldn't even look up. That childish moment of madness between us

317

pushed Dida to a place where no one could reach her and she never really spoke again. Her memories seemed to drain away until all that was left was an empty shell of a person. She didn't leave the house in Doctor's Lane again; she just sat in her room and faded away.

Anjali folds the letter and places it back in the album.

"The rest of the letter is only for Uma. You won't read it?" she says gently, tying the album together.

"I promise," I whisper as she hands Mum's letter album back to me and kisses my cheek. I feel so relieved that, after everything, she's putting this trust in me.

"Maybe she would have lost her memory anyway," Priya says.

"I don't think so." Anjali shakes her head. "Not like that." She has a faraway look in her eyes.

"But, Ma! I don't understand—if you loved the house so much, why did the family sell it?" Priya asks, jogging Anjali back to the present.

"After Dida died, Ma had to go and care for my other grandparents. I think that's why she won't even think about moving in with us. She's spent so much of her life looking after everyone. You know she had a dream to set up a dance school but she was always too busy. We moved from one family home to another but Shudi Uncle stayed on there for many years doing his carpentry until it all got too much for them, just him and Anishka in that enormous house.

"When I married Dinesh we fought hard to set up the refuge there, but the authorities would not give permission, so…the rest is history. Those scoundrel developers bought it, and all they do is wait and watch until the building is so old and decrepit it is ready to fall down itself, or someone burns it down, whichever happens first, and then they can get permission to build something new. So, now their wish has come true. It breaks my heart when I think of how beautiful that house once was, and now it's all gone."

"Why didn't Mum tell me all this?" I ask.

"That's why I've written it all out from the start. Uma couldn't tell you the story, because she never really knew what happened after she left. I refused to answer any of her letters, and eventually I think she gave up trying. Your Granddad Bimal also shielded her from the truth. He came over when Dida died and my ma told him what had happened. Even though she said that no one blamed us, I think he still felt responsible somehow, because after that time he never came back to Kolkata. That's why Ma went to see him when he first fell ill…to make peace."

I feel numb, trying to take everything in. Anjali gets up and walks over to the sari cupboard and lovingly runs her hands over its carved edges. "It used to have doors and a little silver key. But the doors came off the hinges somewhere along the line and the key was lost."

There's no point trying to tell Anjali and Priya about my dreams…that my Great-Grandmother Medini *did* press the key into my palm. And that Granddad sat by my side watching over me.

"Are you feeling OK, Mira?" asks Anjali, frowning at me.

"I think I need to sleep," I tell her.

She nods and strokes my cheek. "I was so afraid that history had come back to haunt us when you were unconscious and you couldn't remember anything, not even your name."

I lie down and Anjali covers me with Nili's quilt.

"So you must give this old sari to Uma, as a present from me. Tell her we bought it in the same Park Street shop we went to with Ma all those years ago," she says, gathering it up off the bed. I nod and smile at her.

"Cholo, help me fold," Anjali orders Priya, walking to the far end of the room. The fine silk wafts between them, like a wave. Anjali and Priya both begin to gather and fold, gather and fold, their bodies twisting and turning, dancing together as the cloth closes the distance between them. I shut my eyes and see lengths and lengths of the brightest-colored sari cloths unfolding. As I'm drifting off something slips from my hand and wakes me.

"Anjali!" I call to her, as she and Priya are leaving the room. I reach down and pick up the tiny piece of carved wood. "This belongs to you!" I say, holding it out to her. "Acha," she says, kissing me softly on the forehead.

"Maybe Janu can mend the cupboard now," I whisper.

"Maybe he can." She smiles as she closes the door behind her.

Janu

❀✿❀

The rain has stopped, the streets are drying out, and Anjali and Priya have gone off to buy presents for my family and a new suitcase for me take all my things home in.

This silence feels so strange after the constant roar of the monsoon rain. I sit on Priya's bed, not quite believing that in a few hours' time I'll be on a plane back to London. I listen to the birds singing in the Kadamba tree and I wait for Janu.

There's a knock on the door. I stand up and go to open it. It feels like so long ago that we stood by the river and kissed, half of me wonders if it will be like opening the door to a stranger. But here he is with his warm smile, reaching out toward my good hand. He leads me through the flat and up the marble staircase to his balcony. It's so good to see him.

"Hold on!" I tell him. "Can you please go back and get my painting?" I breathe in the sweet scent of jasmine as I wait for him.

The balcony is washed clean by the rain. Everything smells fresh and new up here. Janu returns and opens the turquoise door into his room. The jasmine vines cascade through the open window making tiny water droplets, like tears, drip onto his carving table.

He gestures for me to sit down and places my painting on the table to the side of the window.

"It looks like it's *meant* to be there," I tell him. "Anyway, it's for you!" I say as he studies the painting, spotting Chameli in the flower market, and then the two figures running through the crowd.

"You and me?"

I nod. "But it's not finished."

"I think you are right. It is not finished," he looks from the painting to me. "Will it hurt, if I kiss you now?"

"Probably!" I say, leaning toward him and meeting him in the gentlest of kisses. He takes his arms and wraps them round my waist and holds me to him. My head rests in the indent of his neck. We sit still like this for ages just listening to the birds singing. Being this close to him makes my heart ache at the thought of leaving Kolkata, and Janu.

"Did you see the house come down?" I ask him.

"I stood beside Sunil. He cried when the bricks fell. You should have seen him with the street children. It made quite a spectacle, the way they floated that heavy door, like a boat, all the way to the refuge. It's going to be our new front door, you know."

I remember Great-Grandmother Medini's words: "*That door will last for longer than this house.*" The strange thing is, it's not long ago that I learned her name and now I feel as if I've met her.

"And what will happen to Sunil?"

"I'm not allowed to tell you that!" Janu smiles. So he's in on the secret too. "You'll find out soon! But here—Sunil asked me to give you this." Janu reaches under his bed and brings out a thick medical book I've seen before. I open the front page to find the name *Bimal Chatterjee*.

"He told me to tell you, only one page is missing," Janu says. "I have a present for you too. Close your eyes."

I hear him move around the room and then he sits back down beside me.

"OK, you can open them!"

"I don't even have a photo of you," I sigh as I look up into his beautiful eyes.

"I'll send one." He smiles. "But I think this is better to remember me."

He has something cupped between his palms. I start to peel away his fingers, one by one, to reveal the bright turquoise and orange feathers of an exquisitely painted wooden kingfisher.

I trace my fingers over the carving of the little head and the delicate detail of the wings.

"You like it?" he asks, kneeling down and looking up at me.

"The kingfisher on the river," I whisper.

"It can fly home with you," Janu says.

I lean forward and kiss him. I don't know how I'm ever going to say good-bye.

Going Home

✿✿✿

I stare out of the window at the endless passing clouds. I can't get the picture out of my head of my suitcase unopened on my bed. Everything neatly packed exactly as it was. Just as if I had never left and nothing's changed.

"In the air again," Nayan says, looking down at the earth slipping farther and farther away as we climb ever higher.

I understand now what Granddad meant about being "suspended between homelands," because right now I feel as if my heart's being torn in two.

"Looking forward to getting home, I should think, after all your adventures. At least you're in one piece, almost!" Nayan chatters on.

I leaf through Granddad's old medical book. There are hundreds and hundreds of pages, but it's something to keep my mind off leaving Janu, and Jidé coming to meet me at the airport.

"Found the missing page yet?" asks Nayan, a mischievous glint in his eye. "Keep turning!"

Eventually I find a page that has an oval shape cut out of its middle.

"OK! It's time to show you!" says Nayan excitedly as he rummages in his hand luggage beneath his feet and pulls out something I recognize straight away...It's a street wish, but I haven't seen this one before. It's an old paperback book with a new cover on it showing a diagram of an eye. It's obvious that it's been cut out of the book I'm holding. The names "Dr. Bimal Chatterjee" and "Sunil Das" are written at the bottom of the cover where the authors' names usually go.

"What was the wish?" I ask, still hardly believing my eyes.

"It's in the title." Nayan points at the words.

"'My Wish Is to Study Medicine,'" I read.

"We were so touched when we found this in the shop, and then Anjali took us to see the work Sunil was doing with Lal. Anyway, we've decided we're going to find a way to help fund his medical training when he's old enough," explains Nayan.

As I go to close the book, Nayan takes a last look at Granddad's signature.

"You know, Mira, I think maybe fate has intervened. I was already thinking this, when Sunil came to find me," Nayan says, shaking his head, "but when I saw that Kadamba growing outside your auntie's flat, that clinched it for me...it's a holy tree, you know? And I felt then—Bimal must be trying to reach me. Calling in a favor! Is that not so, Iris?" Iris nods.

"You can take the blindfold off now. We're in the air! My wife doesn't like flying," he explains.

"Nonsense! It's only the takeoff and the landing I hate," Iris says, pushing back her mask.

I peer out of the tiny portal window. The sky's on fire with a sunset of yellow and burnt orange.

Maybe some things *are* meant to be. But what if I'd never taken the letters? What if I'd never met Nayan and Iris at the airport? What if I'd never kissed Janu? What if I'd never set eyes on the house in Doctor's Lane? What if…? Then what? Would everything have stayed the same?

"By the way, Mira, do you know the meaning of my name?" asks Nayan.

I shake my head.

"Oh, Nayan! Do you have to?" groans Iris.

"The meaning of Nayan is eye! And this is my Iris!" He grins, wrapping his arm lovingly around his wife's shoulders.

"Now he's going to tell you that we complete each other!" Iris laughs, flicking her long gray plait over her shoulder.

"That is *my* line!" jokes Nayan, patting his wife's knee affectionately.

"Well, excuse me for butting in, but I may just have heard that a few too many times!" Iris winks at me. "Now don't you go boring the poor girl to death. She's been through enough and she doesn't want to hear all your theories! Take my advice, Mira, put your blindfold on, plug yourself into some music, and get some rest!"

～⬦～

I drift in and out of sleep, but I'm haunted by the thought of Jidé meeting me at the airport and how to find the right words to tell him that everything's changed between us, if he doesn't know already, that is. My suitcase might be packed up all neat and tidy but everything else about my world's been turned upside down.

～⬦～

I must have finally dozed off because I wake to the strong smell of coffee and the sound of clanking trolleys. I take off my blindfold to find that I'm lying across Iris's lap, my head resting on a pillow smelling faintly of lily of the valley perfume. The two of them must have swapped places.

"Sorry!" I say, sitting up.

"No problem!" Iris smiles, handing me some juice and a croissant. "We saved breakfast for you."

The bright red light of the "fasten your seat belt" sign has just clicked on above our heads. I adjust the seat into an upright position and as the plane begins to drop through the sky I feel Iris's tension prickling toward me. She closes her eyes and pushes her plump body right into the back of her seat. My stomach knots and I reach for my charm and find nothing but my bare wrist.

Iris takes my hand and whispers in my ear...

"I think, if truth be told, Mira, we're all a bit afraid of landing."

Acknowledgments

To Freda Brahmachari, my mum, and my late dad, Dr. Amal Krishna Brahmachari. To my brother, Dev, and sisters, Shanti and Joya, for sharing the journey through childhood and the many happy memories we hold.

My heartfelt thanks go to my husband, Leo, for his love and support. The individual artistic spirits of each of our three children, Maya, Keshin, and Esha-Lily, are a constant inspiration to me in my writing.

To all my uncles and aunties whose creativity as writers, dancers, singers, and fine artists sparked my childhood imagination.

A special thanks goes to my cousin Jhuma and her late ma, Mira (my character Mira's namesake), whose beautiful dancing is one of my treasured childhood memories. Thank you, Jhuma, for all your encouragement, help with details about Kolkata and Bengali references, and...for your treasured letters.

To my agent, Sophie Gorrell Barnes, for her excellent advice and enthusiasm for the sensory world of *Jasmine Skies* and her jasmine-scented cards!

To Samantha Swinnerton for being such a brilliant, insightful, and enthusiastic editor, for her confidence in my writing and the gentle way she coaxes the story to surface.

To Nihal Arthanayake—DJ for BBC Radio 1 and BBC Asian Network—for helping me to research the character of Priya and her musical influences.

To playwright Tanika Gupta for her Bengali references.

To Trilby and Shelley for their love of Kolkata.

To Maria Levenson for lending me her surname again and helping me to decide on the title of this book, *Jasmine Skies*.